Great Tales
of the
Gold Rush

Great Tales
of the
Gold Rush

Edited by Ted Stone

The Publishers

Lone Pine Publishing	1901 Raymond Avenue SW
10145 – 81 Avenue	Suite C
Edmonton Alberta	Renton Washington
Canada T6E 1W9	USA 98055

This book is a co-publication with Red Deer Press, Red Deer, Alberta, Canada.

Credits
Front cover photograph courtesy of the Provincial Archives of Alberta, B5207.
Cover and text design by Boldface Technologies Inc.
Printed and bound in Canada by Friesens for Lone Pine Publishing.

Editor's Note
To acknowledge the historical significance of the writing styles reproduced in this collection, all originally published spellings, punctuation and grammar have been preserved.

Canadian Cataloguing in Publication Data
Main entry under title:
Great tales of the gold rush
ISBN 0-88995-217-5 (Red Deer Press)—ISBN 1-55105-242-3 (Lone Pine Publishing)
1. Klondike River Valley (Yukon)—Gold discoveries—Fiction. 2. Short stories, Canadian (English)* 3. Short stories, American. 4. Canadian fiction (English)— 20th century.* 5. American fiction—20th century. I. Stone Ted, 1947–
PS8323.K56G7 1999   C813'.01083297191   C99-910344-X   PR9197.35.K56G7 1999

5 4 3 2 1

Contents

Introduction 9

The Spell of the Yukon 12
BY ROBERT SERVICE

The Klondike Stampede 15
BY TAPPAN ADNEY

The Gentleman with the Grindstone 30
BY W. W. MORELAND

At the Dropping-Off Place 53
BY WILLIAM McLEOD RAINE

To Build a Fire 61
BY JACK LONDON

In a Far Country 76
BY JACK LONDON

The Shooting of Dan McGrew 91
BY ROBERT SERVICE

In a Klondike Cabin 95
BY JOAQUIN MILLER

The Test 105
BY REX BEACH

The Weight of Obligation 115
BY REX BEACH

For the Under Dog 134
BY RILEY H. ALLEN

The Ice Goes Out 140
BY ELIZABETH ROBINS

The Cremation of Sam McGee 165
BY ROBERT SERVICE

Luck 169
BY MARJORIE PICKTHALL

Routine Patrol 179
BY JAMES B. HENDRYX

Grist for the Newsmill 192
BY STROLLER WHITE

The Ice Worm Story 199
BY STROLLER WHITE

The Law of the Yukon 204
BY ROBERT SERVICE

Acknowledgments

"The Spell of the Yukon," "The Shooting of Dan McGrew," "The Cremation of Sam McGee," and "The Law of the Yukon" by Robert Service, from *Songs of a Sourdough,* 1907.

"The Klondike Stampede" by Tappan Adney originally published by Harper Brothers, 1900.

"The Gentleman with the Grindstone" by W.W. Moreland originally published in *Overland Monthly,* 1898.

"At the Dropping-Off Place" by William McLeod Raine originally published in *Overland Monthly,* May 1890.

"In a Klondike Cabin" by Jocquin Miller originally published in *Frank Leslie's Popular Monthly,* 1899.

"To Build a Fire" by Jack London, from *The Complete Stories of Jack London,* 1910.

"In a Far Country" by Jack London originally published in *Overland Monthly,* San Francisco, 1899.

"The Test" by Rex Beach originally published by *McClures,* 1904.

"The Weight of Obligation" by Rex Beach from *The Crimson Gardenia* originally published by Harper Brothers, 1916.

"For the Under Dog" by Riley Allen originally published by *McClures,* June 1904.

"The Ice Goes Out" by Elizabeth Robins originally published by McLeod & Allen, 1922.

"Luck" by Majorie Pickthall originally published in *Century Magazine,* New York, June 1922.

"Routine Patrol" by James B. Hendryx originally published in *Western Story Magazine,* New York, 1938.

"Grist for the News Mill" and "The Ice Worm Story" by Stroller White from *Klondike Newsman,* compiled by R.N. DeArmond, 1969, 1990. Used by permission, Lynn Canal Publishing, Skagway, Alaska.

Special thanks to staff at the Walker Library, University of Minnesota, and the Elizabeth Defoe Library, University of Manitoba.

Introduction

By Ted Stone

THERE HAS NEVER BEEN A GOLD rush like it. When George Carmack, Skookum Jim and Tagish Charlie discovered gold on Bonanza Creek, a tributary of the Klondike River, in August 1896, they had no idea of the madness their strike would unleash. It took nearly a year for the news to reach the outside world from that isolated spot, but when it finally did, the impact of their find on people's imaginations was unparalleled.

When the first Yukon miners from the North staggered under the weight of their recently acquired gold down the gangplanks at the docks of San Francisco and Seattle, news of the discovery spread like wildfire around the world. Thousands upon thousands of people abandoned their life in the south and headed for the Alaska and Yukon goldfields. Workers quit their jobs. Men left their wives. Women ran away from their husbands. Everyone was off to join the Klondike Stampede. Factory workers, lawyers, doctors, out-of-work cowboys, debutantes, dance-hall girls, thieves and preachers raced north to the Yukon River and the era's greatest adventure.

Writers, too, joined the rush for gold. Tappan Adney, Jack London, Rex Beach, Joaquin Miller and scores of others found their way north. Popular magazines and newspapers soon began publishing their tales. Even before writers arrived in the North, publishers began selling guidebooks to the Klondike, recommending routes and gear and explaining how to find ore once the reader arrived in the mining camps.

With few exceptions the guides were hastily assembled bundles of wishful thinking and misinformation. Often they suggested dangerous, sometimes virtually impossible routes north, ridiculous routes that were, nonetheless, attempted by naive and inexperienced stampeders. But the public, hungry for news of the Klondike, snapped up the publications as if the pages themselves were made of gold.

As the stampede progressed, more accurate articles about the Klondike emerged from the growing body of writing about the Yukon Valley.

Established writers from around the world, who had traveled north as gold rush correspondents for popular magazines and newspapers, wrote with a more objective hand. Of them all, Tappan Adney, of *Harper's Illustrated Weekly,* was the best. Adney told his stories as if he were one of the stampeders, which for all intents and purposes he was. He started north in the initial wave of the gold rush and reported on life in the camps with a sense of immediacy and drama that brought the Klondike Gold Rush as near to life as anything then being written.

Fiction of the gold rush began almost as early as the guides. Initial tales were mostly dressed-up versions of the standard frontier stories popular at the time, penned by writers who had, with perhaps one exception, never ventured anywhere near the Yukon River. This began to change by 1899, when Jack London published his first Klondike stories in the *Overland Monthly,* after the various nonfiction accounts already published had created a distinct and more accurate impression in people's minds of what life in the North was about.

Gold rush Alaska and Yukon emerged from the literature as a unique place in the popular imagination. Like the cowboy stories that were coming to fill a familiar spot in public mythology at the time, stories of the northern gold camps became a recognizable world in the fiction of the era.

By the turn of the century the public obsession with the Klondike had run its course, but the gold rush to the Yukon Valley had already claimed its spot in the literature of the continent. Biographies, personal reminiscences and fictional tales continued to appear though not with the urgency of the early days. Stories of the northern mining camps became an easily recognized branch of frontier fiction, and while the field was not limited to writers who had taken part in the stampede, Klondike veterans certainly dominated the genre.

Of the stories in this collection, Jack London, James B. Hendryx, Joaquin Miller, Rex Beach and Stroller White, like Tappen Adney, were all veterans of the gold rush. Robert Service, who, next to London, was the stampede's best-known storyteller, failed to reach Dawson City until a decade after the gold rush had passed, but he ended up telling some of the genre's most famous tales.

Service had already published his first book of Klondike poems before he even arrived in Dawson, but he stayed there long enough to be thought of as a legitimate Klondike writer. By the time he finally moved on in 1912, he had even published a gold rush novel, *The Trail of '98.* Still, his tales told in verse of Sam McGee, Dangerous Dan McGrew and other colorful characters of the Klondike remained his most lasting gifts to gold rush literature.

Other writers in this collection might well have ventured north themselves though their travels cannot be documented. Riley Allen was a newspaper reporter during the Klondike stampede and wrote about the gold rush for a Seattle paper. Marjorie Pickthall lived for a time on the British Columbia coast. William McLeod Raine, like James B. Hendryx, was best known for his Western stories, but he wrote several tales about the North as well, and undoubtedly traveled there. W.W. Moreland's story, "The Gentleman with the Grindstone," mirrors a legendary tale of the Yukon, so he, too, was probably a Klondike veteran.

Moreland's story, like so many of the best Klondike tales, rides a thin line between fiction and nonfiction. True stories of Alaska and Yukon in the latter years of the nineteenth and first years of the twentieth centuries were tough to improve upon, and gold rush fiction writers like Moreland, London and others often opted to dramatize a bit on what were probably actual events. Stroller White, the greatest humorist of the gold rush, drifts back and forth between fiction and nonfiction, writing some stories that appear to be straight reminiscences and others that are certainly pure fabrication. But truth or fiction makes little difference in most storytelling. After all, it's the tale that's important. The merging of reality and imagination in these stories only points to the legendary proportion that tales of the Yukon Valley have achieved.

Choosing the tales for this collection, then, was an expansive rather than narrowing exercise, with the final selections ranging from Adney's disciplined tale of the original discovery of gold on the Klondike to White's comic recollections of the resulting stampede. Other stories cover the ground between the harsh realities of the North evidenced in London's "To Build a Fire" and the romanticism at the heart of Hendryx's unswerving and undefeatable North-West Mounted Policeman in "Routine Patrol."

Not surprisingly, many of the tales pit men against nature, but they also pit men against themselves and against each other—or more often bring them together as partners in turn of the century versions of male bonding tales. Women, native people and people of color, on the other hand, come off poorly. All played a big part in the historical gold rush but have been dismissed as secondary, stereotypical characters in most of the literature to emerge from it. In like fashion, the Elizabeth Robins' story "The Ice Goes Out," in spite of its genuinely sympathetic portrayal of a trail-formed partnership between an aging Kentucky colonel and young black stampeder, still suffers from the racial insensitivity too often prevalent in the literature of the time. Despite its shortcoming, though, the story still speaks eloquently of a distant place that has become a legendary part of North America. It is included here because the characters overcome the attitudes of their time even if the author did not.

The Klondike Gold Rush captured the imagination of the world in a spectacular way, but, more surprisingly, it has continued to capture the imagination of generations ever since. The image of the northern miner mushing his dog team from Dawson to the camps is as firmly established in our minds today as the cowboy on horseback. A hundred years have passed since the great stampede north, but the adventure and romance of the Klondike Gold Rush loom just as large and as thrilling in our minds as ever.

The Spell of the Yukon

BY ROBERT SERVICE

I WANTED THE GOLD, AND I SOUGHT IT;
    I scrabbled and mucked like a slave.
Was it famine or scurvy—I fought it;
    I hurled my youth into a grave.
I wanted the gold and I got it—
    Came out with a fortune last fall,—
Yet somehow life's not what I thought it,
    And somehow the gold isn't all.
No! There's the land. (Have you seen it?)
    It's the cussedest land that I know,
From the big, dizzy mountains that screen it,
    To the deep, deathlike valleys below.
Some say God was tired when He made it;
    Some say it's a fine land to shun;
Maybe: but there's some as would trade it
    For no land on earth—and I'm one.
You come to get rich (damned good reason),
    You feel like an exile at first;
You hate it like hell for a season,
    And then you are worse than the worst.
It grips you like some kinds of sinning;
    It twists you from foe to a friend;

It seems it's been since the beginning;
    It seems it will be to the end.
I've stood in some mighty-mouthed hollow
    That's plumb-full of hush to the brim;
I've watched the big, husky sun wallow
    In crimson and gold, and grow dim,
Till the moon set the pearly peaks gleaming,
    And the stars tumbled out, neck and crop;
And I've thought that I surely was dreaming,
    With the peace o' the world piled on top.

The summer—no sweeter was ever;
    The sunshiny woods all athrill;
The greyling aleap in the river,
    The bighorn asleep on the hill.
The strong life that never knows harness;
    The wilds where the caribou call;
The freshness, the freedom, the farness—
    O God! how I'm stuck on it all.

The winter! the brightness that blinds you,
    The white land locked tight as a drum,
The cold fear that follows and finds you,
    The silence that bludgeons you dumb.
The snows that are older than history,
    The woods where the weird shadows slant;
The stillness, the moonlight, the mystery,
    I've bade 'em good-bye—but I can't.

There's a land where the mountains are nameless,
    And the rivers all run God knows where;
There are lives that are erring and aimless,
    And deaths that just hang by a hair;
There are hardships that nobody reckons;
    There are valleys unpeopled and still;
There's a land—oh, it beckons and beckons,
    And I want to go back—and I will.

They're making my money diminish;
    I'm sick of the taste of champagne.
Thank God! when I'm skinned to a finish
    I'll pike to the Yukon again.
I'll fight—and you bet it's no sham-fight;

It's hell!—but I've been there before;
And it's better than this by a damsite—
So me for the Yukon once more.
There's gold, and it's haunting and haunting;
It's luring me on as of old;
Yet it isn't the gold that I'm wanting,
So much as just finding the gold.
It's the great, big, broad land 'way up yonder,
It's the forests where silence has lease;
It's the beauty that thrills me with wonder,
It's the stillness that fills me with peace.

The Klondike Stampede

BY TAPPAN ADNEY

Dame Fortune was never in more capricious mood than when the golden treasures of the Klondike were ripe for discovery. The true story of that time, although so recent, is still obscured by the mists of uncertainty and contradiction, and there are still small points which the long and patient investigation I gave to the matter has not been able to clear up—such as exact dates—and it is doubtful that these ever will be. The first news of the discovery that reached the outside—even the official reports of Mr. Ogilvie—generally gave the credit of the discovery entirely to one Carmack, or "McCormick," as the miners call him. The story is fascinating from beginning to end, and in making this contribution to the history of that time I have been animated not less by a desire to gather together the scattered ends of report and hearsay than that tardy credit may be given to another man whom fortune, never more unkind, has thus far deprived of material compensation for a generous act and years of patient work.

The Klondike River had been known for many years, being only six miles from Fort Reliance, McQuesten's first post. According to Lieutenant Frederick Schwatka, who passed its mouth in 1883, it was known to the traders as "Deer River." Both Harper and McQuesten hunted moose in the present Bonanza Creek on the site of Discovery. Sixteen years ago a party of prospectors, among whom was General Carr, now of the State of Washington, camped on the present Eldorado Creek. Other parties passed down the Klondike from the headwaters of Stewart River about the year 1886, but the river from its general appearance was not considered a gold-bearing stream, so year after year it was passed by for the more favored diggings of Forty-Mile and Birch Creek.

In the year 1890, one Joe Ladue, a French Canadian originally from Plattsburg, New York, an agent of the Alaska Commercial Company, decided to establish an independent trading and outfitting post. Recognizing that his only chance was to grow up with a new region, and having faith that other creeks would be discovered as rich as the Forty-Mile diggings, he built the post, including a saw-mill in partnership with Mr. Harper, at the mouth of Sixty-Mile River, and began recommending all new-comers to prospect the bars or surface diggings of the latter stream, but more especially of Indian Creek or River, a stream entering the Yukon on the right or east side about twenty-five miles below his post, and thirty-three above the now abandoned Fort Reliance. For telling so-called "lies," especially about Indian Creek, Ladue was almost driven from Forty-Mile by the irate miners.

In the summer of 1894, among the crowd drawn in by the glowing reports from the Forty-Mile district was one Robert Henderson, hailing from the mines of Aspen, Colorado, of Scotch parentage, but a Canadian by birth, his father being lighthouse-keeper at Big Island, Pictou County, Nova Scotia. He was a rugged, earnest man, some thirty-seven years of age, six feet tall, with clear blue eyes. From boyhood he had been of an adventurous disposition, with a passion for gold-hunting that showed itself even at his Big Island home in solitary excursions about his bleak fisherman's isle, in which "Robbie," as he was called, was always looking for gold. Henderson had but ten cents in his pocket when he reached Ladue's post. Hearing what Ladue was saying about good diggings on Indian River, he said to Ladue: "I'm a determined man. I won't starve. Let me prospect for you. If it's good for me, it's good for you. "Ladue gave him a grub-stake, and Henderson went upon Indian River and found it exactly as Ladue had said. He could make "wages," working the surface bars. On that account, he did not desert it for the just then more popular fields of Forty-Mile and Birch creeks, but determined to try again. With the experience of a miner, he knew that farther on towards the heads of the tributaries of Indian River he would probably find coarse gold, though perhaps not on the surface, as it was on the river. Accordingly, the next summer found Henderson again on Indian River. He pushed on, and found "leaf" gold on what is now known as "Australia Creek," one of the main forks of Indian River, seventy-five or eighty miles from the Yukon, one piece being, he says, as large as his thumbnail. Had he gone up the other fork sufficiently far he would have discovered the rich diggings of Dominion and Sulphur creeks. He returned to Sixty-Mile, and when winter came he put his goods on a sled, returned to Indian River, and went up Quartz Creek, a tributary of Indian River on the north, forty miles from the Yukon. Having had no dogs to help him, it was a very hard trip. It took thirty days for him to reach Quartz Creek. He worked all winter on Quartz Creek, and took out about $500, another $100 and more being taken out later by other parties from the same hole. In the spring he went back up in the direction of Australia Creek, getting only fair prospects, nothing that warranted the "opening up" of a claim. During this time Henderson was alone, having no partner, and depending mainly on the game that fell to his rifle. Returning from the head of the river he went up Quartz Creek again. This time he cast eyes longingly towards the ridge of hill at the head of Quartz Creek separating the waters of Indian River from those of the then almost unknown Klondike River. Crossing over the short, sharp divide (it is so sharp that if a cupful of water were poured upon the crest, one half would run one way, the other half the other way), he dropped down into a deep-cleft valley of a small stream running northward. He prospected, and found eight cents to the pan! That meant "wages"; such a prospect was then considered *good*. Enthusiastic over the find, Henderson went back over the divide. There were about twenty men on Indian River, working mostly on the bars at the mouth of Quartz Creek, some of them doing fairly well. Henderson persuaded three of the men—Ed Munson, Frank Swanson, and Albert Dalton—to go back with him.

The four men took over whip-saws, sawed lumber, built sluice-boxes, and "opened up" a claim in regular fashion about a quarter of a mile below the forks—a spot plainly visible from the divide—and began shovelling in the gold-bearing dirt.

He named the stream "Gold Bottom." It lay parallel with the present Bonanza Creek and entered the Klondike River about nine miles from its mouth. The amount that they shovelled in on Gold Bottom Creek was $750, *and that was the first gold taken out of the Klondike.* It was equally divided between the four men. Now if a person had stood on the crest of the ridge and looked to the westward, he would have seen the valley of another large creek. That creek had never been prospected, but was known as "Rabbit Creek"; it was so close to Gold Bottom Creek that if one knows just the right spot on the divide, the cup of water would run not only into Indian River and Gold Bottom Creek, but also into the source of this "Rabbit Creek." For in this manner the heads of a number of streams lie together, as the spokes of a wheel around the hub.

Early in August the party ran out of provisions, and, leaving the others at work, Henderson went down Indian River and back to Sixty-Mile. There were about a dozen men at the post and at Harper & Ladue's saw-mill, also a party who were on their way to Stewart River. Henderson told them what he had found. He persuaded the Stewart River party to turn back, telling them they would have to look for it, whereas he had *found it.* Ladue at once sent two horses overland with supplies, and all the others went with them excepting Ladue. Henderson repaired his boat, and with some supplies started down river, leaving Ladue to follow him. On account of low water he was unable to return up Indian River; besides, it was nearer by the mouth of the Klondike River.

It was the fishing season. The salmon in the Yukon are very plentiful in August. Chief Isaac's Indians were taking the salmon in weirs and drying them on racks in the sun.

Across from the Indian village and a few hundred yards below the mouth of the river were the tents of a little party consisting of a white man and some Indians—a squaw, two Indian men, and a boy. The white man's name was George Washington Carmack; the squaw was his wife; the Indian men were respectively Skookum Jim and Cultus (worthless) or "Takish"* Charlie, while the boy was named K'neth—all Takish Indians. Charlie was a big chief of the Takish. Jim would have been chief, being the son of the former chief, but among the Takish the descent is through the chief's sister. Jim and Charlie, therefore, though called brothers, were really cousins, and were called brothers-in-law of Carmack. This Carmack was originally a sailor on a man-of-war, but had taken up his abode with the Chilkoots at Dyea and married a Takish wife. Carmack liked the life with the Indians, and it used to be said that one couldn't please him more than to say, "Why, George, you're getting every day more like a Siwash!" "Siwash George" was the name by which he became generally known. Carmack had made excursions over the pass years before, and both he and the Indians, who were his inseparable companions, knew somewhat of mining, though they could hardly be called miners.

Same as Tagish—pronounced Tah-keesk.

Carmack was outfitted by John J. Healy, who was then at Dyea to trade with the Takish and other interior Indians. Carmack built a post, still called "McCormick's Post," situated on the bank of the Yukon, about twenty miles above Five-Finger Rapids. Any one who took the trouble to stop there might have seen fastened against one of the rude log buildings a paper with some writing upon it: "Gone to Forty-Mile for grub." Under the floor they might have found a bear-skin robe and some other things, left there when he started down river on the journey that was to make the name of Klondike known to the whole world. This notice was put up in the summer of 1895.

The white man and Indians secured an outfit at Fort Selkirk from Mr. Harper. The following spring Carmack dropped down to Forty-Mile, but presently returned as far as the mouth of the Klondike for the fishing, where he was joined by his Indians.* They set their nets just below the mouth of the Klondike, and were drying and curing their catch, Indian fashion, when Henderson came along, on his way to Gold Bottom.

As Henderson's boat touched shore he saw Carmack. "There," he thought, "is a poor devil who hasn't struck it." He went down to where Carmack was, told him of his prospects on Gold Bottom, and said to him that he had better come up and stake. At first Carmack did not want to go, but Henderson urged. At length Carmack consented to go, but wanted to take the Klondike Indians up also, as well as his own. Henderson demurred at that, and, being frank, may have said something not complimentary about "Siwashes" in general. It has been reported that Henderson said he "didn't intend to stake the whole Siwash tribe," and he added, "I want to give the preference to my old Sixty-Mile friends." What effect this may have had on subsequent events I do not know; I can only surmise that it did have some.

Next morning Henderson went on to his claim on Gold Bottom. Carmack with two Indians followed soon, but, instead of taking the circuitous route by the mouth of Gold Bottom, went up "Rabbit Creek." Carmack arrived soon after Henderson, and showed some "colors" of gold that he had found on "Rabbit Creek." "Colors" and "pay" are by no means to be confounded. Traces, or "colors," of gold are to be found almost everywhere. The Indians and Carmack staked each a claim on Gold Bottom. When they were ready to go, Henderson asked Carmack if he intended to prospect on the way

*Another white man, named Fritz Kloke, was also there fishing, and was drying fish under a rough shed of poles covered with canvas, which may be called the first white man's building on the site of what is now Dawson

back, to which he replied that he did. Then Henderson asked him, if he found anything, to send back one of his Indians; saying that he had gold, and that he would pay him for the trouble; which, Henderson asserts, Carmack said he would do.

Leaving Henderson and his partners at work, Carmack returned homeward as he came. A few miles' walk along the bald crest of the divide brought him into the forks of "Rabbit Creek," some distance from its head. Five miles beyond, in the thick spruce-timbered valley, a tributary about as large as "Rabbit Creek" puts in on the left-hand side.

About half a mile below this large tributary the party stopped to rest. They had been panning here and there. Carmack, it is said, went to sleep; Skookum Jim, taking the pan, went to the "rim" of the valley at the foot of a birch-tree and filled it with dirt. Washing it in the creek, he found a large showing of gold. Right "under the grass-roots," Jim said, he found from ten cents to one dollar to the pan. In a little while, it is said, they filled a shot-gun cartridge with coarse gold. A strange circumstance was that this gold was not from bed-rock, which was many feet below the surface, nor even the present creek-bed, but, unsuspected by them, had slid down from the "bench," or hill-side, a kind of diggings which were unknown at that time. Carmack staked off Discovery (a double claim) for himself, and five hundred feet above and below for his two Indian companions, Skookum Jim taking No. 1 above Discovery, and Cultus Charlie No. 1 below. The date of this is variously given as the 16th and 17th of August, the former date being generally regarded as the probable one.

After staking, they hastened to Forty-Mile, forgetting their promise to Henderson, who by every moral right was entitled to a claim near the rich ground they undoubtedly had discovered. They recorded their claims before Inspector Constantine, the recorder or acting gold commissioner, and named the creek "Bonanza."

Carmack's own story of "$2.50 to the pan" was not believed, though it was not doubted that he had found gold. A stampede followed. Drunken men were thrown into boats. One man was tied and made to go along. But there was no excitement beyond what attends a stampede for locations on any creek on which gold has been found. There are always persons about a mining camp ready to start on a stampede simply as a chance, whether good prospects have been found or not. Whole creeks have been staked out in the belief that gold would subsequently be found. So the excitement of this earlier stage was of small significance. It was that of the professional "stampeder," so to speak—rounders about the saloons, some new arrivals, but few old miners, the latter being still in the diggings up the creek.

The first persons to arrive at the scene of the new discovery began staking down-stream. That also was a "stampeder's" custom. The chances were considered better there than above. It is all nonsense, the talk now of persons who would have one believe they "got in on choice locations" by reason of superior foresight. It was blind luck. The staking went on down-stream for six miles, and then began above, and continued for seven or eight miles up-stream before the side gulches, or "pups," as they are called, were thought of seriously.

Ladue, who had started for the mouth of the Klondike behind Henderson, was among the first to hear of Carmack's strike. Ladue staked a town-site at the mouth of the Klondike and started for Forty-Mile, but, meeting a man who wanted some lumber, he sent on his application by another party, returning to the mill at Sixty-Mile, and soon after returned to the mouth of the Klondike with nails, spikes, and lumber, built a rough warehouse, just opposite the present Alaska Commercial Company's warehouse, 22 x 40 feet, and a cabin—the first in Dawson—the name given the new town by the surveyor, Mr. Ogilvie, in honor of his chief, Dr. George M. Dawson, director of the Canadian Geological Survey. The Alaska Commercial Company's steamer *Arctic* having by this time reached Forty-Mile, bound for Fort Selkirk, pushed on through the ice that was running in the river to the new town, arriving in September with a few miners and a very limited amount of supplies. After discharging, she hurried back to Forty-Mile, but was frozen in before she could be placed in a safe place, and the next spring, in trying to get her free of the ice before she was crushed, a stick of dynamite, intended for the ice, destroyed her.

Among the first to hear of the strike were four men from up river—Dan McGilvray, Dave McKay, Dave Edwards, and Harry Waugh—and they located Nos. 3, 14, 15, and 16 below Discovery. These men did the *first sluicing* that was done on the creek, and they made the first clean-up, with five boxes set. The figures are lacking for their first shovelling, but on the second they cleaned up thirteen and a half ounces of gold ($329.50), being five hours' work of one man shovelling. The gold varied from the size of pinheads to nuggets, one of $12 being found. Now the Klondike magnifier began his work, with this curious result, that the "lies" of to-day were surpassed by the truth of to-morrow, until it came to be accepted that, "You can't tell no lies about Klondike." McGilvray and the rest had perhaps $1500—surely a large sum for the time they had worked. Ladue weighed the gold, and as he came out of the store he said to some assembled miners, "How's that for two and a half days' shovelling-in—$4008?" The liability to exaggeration about a mining camp is so great that it is impossible for any one to escape who writes or speaks in the midst of affairs concerning any specific find. A man with a town-site must also be allowed a great deal of latitude in such matters. But soon the joke was on the other side. Men actually on the spot would not believe anything they heard. Two of the men working on Indian River came down and heard of the strike. Said one to his partner, "Shall we go up and stake?" Replied the other, "Why, I wouldn't go across the river on that old Siwash's word" (meaning Carmack). They went on down to Forty-Mile. Another party, one of whom was Swan Peterson, who bought in on No. 33 Eldorado, came along at the same time, and argued for three hours at the mouth of the Klondike whether they should go up, and finally went on to Circle City.

There were few old-timers in the procession. *They* knew all about Klondike. It was nothing but a "moose-pasture." It was not like other places where they had seen gold. They climbed the hills and walked along the divide until they could look down into the valley of Bonanza. Here many of them stopped and threw up their hands in disgust. Others went the round of the creek, cursing and swearing at those who told them to come there. One old-timer got up as far as No. 20 above, where the last stakes were. He surveyed the prospect, and as he turned away remarked, "I'll leave it to the Swedes." (The Swedes were supposed to be willing to work the poorest ground.) Another, or it may have been the same, is said to have written on the stakes of No. 21, not the usual "I claim," etc., but, *"This moose-pasture is reserved for the Swedes and Chechahkoes."* Louis Rhodes staked it right afterwards. After he had written his name he said to his companions, being ashamed of staking in such a place, that he would cut his name off for two bits (25 cents). The next summer he took out forty-four thousand and odd dollars.

But all that and much more was hidden in the future. A Klondike claim was not considered worth anything. One-half interest in one of the richest Eldorado claims was sold for a sack of flour. A few thousand dollars could have bought up the creek from end to end.

Some who had provisions remained to prospect, others returned to Forty-Mile, just as the miners were coming in from the diggings, to learn for the first time of a strike on Klondike. Among these was a Swede by the name of Charlie Anderson. By the time Anderson reached the new diggings there was nothing left. After a fruitless attempt to reach a distant creek from which gold had been reported, he returned discouraged to Dawson. There a gambler approached him and said, "Charlie, don't you want to buy a claim?" "I don't care if I do. How much do you want?" "I'll let you have No. 29 on Eldorado for $800." "I'll take it," replied Anderson, who had taken out a considerable sum that summer from a claim on Miller Creek, at the head of Sixty-Mile River, and he weighed out the dust. The enterprising salesman went about boasting how he had played Charlie for a "sucker," only he wanted some one to kick him for not having asked him $1200. He believed he could have got it just as easily as he did the $800. The man who sold the claim is still a poor man. When Eldorado began to "prove up," even Anderson could not realize the enormous value of his claim, from which there will come out $400,000, if the remaining two-fifths are as rich as the three-fifths that have been worked thus far. Eldorado was not liked as well as Adams Creek, just below it. A late-comer went up Adams, found a man staking for himself and family (by this time the real excitement had begun). Said the late-comer: "I've come a good way. What you are doing is illegal, and I want a claim and mean to have one." The man who was staking told him he would like to have his friends near him, and offered him the stakes of No. 15 Eldorado, if that would do as well. It was accepted. Nothing more than "wages" has yet been found on Adams.

How was the news of the Klondike discovery received on the lower river? Forty-Mile, the seat of the recorder, was of course the first to hear all the reports and rumors. This can best be told in the words of one who was in Forty-Mile town at the time. "Nobody believed any of the first reports about gold on the Klondike. You see, there never was any money in the lower country. A man would come in after a hard summer's work with a 'poke' *sack* that a man would be ashamed of here in Dawson. They owed the stores for their last year's outfit, and they'd pay for that and get credit on next year's outfit. The stores had rather have it that way than not. They were sure a man would not leave the country without paying, or with a small stake, so they'd be sure sooner or later of getting all he made. They were a pretty good class of men in the lower country, and most of them could get credit. A man would come into a saloon, and all he'd have would be one drink or one dance. You'd never see them asking up three or four at once to drink. Why, there weren't but three men in Forty-Mile that could afford to get drunk. They did nothing all winter but sit around where it was warm, playing pedro, solitaire, and casino. Word came to Forty-Mile that Louis Rhodes had two men working for him, and was getting good pay. 'That's a lie,' said one man. 'Louis Rhodes! when was *he* able to hire two men?' Next word came down that Ben Wall was getting two-bit dirt. 'Hell!' says Nigger Jim; 'I've known Ben Wall these ten years, and he's the all-firedest liar in the Yukon.' When they heard that Berry was getting $1 to the pan, they laughed. Klondike was a bunco—nothing but a bunco." These words were spoken in what the miners called "josh," but they were true, nevertheless.

Circle City, 170 miles farther away than Forty-Mile, did not get the news so soon. The first report that reached Circle was of a discovery on Klondike—an ounce to the "shovel," shovelling off the surface. This, in miners parlance, meant that one man had shovelled into the sluice-boxes gold to the value of one ounce ($17) per day. The next news was when Sam Bartlett came down with a raft of logs which he had failed to land at Forty-Mile. Bartlett said it was a "bilk"; that Joe Ladue was only trying to get men up to his town-site—he had stopped there, but would not stake. The next news came to Oscar Ashby, a saloon-keeper, from a friend, about the middle of November. The river was then closed, and the letter came down over the ice.* There were about seventy-five men in Oscar's saloon when the letter was read. It was somewhat to this effect, telling Ashby to buy all the property he could on Klondike, it did not make any difference what the prices were: "This is one of the richest strikes in the world. It is a worldbeater. I can't tell how much gold we are getting to the pan. I never saw or heard of the like of such a thing in my life. I myself saw $150 panned out of one pan of dirt, and I think they are getting as high as $1000." The crowd in the saloon had a big laugh, and thought so little of it that they never spoke of it again. "It disgusted them that men were so crazy as to write that way," to quote the words of one who was present. Soon after another letter came. This time it was to Harry Spencer and Frank Densmore, from a party with whom they

*Tom O'Brien and the general manager of the Alaska Commercial Company made the 250 trail-miles or more in a few hours over five days, travelling light, with basket sleigh and dogs—a record trip.

were well acquainted. Densmore at once fitted out a dog-team and went up. After he got up he wrote back to Spencer, relating all the particulars. He repeated the words of the others—namely, that he really could not tell what they *were* finding: it was immensely rich; he had never seen anything like it. Now Spencer and Densmore had large interests in Circle City, so the men knew it could be no lie; they were compelled to believe it. The wildest stampede resulted. Every dog that could be bought, begged, or stolen was pressed into service, and those who could not get dogs started hauling their own sleds, men and even women, until in two weeks there were not twenty people left in Circle, and of those some were cripples and could not travel. In a short while there were not even that number left, a report giving the actual number as two men and one woman. Those who had claims deserted them, and those who had outfits took what they could haul and left the rest in a cache, where they are to this day. One man, William Farrel, of No. 60 above on Bonanza, left a thousand dollars' worth of provisions, five full claims on one creek, and fully a dozen other interests, all considered good prospects; and, says he, "I haven't paid any attention to them since." By the time the Circle City crowd arrived Bonanza was staked to No. 60 below and into the 60's above, and also the side creeks, Eldorado and Adams. So that the late-comers had to go into the side-gulches, or else buy in, which latter many of them did, so that on such as Eldorado it soon came about that few of the original stakers were left, having sold out at ridiculous prices.

There were from three to four hundred miners at work about Circle City, and nearly all had money, the United States mint returns giving the amount of gold cleaned up that season in Birch Creek as $900,000!

The first mail that went outside by dog-team carried letters to friends and relatives, advising them that a big strike had been made. It reached them in January and February, and they started. Crossing the pass in spring, they came down on the high-water in June, and, though unable to get in on the main creeks, many of them located other creeks that are showing up rich. That the report of a strike of this magnitude should have been common property outside six months before the excitement is clear proof that the world's acute attack of insanity was caused by the adroit manipulation of the story of the miners' arrival by sensational newspapers, as the result of rivalry and to boom the Alaska outfitting business.

But where were Henderson and his partners while Bonanza and Eldorado were being staked?

Bonanza was staked into the 80's above and Eldorado to No. 33—or over three miles—when a party of miners, including George Wilson and James McNamee, went over the divide to Gold Bottom, where Henderson was still working.

Henderson asked them where they were from. They replied, "Bonanza Creek."

Henderson says that he did not want to display his ignorance. He had never heard of "Bonanza" Creek. At length he ventured to ask where "Bonanza" Creek was. They pointed over the hill.

"'Rabbit Creek!' What have you got there?"

"We have the biggest thing in the world."

"Who found it?"

"McCormick."

It is said Henderson threw down his shovel and went and sat on the bank, so sick at heart that it was some time before he could speak.

There was nothing left for Henderson. Many another man would have been utterly discouraged. It is true, however, that there was very rich ground for a mile farther up on Eldorado, but the extent of the richness of the new creeks was not then suspected. Nor did Henderson's ill-fortune end here. He had been over the ridge, upon a large fork of Gold Bottom, and made discoveries, one of which amounted to 35 cents to the pan. He staked a claim there, according to the law then in force—one full claim, and another to which he was entitled by virtue of discovery. After cleaning up on Gold Bottom and dividing the money between his partners, he staked a discoverer's double claim and started for Forty-Mile, as winter was coming on. On the way he met Andrew Hunker, a German by birth, who had staked and recorded No. 31 below on Bonanza Creek, and Charles Johnson, an Ohio man, who had staked No. 43 below on the same creek. They told Henderson that they had made a discovery of $3 to the pan on the other fork of Henderson's "Gold Bottom." They had staked between them Discovery and No. 1 above and No. 1 below, on September 6th. This was two miles below Henderson's discovery. They told Henderson they thought he could not hold Discovery as against them, and as their new find was apparently better than his own, he staked No. 3 above. This fork was first called Hunker's Fork of Gold Bottom, and was so shown on maps of that time. But as the subsequent staking began at Hunker's discovery, the whole creek to its mouth at the Klondike was recorded as Hunker Creek, Gold Bottom becoming a fork of Hunker Creek. At Bear Creek, between Hunker and the Yukon, where Solomon Marpak, a Russian Finn, had just made a discovery, Henderson stopped and staked a claim. When he reached Forty-Mile, Henderson learned that instead of being allowed a claim on each separate creek, a new mining regulation just received from Ottawa provided that no person could hold more than one claim in a mining "district," the Klondike River and all its tributaries being considered a "district." Sixty days from the time of staking was allowed in which to record, and Henderson applied, he maintains, within the time, and there is no reason for doubting his general statement. Although his record is imperfect, much latitude must be allowed men who are isolated for months and necessarily have hazy ideas of dates. In general there is no doubt but that at the time Henderson drove his stakes he was entitled to either four or five claims, according as he chose his locations, on Hunker Creek, and the law which thus deprived him came into force between the time he staked and the day he reached Forty-Mile. And, I would ask, how could Henderson— and I would include all of his class, the hardy prospectors who were the real developers of the Yukon, who have given to Canada all that is at present shown to be of value there—how could he have made the original discoveries, that paved the way for the development of the great riches of Klondike, if he had remained, say, at Forty-Mile town, where he could have kept posted on changes in the mining law made from time to time at Ottawa?

Hunker's discovery being better than his own, Henderson recorded No. 3 alone. He was laid up that winter, unable to work, from an injury he met with on Indian River. In the spring, far from being disheartened, and with energy and faith characteristic of the man, he took his tools, boat, and some provisions and went up the Klondike forty miles, to a large tributary then called "Too Much Gold," but known now as "Flat" Creek, prospecting. He soon returned and proceeded to a large creek, two miles below the mouth of Stewart River, and, eleven miles above the mouth of the creek, made a discovery of 10 cents to the pan, the creek being subsequently named "Henderson" Creek. From there he ascended the Stewart River a long distance, prospecting. Being favorably impressed by the outlook, he staked a town-site at the mouth of McQuesten Creek, eighty miles from the mouth of Stewart, and on his return made an application for the same to Ottawa. For some cause he received no reply to the application. (The town-site has since been taken up and stores built there.) Returning to the new camp which had sprung up at the mouth of the Klondike, he took steamer, intending to leave the country, but was frozen in with the rest of the refugees at Circle City. He was under the doctor's care all winter. Obliged to realize some money, he sold No. 3 above Discovery on Hunker Creek for $3000— a mere fraction of its value. Henderson, miner that he is, would have worked this claim had he been able to do so, and he would still have found himself in possession of a comfortable fortune, and thereby received some compensation for his many discouragements.

Although he did not himself make the discovery on Bonanza, he was yet the direct cause and means of that discovery being made. He was not the victim of his own negligence or failure to grasp an opportunity. He created the opportunity, and was prevented from profiting by it. It is beside the point, but yet of interest, that I have it, on Henderson's own word, which I am not disposed to question, that it was his intention, when done with Gold Bottom, to go down Rabbit Creek prospecting. When the news of the wonderful richness of Bonanza burst upon the world, Henderson was forgotten. Mr. Ogilvie, then at Forty-Mile, kept his government posted concerning the developments of that fall. Mr. Ogilvie gave the best information at his command. Carmack had made the discovery on Bonanza Creek: Henderson's part was not then understood, and Henderson was no man to press himself forward. But later Mr. Ogilvie gave the man full credit in the following words:

> "The Klondike was prospected for forty miles up in 1887, without anything being found, and again in 1893, with a similar lack of result; but the difference is seen when the right course is taken, and this was led up to by Robert Henderson. This man is a born prospector, and you could not persuade him to stay on even the richest claim on Bonanza. He started up in a small boat to spend this summer and winter on Stewart River prospecting. This is the stuff the true prospector is made of, and I am proud to say he is a Canadian."*

Extract from Victoria Colonist, November 6, 1897.

When I first met Henderson I was impressed by the earnestness of the man. I asked him if he was not discouraged by all that had happened.

"No," replied he, "there are as rich mines yet to be discovered as any that have been found."

I was not quite sure that he believed that, but it was characteristic of the man to say so.

In October, 1898, I saw Henderson for the last time. He had just reached Seattle from the Yukon. Unsuspicious and trusting, he had been robbed on the steamer of all the money he had—$1100. He had one thing left. It was the golden (carpenter's) rule and myrtle-leaves badge of the Yukon Order of Pioneers, of which he was a member. For some reason he insisted on pinning it himself upon my vest, saying, "You keep this. I will lose it too. I am not fit to live among civilized men." He returned to Aspen, where his wife and child were, to work again at the same mine where he worked six years ago, before he went into the Yukon. Surely, if the Minister of the Interior could from Ottawa grant hundreds of miles of claims, supposed to be of great value, to men who never saw and never will see the Yukon, surely it would be a graceful act for him yet to do something for this man, who scorns to be a beggar and to whom the offer of a pension would be an insult as long as he can tramp and dig and look. Canada owes not less to Henderson than California to Marshall, the discoverer of gold at Sutter's mill.

The miners who knew have always given Henderson credit. "Siwash George would be fishing yet at the mouth of the Klondike if it hadn't been for Bob Henderson."

The Gentleman with the Grindstone

BY W. W. MORELAND

THERE WAS GREAT BUSTLE and activity at the ocean steamship wharf in Seattle, Washington, one afternoon about the first of April, 1896. The restless vessel which lay at the dock with steam up and hissing, with screw turning, and with the stem and stern lines alternately tightening and loosening, was about to start to the southwest coast of Alaska, the voyage to end at a point about one hundred miles above Juneau; and most of the persons who were collected on the ship and dock were to become passengers at that point. The end of the sea voyage was not, however, the final destination of the passengers. It was only to be the first and easiest stage of their Journey. From that port they were about to seek their fortunes over the mountains and in the interior of that little known land. They were bound for the mythical land of gold.

For a good many years it had been known that gold existed in placers along the coast; in some places in sufficient quantities to pay for the working; and during the same period of time, vague and uncertain rumors of the existence of the precious metal in mines of fabulous wealth along the banks of the Yukon and its tributaries, had periodically found their way to the outside world. Undeterred by the stories of hardship and starvation suffered by others, the first of which must, and the second might await them, these restless men were willing to brave the dangers of the mountain pass, of the river rapids, the cold and severity of an Arctic climate, and more than all, the possibility of starvation should their stock of provisions become exhausted before the return of the short summer. It was a motley throng. The boy just out of school, the bewhiskered man of middle age, the large and strong, the small and delicate looking, the learned

and the illiterate, elbowed and jostled each other or
ship. Though their ages, their appearances, and then
were so diverse, there was a similarity in their "outfits" and the
plies." The freight, nearly all of which at the time our narrative open
had passed over the ship's side, consisted almost altogether of flour,
tea, sugar coffee, bacon and beans, and of miners picks, shovels, pans,
and axes; and from the character of the baggage, lugged and carried
aboard with difficulty by the passengers, it seemed that each had,
beside what he wore, a heavy overcoat, boots, an extra suit of heavy
clothing, three pair of blankets, and underclothing to match. Before
depositing it on the ship, each passenger brought his baggage to the
scales to have it weighed. In nearly every case the weight went to the
full limit,—one hundred and fifty pounds. Toward the last, when
nearly all had been weighed and disposed of, a much smaller package
was placed on the scales by the expressman who had brought it to the
wharf. It weighed scant sixty pounds.

"You travel light for a man who is going to the Arctic," said
the weigher.

"The baggage does not belong to me, but to the gentleman
over there," pointing to a man who was standing a short distance
down the wharf, calmly smoking a cigar, and looking up the street.

The person designated was alone; no friends were taking
leave of him; and like many others, he was to all appearances only a
casual spectator who had, in passing, been attracted by the unusual
sight, and was idly looking on to while away the time. His face was
fresh and smoothly shaven, his hands were small and white; he seemed
to be well preserved, apparently, had never been enured to hardships,
and was too neatly dressed for a man who proposed to "rough it." He
seemed also to have the aspect and bearing of one of those few persons
whom fortune, good or bad, could neither exalt nor cast down.

"If he is the owner, let him come forward and present his
ticket," said the weigher.

At this the smooth faced gentleman came forward, deliberately presented his ticket, and very quietly said, "Please mark the
weight of my baggage on the back."

This done, though it was hardly "regular," he said to the
expressman, "Take the baggage on the ship."

That gentleman, with an inward remonstrance at being
asked to do more than his contract required, carried it up the gang-

plank and deposited in the bow with the other baggage. The smooth faced gentleman resumed his position on the wharf, together with his far-away look up the street. At least the noise and confusion incident to the departure of a vessel on a long voyage, with an unusual purpose, had died out; those "not going" had been warned by the gong to go ashore; leaves had been taken, and apparently the last passenger was aboard and the lines were about to be cast loose. The gentleman on the wharf was still looking up the street, with a trace of anxiety and impatience in his countenance, when an express wagon came dashing toward the steamer with extraordinary speed, and the driver was hastily about to deposit at the feet of the silent gentleman a grindstone and a small box which it was afterward ascertained contained an ax, an auger, and about one half pound of assorted wire nails.

"Hold on; take them on board the ship!"

The driver, thinking no doubt to make amends for his tardiness, started up the gangplank with his heavy burden.

"Take that back!" came in stentorian tones from the officer in charge. "We want no grindstones on board this vessel."

The imperturbable man, who was just behind the expressman, said in a soft and quiet voice: "Go ahead; I will make it all right"; and turning to the mate, he said: "Your rules allow one hundred and fifty pounds of baggage to each passenger; what I have had put on board weighs only sixty pounds. I claim this grindstone, which only weighs eighty-five pounds, as you can see by the mark on it, as a part of my personal baggage."

The officer in charge, astonished by this unexpected proposition, was about to enter into an argument as to whether or not a grindstone was personal baggage, when the captain, who was on the bridge, and impatient at the delay, shouted, "Why don't you cast off?"

The mate solved the question by dropping it, and calling back to the captain, "Aye, aye, sir," the lines were cast off, and the expressman leaped ashore.

It is proverbial that acquaintanceship on a sea-going vessel on a long voyage, is quickly formed and made. The proverb was more than justified in this instance. It is true that on our vessel there were a few parties, of two or three, who came from the same town or vicinity. These of course needed no introductions. But our passengers being all men, and generally from the West, with a common object in view, and expecting to meet and overcome the same obstacles and endure the same hardships, it is not surprising that soon everybody knew everybody else. The thin ice of reserve began to break even while the baggage was being stored away. It began in each stateroom between those who had been assigned to it. It commenced by the lower berth saying, "How do you do?" to the upper. The upper not only recognized and answered the salutation, but further ventured to say, "I think we are going to have a fine trip." Then the middle chipped in and proved itself to be an ice-breaker, by saying, "I suppose you two gentlemen are starting out to seek your fortunes the same as myself?" These observations, and such as these, were ordinarily commonplace enough, but they served the useful purpose of paving the way to the more important plans and communications which followed.

After a bit, when they began to leave the rooms and come on deck, the gregariousness of the human kind manifested itself by the passengers gathering in little knots; the occupants of one stateroom introducing themselves to those of another; and it was not a great while before nearly every person on board was acquainted with every other. On the second and third days out, parties of four and five were formed who were to travel together; and before the voyage was ended many partnerships to live, prospect, and mine, together were entered into.

"It's no trick at all," said Mr. Sandy Dalton, formerly of Mokelumne Hill, "to get acquainted."

Mr. Jagsey Smith, whose proper, if not baptismal name was Aaron, and who since he has been raised to the dignity of a "grub-staker" by the favor of a well-to-do brother-in-law, had had his name inscribed on the passenger list by the latter cognomen, concurred in the truthfulness of the observation, with an exception.

"Blame my skin," said Jagsey, "I can't tumble to thet feller with th' smooth face. I passed him as we was comin' out o' th' Straits an' I says to him, 'How d'y do?' an he on'y nodded his head. An' th' nex' day as we wus a settin' at th' table an' I wus a tryin' to show my p'liteness, an' seein' th' biled meat wusn't on his side, I kinder keerless like ast him if he would hev some, an' he on'y drapped his coconut as befor'. He's a queer duck, I'm a-tellin' ye."

"Yes," said Judge Sinclair, formerly of San Bernardino, "he is a peculiar character; he appears to be very diffident; yet I dare say he would like to make friends. We must try to make it as pleasant for him as possible; we must cultivate his acquaintance. Every man has his good points, and we must try to find his."

Whereupon Judge Sinclair was deputed to interview the gentleman, and bring him into the fold of goodfellowship. This task the Judge was not long in undertaking. Strolling along the deck in a careless manner, he met the gentleman referred to, and casually bade him good morning. The stranger returned the salutation. The Judge then ventured to make the usual remark about the weather; the stranger assented.

The Judge still persisting, said, "I suppose you have the same object in view that the rest of us have, and that you expect to find a rich claim?"

The gentleman replied that he did not expect to engage in mining, yet he hoped to make some money before his return.

"The fact is," he said, "I have never worked, and I would not know how to go about working in a mine, or do any other kind of labor, for that matter."

The Judge pursued the conversation further, but did not acquire much information. The gentleman was polite and agreeable, in his way, but did not seem to be communicative on the point on which the Judge wished to draw him out, and on which all the others were very loquacious. When the Judge reported the result of the conversation to the group, the consensus of opinion was that he was a gambler, and that he was following the crowd for the purpose of plying his vocation.

During the remainder of the voyage, when he was spoken of, he was called the "Stranger." Out of this throng of more than one hundred men; coming from all parts of the country, and who had met but four days ago, there was but one who was a stranger. All the others were acquaintances, and many were already warm friends.

The shore at the head of Lynn canal was strewn with tons of freight, stores, baggage, and impediments of various kinds. A semblance of order had been evolved out of the great mass of personal belongings, but they were still badly mixed. Tents had been erected, and some were engaged in cooking their first meal ashore, or for that matter, at any other place. Others were still seeking to disentangle individual stores from the great mass on the shore. The outline of the vessel, which had left them on this spot, and the only thing which bound them to home and friends, had disappeared on the horizon. The spot on which they were encamped was a fairly good stopping place, though they were somewhat cramped for room. Snow covered the towering mountains in the immediate rear, and the inlet was in front, with a narrow fringe of comparatively level between.

Amid all this stir and preparation in the camp, there was one who did not seem to be troubling himself about meals or camping facilities. The "Stranger" whom we met on board the ship, as night came on, had settled himself down to rest under an Alaskan spruce, where his personal belongings, including the grindstone, had been first placed. It is true that a few Alaskan Indians, many of whom were circulating about the camp, had been seen talking to him; but otherwise he had no communication with any human being.

As night and darkness drew on, the noises, except the baying and fighting of the Kamchatcan dogs in the immediate vicinity, had died away, and the adventurers slept the sleep of the tired. After many days of tossing on the ocean it is sweet to enjoy the rest which only mother earth can afford. With the dawning of a new day, however, all was work and activity. Every group and "partnership" were preparing for the journey up the stream and over the dangerous pass, which would lead them to the waters of a succession of lakes whose final outlet was the great Yukon river of the Northwest.

As breakfast was about to be announced Judge Sinclair remarked to those about him, "Boys, I don't like to see the 'Stranger' over there all alone. Last night as I passed his camp he was eating dry crackers, and I believe that is the only grub he has. I propose we ask him to breakfast."

It was so agreed, and the Judge went over with the invitation. It was quietly and politely accepted, and the stranger took his seat on the ground around the coffee pot and frying pan, with the others.

It was a plain but substantial camper's meal; and as they warmed up under its influence, conversation began to flow. It very naturally turned upon the work before them, the difficulties of the mountain pass over which they proposed to travel, and whether they should employ Indians to carry the goods.

Sandy Dalton thought they should try to transport the goods themselves "Of course, boys," he said, "we are not as expert at that kind of business as the Indians, nor as hardened; it may go a little hard with us at the first, seeing that we are soft, but we shall have to get used to this kind of work, and many other kinds, and we might just as well commence now. I am willing to do my part, and to shoulder as much as I can reasonably carry and start up the hill."

"Leadville Joe" was of the opinion that if they would take their time, carry a moderate load a short distance and then rest, and go on again, they would get the stuff over the mountains almost as quick as the Indians could do it. "By doing the work ourselves," he said, "we will save a whole lot of money, and you all know it might come in handy before we get back."

And so it fell out that they would at least make the attempt to transport their goods over the pass.

While the foregoing discussion was being carried on the "Stranger" had remained silent, except to acknowledge politely the invitations to partake of the dishes which were pressed upon him.

Jagsey Smith, who between the satisfaction of his appetite and the deference due his superiors, had heretofore no opportunity to join in the conversation; but now being unable to restrain himself longer, turned to the "Stranger" and addressed to him this preamble, followed by an interrogatory:—

"Mister, we all com' up on th' ship, includin' yerself; an' we got so well acquented that we know purty near everybody's name; 'xcept yourn. What may it be?"

The "Stranger," not directing his remarks to Jagsey in particular, but to the group, and speaking as though it were a matter on which they were entitled to information, and on which, in view of the relations which they now sustained, and which they might hereafter sustain toward each other, he evidently thought it his duty to enlighten them, said quietly and deliberately: "Gentlemen, my name is Whizzer, Nickelby Whizzer. My parents gave me a fair education but little else. I am a native of Connecticut, but came West several years ago to seek my fortune. Since then I have been thrown mainly on my own resources I have not been an entire failure, neither have I forged ahead to any great extent. The rumors of gold mines somewhere in the interior of Alaska coming to my ears, as it has to yours, I thought I would try my luck there. I have brought no supplies and but little clothing with me; and I had hoped to attach myself to a party and pay it what it was reasonably worth for my board and transportation while on the trip. It would be useless for me to have provisions, for I do not know how to cook, and don't think I could learn. I have never worked, and know but little about it."

It was an ill-advised thing for Mr. Whizzer, as he had just introduced himself, to proclaim his inability, if not his aversion, to labor, to men in their situation; and no one realized this more than Mr. Whizzer. But he thought it best to tell the truth at the start. He reasoned that it were better for them to know it now than to find it out afterwards.

After a long silence, produced by the novelty and boldness of the proposition, Judge Sinclair, not assuming to speak for the company, as he expressly declared, replied: "Your proposition, sir," he said, "is a very extraordinary one. This company will have great difficulty in getting over the pass with its own goods, and could not, in my opinion, think for a moment of assisting one who asserts that he is unable, and I might say unwilling, to do his part. I can conceive of no place in a camp, or in a new country, for a man who is unable and unwilling to labor. Every man in this company has agreed, as you have heard, to do his full share of the work; and from the size of our packs and the height and steepness of yonder mountain there will be plenty of it, God knows."

The rest of the party warmly concurred in the sentiments which the Judge had just expressed, and Mr. Whizzer's proposition was thus unanimously rejected.

After the sense of the meeting had been taken in the manner above stated, Mr. Whizzer said, "Gentlemen, I think you have partially misunderstood me. I did not expect you gentlemen, nor any one else, to carry my pack without pay. The objection the Judge has made is a very reasonable one and I have anticipated it. I have employed three natives to carry my meager belongings to the lake on the other side. One of them will carry my blankets and clothing, and the others will transport my grindstone,—"

Sandy Dalton: "Grindstone?"

Leadville Joe: "What, a grindstone?"

Jagsey: "Well, blame my skin if—"

The Judge had been trained in a profession where he had learned not readily to give way to surprises, and he said nothing; but notwithstanding his self control, his jaw dropped, and he stared at Mr. Whizzer with a look of astonishment.

Just at the very moment that Mr. Jagsey Smith was calling down imprecations on his cuticle, as above, a team of untrained dogs which had been brought up on the steamer, and which at an adjoining camp were being given their first lesson in the traction of a sled, bolted and ran pell-mell into our group, tripped up Jagsey and piled up, one confused mass of harness, sled, and growling, fighting, and writhing dogs, in and about the remnant of the fire which had shortly before served the useful purpose of cooking the breakfast. This diversion turned the thoughts of the crowd into other channels, and the mystery of the grindstone was unsolved.

When quiet had been partially restored Mr. Whizzer took his departure, and turning to the group said, "I suppose I shall meet you again at the lake on the other side."

The transportation of the grindstone over the mountains was the great problem which had disturbed the equanimity of Mr. Whizzer since the evening before; at which time the Indians had declined to carry it. They argued, with great truth and plausibility, that owing to its peculiar shape and cumbersomeness it would be impossible to get it over the mountain unless it were broken into two parts. Now the breaking of the stone was the one thing Mr. Whizzer would never consent to. So, after due reflection and consideration, Mr. Whizzer, by the aid of his small ax, into which he had put a temporary handle, cut and fitted a ten foot pole of tough wood into the square hole in the middle of the grindstone, and tightly wedged it so that five feet of the pole would be at each side. By this means, one Indian could shoulder the end of the pole in the front and the other behind, and thus dividing the weight, transport it without difficulty.

The exodus of Mr. Whizzer from Lynn canal was the most picturesque that had ever been witnessed at that place. The two natives carrying the grindstone in the manner above described, reinforced with about twenty five pounds each of flour and bacon, which Mr. Whizzer had purchased at the landing, followed by the Indian with the clothing and blankets, and the rear brought up with the box containing the ax, auger, and nails, which Mr. Whizzer in defiance of his resolution not to labor had himself concluded to carry, presented a picture at once unique and interesting in that section.

It is useless to narrate the numerous perils and difficulties encountered by the party in reaching Lake Lindeman. Suffice it to say, that in the afternoon of the third day they reached the navigable waters of the lake; and Mr. Whizzer being the first arrival for the season, selected the most eligible camping place. Finding a piece of rough board near by, which no doubt had been left by some party of the previous year, he marked upon it with charcoal "Camp No. 1" and nailed it to the nearest tree.

The natives, after initiating Mr. Whizzer into the mysteries of ash cake and bacon broiling, returned to Lynn canal in search of more business, and Mr. Whizzer was left alone.

It was certainly not a very desirable situation. The earth was covered with snow, the lake was frozen, the wind was blowing and it was bitterly cold; but Mr. Whizzer, philosopher that he was, set about to make himself as comfortable as possible under the circumstances.

He was not long, however, in a state of single blessedness. The next day others began to arrive in parties of two and three, foot-sore, backsore, and fagged out, and after selecting a place of deposit for their goods and taking a short rest, would leave one of their number to guard the camp, and return for a further supply. And thus the various parties would come and go.

In the afternoon of the third day who should Mr. Whizzer see but Sandy Dalton coming slowly and laboriously down the trail under a heavy load. Mr. Whizzer met him and invited him to leave his burden at "Camp No. 1" and to make that spot the headquarters of the party. This, Sandy was very glad to do; and the spot not only became their stopping place at the lake, but the party was thereafter known as "Camp No. 1" wherever they were found in the Northwest Territory. Mr. Whizzer offered to take charge of the camp while the others finished the packing, and thus it happened that all the supplies belonging to "Camp No. 1" were transported to the lake before those of the others.

Soon the sounds of the ax, the whipsaw, and the hammer, were heard in the land. Each company was engaged in building boats in which to float down the river as soon as navigation, such as it was, opened. About the middle of May our party, having finished their boat, launched it and stored their goods in it. There was some difficulty in providing for Mr. Whizzer, but it was finally agreed that in consideration of the sum of four dollars per day to be paid by Mr. Whizzer, they would board him and carry him and his goods to their final destination. It was stipulated, however, that Mr. Whizzer should carry his belongings around all portages that might have to be made on the journey.

Owing to the floating ice, and the shallowness of the water, their progress was at first very slow; but after many adventures, more or less thrilling, they finally reached the dreaded White Horse rapids, around which a portage must, of necessity, be made.

Here arose another difficulty. It had been stipulated that each person should carry his own property around the rapids; but it was impossible for Mr. Whizzer to carry the grindstone, owing to its shape and weight. That gentleman argued that as the boat was too heavy to carry around the falls, it must of course be allowed to float through; that it required some ballast to keep it steady, and that the grindstone placed in the bottom was just the thing they needed. These representations being considered reasonable, it was allowed to remain in the boat, provided that Mr. Whizzer was willing to take the chances on its loss. Mr. Whizzer was willing; and tossing his bundle of blankets on top of the grindstone, said, "I will take the chances on that too."

Leadville Joe, who had had considerable experience in shooting the rapids on the upper Arkansas and Colorado, insisted on getting into the boat and steering her down, "because," he said, "I think I can keep her off the rocks and bring her through all right."

All, except Joe, went to the end of the portage at the lower portion of the rapids. Sandy was prepared with a rope in his hand to throw to Joe when be emerged, and thus bring the boat on the right side of the river and at the proper landing. When the latter observed that the others had reached and stopped at the place agreed upon, he jumped into the boat and pushed off into the current. Sitting low on Whizzer's grindstone, he dexterously kept her straight and off the rocks. She rushed down the stream, through the foam and waves, with incredible swiftness. Barring the excitement of the passage, everything went right, until, when within about fifty yards of the group on the shore and as he was passing out of the mouth of the rapids, there was a sudden jar and stoppage. The boat seemed for a moment to be lifted in the air. Then it whirled broadside on, and turning over and over, rapidly floated down the stream, keel up. It was all done so quickly that no one seemed to know just how the disaster occurred. Those on shore appeared transfixed with horror, and incapable of thought or action,—all except Mr. Whizzer. With the quickness of a flash he snatched one end of the rope from Sandy's hand, and taking two half hitches around his left arm above the elbow, and shouting, "All hold on to the other end as you value your lives!" plunged into the stream to meet the coming Joe. Once he was thrown off his feet, but quickly regaining them, went farther into the stream. Joe was now scarcely ten feet away, rolling and turning helplessly in the angry waters. Mr. Whizzer arrived at the point where Joe would pass in the nick of time, and succeeded in getting a firm grip with his right hand on his leather belt. Now began a gallant struggle to save Joe's life, and incidentally the life of Mr. Whizzer. Sandy wound the end of the rope around himself as the anchor man in a tug-of-war contest, while the other two braced themselves and held on with all their strength. Although the tightening of the two half hitches on Mr. Whizzer's arm gave him indescribable pain, he grimly retained his hold on Joe's belt. The consequence was that the strength of the current soon swung those in the water around to the shore, where they were rescued, Mr. Whizzer exhausted, and Joe more dead than alive. As to Joe, the above is no figure of speech. He was entirely helpless, and his breathing could hardly be distinguished. They rolled, rubbed, shook, and walked him up and down the bank, until he was able to speak a few intelligible words. Then the Judge produced a flask from some mysterious source and gave him a portion of its contents; whereupon his life and strength slowly returned.

Notwithstanding their serious surroundings, Jagsey's attention was so distracted by the sight of the flask, and with speculations as to where the Judge had kept it all this time, that he forgot his charge and sat down on a near by stone, stroked his beard, and rubbed his head in deep meditation. After sitting there for some time, and being apparently unable to solve the problem under consideration, he suddenly sprang to his feet and exclaimed, "I don't know wher' the Jedge got that ther' bottle and I don't know wher' he put it after he give Joe the drink, but ther's one thing I do know. I know that Whizzer's a dead game man; and don't you forget it."

Nobody dissented from Jagsey's statement, and it was enthusiastically conceded by all that Whizzer was a hero, and no mistake.

As to poor Whizzer's physical condition, he was indeed in a bad way. His arm was sore and badly swollen. He made no complaint, though it was plain to be seen he was suffering acutely. His friends, true friends now, did all they could for his relief; but his thoughts were not all on his physical sufferings. His grindstone was at the bottom of the river, and he could barely think of anything else.

It was plain to him that the object of his trip to this remote and inhospitable region must now be abandoned, and he must return to the "States" unless the grindstone could be found and recovered. Seized with this idea, which, it must be admitted, was a remote and unsatisfactory one, he went down to the river and walked up and down its banks, peering intently into its waters. Useless. The water was muddy from melting snow and ice and its recent rapid rise, and he could hardly see an inch below the surface.

Finally he returned to the camp discouraged and found his companions talking about a subject which had not yet entered his mind, the loss of the boat and the chances of finding it. It had been arranged during his absence that the Judge should remain in camp and prepare the supper while Sandy and Jagsey would go down the river and search for the boat.

During their absence Mr. Whizzer was not communicative, but sat apart from the others seemingly abstracted in his thoughts. He at last arose, and coming to where the Judge was working, quietly announced that in the morning he intended to return to the coast.

The Judge tried to cheer up Mr. Whizzer, and to dissuade him from carrying out his intention to leave them. "I have noticed," said the Judge, "that you are worried about the loss of your grindstone, and that you have been trying to find it in the water. Do not allow the matter to disturb you at the present time. Tomorrow morning early we can search for it under more favorable conditions. I think, from the feeling in the air, that tonight will be cold. If so, the thawing of the snow and ice will cease, the river will fall considerably, and the water will be clear in the morning. Then if it is possible to see the grindstone lying at the bottom of the river we can do so. Beside, Mr. Whizzer, we have all taken a liking to you and don't want you to return. We desire that you remain with us."

Consoled by these manifestations of friendship, and the prospect of recovering the grindstone, no matter how remote, Mr. Whizzer assumed a more cheerful bearing, and actually rendered some assistance in the preparation of the meal.

At the coming of twilight, Sandy and Jagsey returned and reported having found the boat about two miles below, bottom up, and wedged between the shore and a root which. projected out of the water. They were unable, however, to do anything more than to pull it up on the beach, and fasten it to an adjoining tree.

When the hour of retiring came, Mr. Whizzer, having lost his blankets in the boat wreck, the party divided theirs with him; and Joe and Mr. Whizzer having been made comfortable, they were soon enjoying that repose their labors had earned. The next morning at early dawn Mr. Whizzer was on the bank of the stream anxiously gazing into its depths. The night had been cold, as the Judge had predicted. The water was clear, and the river much smaller than on the previous evening. But notwithstanding Mr. Whizzer's anxious search he could see nothing.

"Wait," said the Judge, "till the sun rises and shines upon the water. From our position it will cast its rays in the right direction to see anything on the bottom, if it can be seen at all."

The rising of the sun found the whole party on the river bank where Joe had been rescued. From that point the Judge and Sandy went up the stream, while Jagsey and Mr. Whizzer went down. They had not been long separated till a great shout was heard from Jagsey.

"Blame my skin, if I don't b'l'eve I have found it. Come here, boys."

They immediately gathered around Jagsey, and there, sure enough, resting against another rock at an angle of about forty-five degrees from the current; appeared the dim outlines of the round grindstone.

That it was the grindstone there could be no doubt; but how to get it out of the river was the question. Many methods were proposed, but after discussion were rejected as impracticable.

Mr. Whizzer, however, was equal to the occasion. He sent Jagsey to the camp in haste for one of his augers, a stout piece of small rope, and an ax. Upon his return he requested Jagsey to cut a long, small pole; and into the end of this pole a hole was bored about two inches in depth; and one end of the rope was tied around the auger about the middle so that the two ends would balance and remain in a horizontal position when held by the rope. Then Jagsey, under the direction of Mr. Whizzer, tied the other end of the rope to the pole above the auger hole so that there would be considerable slack of the rope between the two places where it was tied and inserted the auger, loosely, in the hole in the end of the pole. Jagsey was then directed to push the pole slowly and carefully into the water and through the hole in the middle of the grindstone.

"Now shake the pole," said Whizzer, and the auger dropped out on the under side of the grindstone.

"Now all pull," said Mr. Whizzer; which they did, and the grindstone was once more on terra firma.

On the same day the boat was rescued from its position and

towed up the river to the camp; and the two following days were employed in caulking, repairing, and repitching it. On the morning of the third, the boat now being as good as new, it was loaded with the baggage and supplies, and the party again turned its prow down the stream.

The convalescent Joe, being as yet unable to perform any labor, was allowed to sit in the bow and act as the lookout. In the afternoon he saw something in the river which seemed to have been caught and retained by an overhanging bough. On inspection it proved to be the bundle of blankets and clothing which Mr. Whizzer had thrown into the boat before it went through the rapids. The package was uninjured, but of course very wet, and the whole of the next day was spent in camp, drying Mr. Whizzer's baggage and clothes.

The voyage was then resumed, and nothing of importance occurred, except that they made frequent stops to prospect for gold along the banks of the adjacent creeks. In this way they leisurely floated down the stream till they came to an embryo town called Dawson, or Dawson City, situated at the junction of the Yukon and the Thron-Duick, the English pronunciation of which is "Klondike."

Here Mr. Whizzer concluded to remain, for a time, at least; and the water journey of the rest of the party also terminated at this point. The boat and the greater portion of the supplies were left in charge of Mr. Whizzer, and the others, taking as much as they could each conveniently carry together with the mining implements, struck out into the interior.

Mr. Whizzer engaged board at the only restaurant, and made a little camp on the river bank where he might sleep and watch the boat and its contents.

The time thus passed until the summer was nearly over, Mr. Whizzer not hearing from his party but once, when they had sent in for more provisions. They reported that they had not found gold in paying quantities, were becoming much discouraged, and announced that if they did not locate a claim before the first of September, they intended to return to Dawson, take the boat and go down the river as far as Circle city.

It has always been a mystery how news, in a sparsely settled country where there are no mail routes, telegraph lines, or other means of rapid communication, travels with such celerity and certainty. Uncivilized tribes appear to have means of communicating with each other, at long distances and over mountains and deserts, with a speed which is astonishing; and to civilized people, when surrounded by the same environments, the same facility seems to come as a necessary part of their isolation.

One day in the latter part of August a man came into Dawson and said he had heard that a mine of wonderful richness had been discovered about forty miles above the town on the "Klondike."

The same afternoon another man came from an opposite direction, and said, "As how he had hearn tell at his camp down the river that a feller had made a rich strike over on the 'Klondike.'"

The next morning early a party of four passed through the town announcing that they had heard down at Forty-Mile, where they lived, of great finds on the "Klondike," and the same afternoon a part of tenderfeet from the "States" came down the river and wanted to know whether the report was true about rich gold mines on the "Klondike."

The following day the village was almost deserted of its inhabitants and people were passing through in parties of two, four, six, and eight, all headed toward the east and bound for the "Klondike." On the same day a messenger arrived with a letter from Judge Sinclair stating that "Camp No. 1" was at the new diggings; that they had located and prospected a good claim near that of the original discoverer, and that they had used Mr. Whizzer's name in their notice as one of the original locators and owners; and concluded with a request that Mr. Whizzer, immediately on the receipt of the letter, employ a sufficient number of packers to transport their goods and supplies to the claim. It further said that two of the number from the claim would follow the bearer of the letter on the next day to assist in packing the supplies.

Mr. Whizzer at once went to the Indian village on the opposite side of the river and engaged a sufficient number of packers, not forgetting to hire a couple of likely looking fellows on his own account to carry the grindstone to the newly discovered mines.

In due time Mr. Whizzer, Sandy, and Joe, with a long line of well loaded packers took the trail leading from Dawson to the mine. Their arrival at "Camp No. 1" was heralded with joy; Jagsey not being the least demonstrative of the lot. The mine, and the nuggets picked up and panned out were shown, and many things were talked over.

"And just to think," said the Judge, "we are all together again, and with an almost certain prospect of becoming rich. We have now prospected the mine sufficiently to know that it contains enough of the precious metal within its boundaries to satisfy any five reasonable men in the world. We have made you one of the owners, having an equal share with the others, but we do not expect you to do any of the hard work. We have talked the matter over, and all we ask of you is to look after the camp, keep things straightened around, and do only what you feel like doing."

Mr. Whizzer demurred to owning any part of the mine. "It would be neither fair nor right for me to have any interest in the mine. It was neither through my labor or enterprise that it was discovered. To you who have undergone the hardships and performed the labor, it rightfully belongs; and I cannot accept any share of it. I thank you, however, for your kindness. I would like to remain with you during the winter, and promise to look after the camp, during your absence, to the best of my ability."

Mr. Whizzer was so firm in his refusal of any share in the mine, that the matter was not pressed further, and was not afterward alluded to.

The following morning, after the other members of the party had gone to their daily labors at the claim, Mr. Whizzer did a very unusual thing. He got out his ax, put a temporary helve in it, and went to the woods on the side of the mountain. In the afternoon he returned with as much split timber as he could comfortably carry, and out of the timber he constructed a frame for the grindstone, and put it together with the nails he had brought with him. Then, by means of the auger and ax he fitted a shaft to the grindstone, and made a crank and handle. The bearings, which he had been very particular about, he greased with bacon rind. After hanging the grindstone, he made and nailed a small shelf on the side of the cabin and put on it a fruit can which he had found around the camp, and placed beside it an iron teaspoon. When the whole was completed it was no ordinary piece of work, as Mr. Whizzer was no mean amateur mechanic.

After he had carefully put away his tools he went into the cabin. From his actions it would appear as if his task was done, and his work finally completed. He washed himself, changed his clothing, lit his pipe, and sat down, and shut his eyes in contemplation, as if to say, "I never intended to work, but circumstances compelled me to do so in this instance, but now my work is finished for life. I will never do any more," and then settled back against the wall for a nap.

How long Mr. Whizzer slept we have no means of knowing;

but he was wakened from his reverie by the sudden and unexpected appearance of Jagsey. To that gentleman had been delegated the task of supplying the mine and cabin with wood; to the mine for thawing purposes, and to the cabin for heating and culinary purposes. He had diligently and cheerfully performed his appointed employment since the mine had been first discovered to the entire satisfaction of the company; but on this occasion he came home very much out of sorts. He was almost ready to throw up his job.

"Blame my skin if I'll try to cut any more wood. I have used this old ax' till it's as dull as a frow."

Mr. Whizzer, although somewhat discomposed by his sudden awakening, listened to Jagsey's lamentations, and when he had finished, quietly said, "Jagsey, there's a grindstone outside, ready for business. Grind your ax."

As Jagsey could not grind it alone, and as Mr. Whizzer did not offer to help him, he had to await the return of the rest of the party. Jagsey spent the intervening time in the inspection and admiration of the stone and the frame on which it hung. Even the can and spoon on the shelf did not escape his attention. He asked no questions, but he could not have been more delighted and surprised if he had discovered another rich claim. Of course he had known of the grindstone, but he had not before thought of the possibilities. In a short time, after the return of the others, the ax was in excellent condition, and Jagsey had exacted a promise from his partners that he was to continue the woodsman of the camp. His voluble tongue soon spread the news of the grindstone over the immediate district, and the next morning several miners appeared with axes to grind. When they asked of the owner the terms for using the stone, he replied, "To 'Camp No. 1' it is free; to all others the terms are a spoonful of gold dust for each hour you use it. After you have used the stone, put a spoonful of dust in the can for each hour."

The next day a delegation called to see whether they might grind their picks. It was agreed that they might do so, on the same terms.

"Grind fair, and don't bear down too hard."

In a few days the knowledge of the existence of the grindstone had spread to the remotest parts of the district, and every miner used it, or wanted to use it; some even standing, in line for hours, each waiting his turn and so it came around that all through the short winter days and the long Arctic nights the grindstone was kept turning,

turning; and as the circumference of the stone grew smaller, the moose-skin sacks containing its earnings, grew fuller and heavier. The end of every twenty four hours saw twenty four spoonfuls of bright yellow gold dust in the can. The can was a veritable cornucopia to Mr. Whizzer. Every day at high noon he would empty the contents of the can into his mooseskin sack; and this effort on the part of Mr. Whizzer comprised the total of his labor during the winter. As there was no blacksmith shop in the whole region nearer than Circle city, the miners were glad to have the opportunity of using the stone, and thought it a favor and a condescension on the part of M. Whizzer to allow them to do so. The price asked and paid was only an incident, and was not taken into serious consideration.

The long winter at last wore itself out; the days were percep-tibly lengthening; the snow and ice were rapidly disappearing; a few shrubs of the hardier kind began to put forth buds and blossoms; the waters began to flow and the miners were busy making ditches and diverting it into their sluices for their summer's work. Spring had come with all its Arctic suddenness.

About this time Mr. Whizzer announced his intention of going to St. Michaels by the first steamboat which came up the river, and from thence to the "States." That gentleman had been so manly during his stay with them, and had conferred such an inestimable boon on the miners by bringing a grindstone to the district, that they deter-mined the best methods of showing their appreciation of him before his departure was to call a public mass meeting, and pass resolutions expressive of their feelings toward him as a man and public benefactor.

The meeting which assembled at "Camp No. 1" a week later was unique in character. Nothing like it had ever before been seen in that or any other country. The district was populated by all classes and conditions of men. Among them could be found the gambler, the hardy but illiterate son of the frontier, and the man who had been rec-ognized at home as an educated professional man of the highest stand-ing. Shut out, as they had been from civilization for eight months they were bearded and unkempt, not too well dressed. Their appearance was not prepossessing; but when a person looked beneath the surface, and saw their actions, and heard them talk, the opinion of them changed. They came from all the region round about. Every creek, gulch, and cañon contributed its quota.

In view of his experience and popularity, Judge Sinclair was elected the chairman of the meeting, and Mr. Robinson of Bonanza Creek, a graduate of Harvard, was selected to act as the secretary.

The chairman then stated the object of the meeting, and dilating at some length on the many virtues of Mr. Whizzer, concluded by asking for the further pleasure of the assemblage.

Mr. Asahel Shinn of Sand Bottom creek, elaborated on what the Judge had just said; and moved that the chairman appoint a committee of three to draft resolutions suitable to the occasion.

This motion having been seconded and carried, the chair appointed Mr. Shinn of Sand Bottom, Mr. Puckett of Last Chance, and the Secretary, as such committee.

The Chairman now declared an informal recess until the report of the committee was ready to be submitted, and remarked that during that time if any gentleman had any remarks to make the meeting would, no doubt, be glad to hear him.

Immediately there were cries of "Whizzer!" "Whizzer!" and that gentleman, in spite of his resistance and protestations, was forced to the front. He began by saying that he was no speaker—could not make a speech if he tried; that he appreciated the honor of being their guest on this occasion; and that he would always hold in kindly remembrance his associations with them. He further said he would like to leave with them some token of his appreciation of their uniform kindness; but had nothing he thought they would esteem more highly than the remnants of the grindstone, that it was now very small,—only weighed eleven and one half pounds,—but with their permission he would leave it as a legacy to the District. He concluded by saying that he would be glad to take them all by the hand and bid them farewell.

At the height of Mr. Whizzer's impromptu levee, which had been quite enthusiastic, the chairman rapped for order again, and announced that the committee on resolutions was ready to report.

When quiet had been restored, the secretary, by direction of the chairman, read the following report, which was received with vociferous applause:—

"Mr. President:—Your committee on resolutions do report the following, and ask the meeting to adopt them:—

WHEREAS, we have heard with deep regret of the intended departure of Colonel Whizzer from this District, and

WHEREAS, the association of the people with Colonel

Whizzer during the entire time of his residence with us has been of the most pleasant character, therefore,

RESOLVED, That the thanks of the miners on the Klondike are due, and they are hereby tendered to Colonel Whizzer for the great service he has rendered them during the past winter.

RESOLVED, FURTHER, That the good wishes of those who are here assembled, for the health and continued prosperity of Colonel Whizzer will attend him to whatever land he may go, and in whatever spot he may hereafter reside.

RESOLVED, FURTHER, That an engrossed copy of these resolutions, signed by the President, and countersigned by the Secretary, be presented to Colonel Whizzer before his departure.

The secretary having concluded, the chairman arose and said the resolutions were so apropos he would take the liberty of calling for a vote on them without the formality of a motion for that purpose; and then said, "All who are in favor of the adoption of the resolutions which have just been read, please say 'Aye.'"

The vote in favor of the adoption seemed to be unanimous, but the chair, as a matter of form, was proceeding to take the negative, when "Battle Axe Bowers" of Freezeout Diggings, a tall, uncouth-looking man with a sweeping white beard, arose and commenced talking incoherently and gesticulating wildly.

"I don't agree with them reserlutions," he protested. "They air too soft. What's a man a comin' to this kentry fer, an' a payin' his own ixpenses, ef soft soap's all he's a goin' to git? No, sir, they won't do."

The Chairman: "Does the gentleman intend to make a motion?"

Mr. Bowers: "Do I intend to make a motion? Not much. I hev lived in Tombstone an' Deadwood too long, before I kem to this blasted kentry, to make a fool of myself a makin' motions unless I've got the drop on the other feller; which I have n't got in this case."

At this point a smooth shaven gentleman from Bear Creek, with his hair neatly combed and parted, and whose name in the noise and confusion the chair did not catch, called Mr. Bowers to order, "on the ground that he was not speaking to any question before the house."

Mr. Bowers: "Call me to order, do yer? Well, I'm not as smart es some dudes I've seen. I can't do pen writin', an' I hev n't got es much book larnin' es some people, but I'll bet fifty ounces—"

At this juncture, when everything seemed to be getting into

a condition of sixes and sevens, and the meeting liable to break up in a row, Mr. Ransom Quigley of Skookum Gulch, a pleasant appearing young man, arose, and said: "Mr. President, I think I understand the gentleman from Freezeout. His heart is right, and his ideas are right; but he does not appear to have the faculty of expressing them to the meeting. I, therefore, move as an amendment to the resolutions, that the meeting contribute to Colonel Whizzer the sum of one hundred ounces for the purpose of assisting him to defray the expense of bringing his grindstone to this country."

Mr. Bowers: "That's right, sonny. That's just what I want, an' I couldn't 'a' sed it better myself."

The resolutions and the amendment were now adopted with a rush, and the meeting adjourned with everybody in a good humor.

On the third day after the meeting Colonel Whizzer set out for Dawson to meet the boat, which was expected daily. Joe and Sandy insisted on accompanying him, and carrying his dust. The arrival on the upper Yukon of the first steamboat of the season is a great event; and when, after much weary waiting and watching, it was soon steaming up the river in the middle of June, 1897, the population went wild. Every man, woman, child, and dog, in Dawson rushed pell mell to the landing to meet it. Who can blame them? Shut up as they had been on the Arctic circle for nearly a year without a word or whisper from the outside world, it is no wonder they became excited at the prospect of learning of what had happened during their imprisonment.

Colonel Whizzer took an affectionate leave of Joe and Sandy; and the boat turned its prow down the stream toward home and civilization.

On the 18th day of July there was great excitement in Seattle. For several days vague rumors had been coming from the far North telling of wonderful discoveries of gold at some remote mining center in Alaska; but these rumors appeared to be too exaggerated for belief. On this particular day, however, the newsboys were running up and down the streets selling extras which announced that a steamer was then coming up the Sound, and would arrive within two hours, and that it had on board seventy miners with tons of gold from the newly discovered mines. When the steamer arrived it was met by an immense concourse of people; and when they saw the gold in canvas and mooseskin bags, in blankets and tin cans, the rumor materialized into certainty; and when the onlookers saw the gold loaded into express wagons for transportation to some safe place in the city, they simply went wild.

After the departure of the crowd, Colonel Whizzer, who had remained in the steamer, called to an expressman and told him that he had some gold which he wished taken to the office of the Northern Pacific Express.

"All right," said the expressman, "bring it down."

"No," said the Colonel, "you come up and get it. It is too much like work for me to bring it."

When the gold had been weighed at the office the Colonel tarried at the counter for his receipt, but the clerk appeared absent-minded and did not attend him. He bent over the desk, making figures, and rubbing his chin, and stroking his hair, until finally the Colonel called his attention to the fact that he had not yet handed him the customary receipt.

"O, I beg your pardon, but there is something very peculiar about your package," said the clerk. "As I estimate its value there is exactly twenty thousand dollars worth of coined gold; no more, no less."

Colonel Whizzer took his receipt and went out to the street and did some figuring also. When he finished he put his book in his pocket and said to himself, "Well, that is strange, very strange. Exactly seventy-three and one half pounds were ground off of that grindstone, and twenty thousand dollars in coined gold weighs just seventy-three and one half pounds. Very strange." And the Colonel walked up the street and disappeared in a Puget Sound fog.

At the Dropping-Off Place

BY William McLeod Raine

In the cabin situated on Lot 10, Block E, Water Street, Eagle City, Alaska, four men were striving to wear away the torment-laden, sleepless Yukon night. It was twelve o'clock by the Waterbury watch which hung on the wall, but save for a slight murkiness there was no sign of darkness. The mosquitoes hummed with a fiendish pertinacity that effectually precluded sleep. The thermometer registered one hundred degrees of torture. A thick smoke from four pipes and a smudge-fire hung cloudlike over the room, but entirely failed to disturb the countless pests.

The torture of the hour fell heavily on the four outcasts, and they writhed with silent curses and futile nausea of the soul. One of them lay on the floor, rolled in his blankets, damning the mosquitoes, the country, his luck,—anything that he could lay a name to. The poor living, the heat, lack of sleep, and the endless sunshine had worn his nerves to the danger-point. He was in that condition in which the merest word of his best friend would drive him into a rage. By birth he was an Englishman, though the uncivilized ends of the earth had long claimed him for their own. He had been a soldier of the Queen in India and a beachcomber in the South Sea islands. He had mined at Ballarat and at Cripple Creek. The music-halls of London and the Chinese Quarter in San Francisco were alike familiar to him. To-night the memories of the past were torturing him, and he felt impelled to cry out like a whipped boy.

Another man was sitting on his bunk patching his nether garments, whistling softly to himself the while. He wore a jumper made from a flour-sack with the lettering "EXCELSIOR XXX" stretched across his breast, like a baseball player. The rest of his costume was, for the present, meager; it consisted of a frown.

Just outside the hut, leaning over a camp-stove, was a third man, Grover by name. Between two frying-pans, thrust into the coals, he was cooking sour-dough bread.

The fourth man was writing to his wife back in the States.

Judged by ordinary standards, they were a disreputable lot—dirty, unshaven, unkempt. Among them was only one respectable article of wearing apparel—a mackinaw coat, owned by the man writing home, who in consequence had been dubbed by the Englishman, "the *swagger* swell." In point of fact the coat served as a dress-suit for any of the men in their occasional trips to Dawson. If the rest of their clothing was hopelessly nondescript and ragged, at least they had the consolation of knowing they were no worse than their neighbors. Yet one of them—the one patching his mackinaw trousers—was in all probability a millionaire. A year before he had been a railroad navvy. And the cook was a graduate of one of the greatest of American colleges. He was a clever cook, too, which was much more to the point. When one is reduced to bacon, beans, and flour, the *cuisine* possibilities are limited; but Grover was a man of imagination, and could produce a greater variety than any man in Eagle City. His cooking would have reduced a woman to despair.

The writer finished his letter and read it over. It was a bright, cheery letter, filled with love and hopes for better times after he should make his strike. He touched with characteristic American humor on the life he was leading, and described his companions with genuine dramatic ability. The letter gave no hint of soul-weariness.

"Finished your letter, Wood?"

"Yes. Been writing her we have a blamed good time. Been writing lies to keep her from worrying."

The man on the floor rolled over with a groan.

"What's the matter, Jones?"

"Matter?" he shouted. "Matter? What ain't the matter? I'm wondering why I was such a fool as to come to this God-forsaken country. If I stay here much longer I'll kill somebody,—myself or one of you!"

Grover, seating himself in the open doorway, took in the bloodshot, sleepless eyes and the haggard appearance of the man, and mentally agreed that he was traveling fast in that direction. There was a look in his eyes that might have been the beginning of madness.

"In another month we shall be past the worst of it. I don't believe the mosquitoes are as bad as they were last week," said Grover soothingly.

Jones felt that the other was treating him as he would a sick child, and resented it with unspoken rage and grinding teeth.

"When the first steamers break through the ice the mosquitoes—"

Jones sprang to his feet in a sullen fury, his eyes blazing. The longing for a fight was on him, but the pretext was lacking. Before he could speak, Wood interrupted. The sickness for home was eating his heart and had to break through, now that the floodgates of speech were opened.

"Jones is right," he said. "The Lord made the rest of the earth, and when he got through he had some rocks left and piled them here, hit or miss, because he thought folks had sense enough to stay away from here. It's no white man's country."

"It's a frozen fact that I haven't slept a wink for three nights," cried Jones. "Half the year, it is the eternal cold, and the other half it is infernal heat and mosquitoes.

Grover shrugged his shoulders and began to hum "The Star-spangled Banner." His selection appeared to be unfortunate.

"Drop it!" cried Wood. "Do the people in hell sing about heaven?" Then he continued a little shamefacedly, "It is all very well for you Grover; but I've got a wife and two little kids down in God's country. If you've got to sing, sing something else. You make me homesick."

"Well, I'm a little that way myself," remarked the millionaire, holding his trousers out before him and viewing the artistic patch critically, his head slowed round a little to one side. "But I never know you to kick before, and thought you didn't mind it, Wood."

"Did you?" cried the other bitterly. "Well, I do. A man may be sick without shouting about it all the time. And I'm sick—damn sick. I haven't sat down once in the last six weeks to these soggy beans and sour bread without thinking what a fool I was to come. Good Lord!" he groaned, "I might have been sleeping in a bed to-night—a bed with springs and a soft mattress; nothing to do but reach out my hand to touch my wife, and the kids in a crib not three feet away from me. I might have got up to-morrow morning and eaten eggs for breakfast and beefsteak that your teeth sink into. I might have had strawberries and cream from my own ranch. But the best wasn't good enough for me. O no! I wanted the earth, hooped round with a barb-wire fence or handed me on a silver platter. Think of it, men! Down in the States they are eating peas and beans—fresh beans, not this moldy mess—and cabbages and corn, and strawberries and watermel-ons—no, watermelons aren't ripe yet, but bottled beer is on tap all the year round."

"You two fellows had better run down to the States for the summer. The magnate and I will stay and look after things," said Grover gravely.

"That's right. I've been roughing it twenty years and don't mind it much," acquiesced the millionaire tailor.

"I'm no more a *chechocho* than you fellows," Jones respond-ed. "I've worked as long hours and risked as much and lived as hard. I've worked all winter underground and asked no odds of anybody. You have never heard me squealing for the windlass end, I reckon. But I'm sick of it. By God! if it were not for my mother I'd—"

He set his teeth with a click and an expression on his face that was not good to see. It was as if the veil had been lifted and his soul stood naked for a moment.

"You're all right, Jones. But you two fellows have a touch of fever. There really isn't any reason why you shouldn't go home for the summer," continued Grover, noting the look which had swept over the face of the other man when he let the bars down. A man does not look like that unless he has thought of *harikari*.

"You make me weary," cried Wood. "I'm not going home till I make a strike, if I stay till I rot."

"I'll tell you where I wish I was," said the Englishman, harp-ing on. "I wish I was in 'Frisco. I'd have a new rig-out, swell as they make 'em,—patent-leather shoes, ice-cream pants, gaudy necktie, and a billycock to top off with. My word! then I'd get a girl! You bet she would be a high-flyer, and we would go together to a feed-shop—best in town. It wounldn't be beans and bacon I'd order. I'd have oyster stew and hot tamales to start the show, then go down the line and finish off with chamnpagne fizz—in buckets, mind you. Then we would go down to the Cliff House and listen to the bands play, and see the what-d 'ye-call-'em-scopes that shows moving pictures. There'd likely be thousands of people moving about and electric lights galore. Gad!

but we'd have a boat and sail out on the bloomin' Pacific while the band played 'Mandalay' and 'Tommy Atkins'!" and Jones broke into boisterous song:—

Bloomin' idol made o' mud—
What they called the Great Gawd Budd—
Plucky lot she cared for idols when I
    Kissed her where she stud!
On the road to Mandalay,
Where the old flotilla lay,—

Then as if there were no break in the song:—

But that's all shore be'ind me—long ago an'
    fur away
An' there ain't no 'buses runnin' from the
    Bank to Mandalay.

"I used to be a 'Tommy' myself, ye know. It would be a balmy, velvet time I'd have. I'd paint the town red P. D. Q. My word!" He ended with a long-drawn sigh and fell into ecstatic reverie, and Wood took up the burden of speech:—

"I believe you. Guess we'd all blow ourselves one way or another. I'd stop at Seattle and go round to some bank and cash up my chips. Then I'd clean out some toy-shop for the kids and get my wife the best dress I could find. After that I'd charter a special boat and go across the lake—Lake Washington, you know—to my ranch. I reckon they'd never quit hugging me, those blame little kids." And the man drew a deep breath that was more than half a sob. "Gee! but I'd like to see little old, hilly Seattle again, with its dirty water-front and its six-month rains! But what's the use of talking? D'ye s'pose Dives enjoyed seeing Lazarus in Abraham's bosom?" concluded Wood, lapsing into silence and holding himself in tightly.

All this proved too much for the millionaire, and he now took up the strain. "I'll take Denver in mine," said he, waving his nether garment excitedly. "I've railroaded and mined there twenty years, and it's the best State there is. You can't tell the truth about it without lying. There's a saloon on Arapahoe Street that used to be my headquarters. I know all the boys about town, and I guess I would be strictly in it. You can get more fun for your money in Denver than in any town I know. I'd go up to the First National Bank, just as I am in these duds—"

"Then you'd be arrested," broke in Grover; "for—"

"Shut up! You know what I mean. I'd wear this same old mackinaw suit. I'd tell the cashier I wanted to deposit some money, and he'd say 'How much?' Then I'd say, kinder casual like, 'Well, I haven't counted it—about a million, I guess—or maybe two. It's down at the express-office. You'll need several teams to get it up.' He'd size up my duds and think I was crazy, or maybe only drunk. About that time I'd hand out the express receipt, and if that didn't paralyze him it would be because he was lightning-proof. I think I see him wilt."

"What would you do, Grover?" asked Wood.

"Take a Turkish bath first thing; next have some clothes made by a decent tailor. Then I would run on to my class reunion at old Yale. After that—"

The figure of a man blocked, the doorway—a man in new brown boots laced up his legs, new mackinaw suit, new broad hat, in fact a brand new man just off the St. Michaels boat. Not a tear or a rip about him—*chechocho* written all over him from head to foot.

"Good evening, or perhaps I'd better say, 'Good-night,'" he began jauntily. "I just came up from St. Michaels. Our boat is stuck on a sand-bar five miles down, so I and another fellow rowed up."

"The deuce you did!"

Imagine Livingstone when Stanley first showed on the horizon, and you have some conception of what it meant to these outcasts to see a face fresh from civilization. For seven months they had been cut off from news of the outside world, and here was a man fresh from the States, as if sent especially by Providence to enlighten them.

They began promptly, forgetting everything around them and asking a thousand questions about the war, about politics, about crops,—anything and everything they could think of. Then they made him sing the latest songs over and over until they had caught the air and learned the words. He promised them some old magazines he had on board. They had been restricted to a tattered copy of the Bible and a fragment of "The Origin of Species" for twelve months, so they naturally hailed him as a public benefactor. They made him talk—talk—talk! At first he enjoyed it; then it bored him; finally he rebelled.

"Say, have you fellows got anything to eat?" he asked. "There's nothing worth eating on the boat—nothing but canned goods and truck. You don't know what hardship is until you take the St. Michaels River trip."

"I presume that's so," said Grover, never twitching a muscle. "Well, you are through that hardship now, thank Heaven! You shall have a good square meal to start with—the best we have got."

They put it before him. He looked in pained surprise at the musty beans, the soggy bread, the fat bacon, and then asked for coffee.

"Haven't had any for two months," said Jones.

"Tea, then."

Grover shook his head. "Not in stock."

"But is this what you eat every day?"

"Yes. I thought it would be a pleasant change for you from the canned stuff on the boat."

"I don't believe I'm hungry after all," he said at last.

They shouted with laughter and stamped up and down and slapped each other's backs in an ecstasy of joy till the tears rolled down their cheeks. They had had their revenge. They, who had endured the horrors of the trail, the dangers of the river with its cañons and its rapids, the hardship of a Klondike winter in the frozen North, with its stampedes over snow-clad mountains, its arduous work in the frozen ground, and its poor food and wretched shelter,—they, who had risked death from drowning, from fever, from starvation, from freezing,—they had been told by a dapper young clerk from the States, with the creases not yet out of his trousers, that they did not know what hardship was! It was too good!

The newcomer interrupted their laughter to make inquiries as to how far Ladue's claim was from Dawson.

"I mean to stake out one near his," he said. "It stands to reason that some of those around must be as rich as his."

His profound penetration sent Jones off in another shout of laughter. Grover explained that every river claim within fifty miles of Ladue's had been staked long ago.

"That can't be! The company told me there were plenty to be had."

"Of course the steamboat company told you that. These companies are the biggest liars on the face of this frozen earth. We tell you that there aren't any to be had near his."

"It may be to your interest to tell me that," he said stiffly.

"All right, my son. No teacher like experience. Better go and see. You'll be a wiser man in a couple of weeks. My word!" And Jones flung himself on his bunk, threw out his arms and legs, and kicked in a frenzy of appreciation of what was before the new-comer.

At this moment a whistle blew, and the inhabitants of Eagle City adjourned *en masse* to the banks of the Yukon; for an echo of this wicked but delightful world was coming up the river to meet them in the form of a shallow river flatboat.

To Build a Fire

BY JACK LONDON

Dᴀʏ ʜᴀᴅ ʙʀᴏᴋᴇɴ ᴄᴏʟᴅ and gray, exceedingly cold and gray, when the man turned aside from the main Yukon trail and climbed the high earthbank, where a dim and little-travelled trail led eastward through the fat spruce timberland. It was a steep bank, and he paused for breath at the top, excusing the act to himself by looking at his watch. It was nine o'clock. There was no sun nor hint of sun, though there was not a cloud in the sky. It was a clear day, and yet there seemed an intangible pall over the face of things, a subtle gloom that made the day dark, and that was due to the absence of sun. This fact did not worry the man. He was used to the lack of sun. It had been days since he had seen the sun, and he knew that a few more days must pass before that cheerful orb, due south, would just peep above the sky-line and dip immediately from view.

The man flung a look back along the way he had come. The Yukon lay a mile wide and hidden under three feet of ice. On top of this ice were as many feet of snow. It was all pure white, rolling in gentle, undulations where the ice-jams of the freeze-up had formed. North and south, as far as his eye could see, it was unbroken white, save for a dark hair-line that curved and twisted from around the spruce-covered island to the south, and that curved and twisted away into the north, where it disappeared behind another spruce-covered island. This dark hairline was the trail—the main trail—that led south five hundred miles to the Chilcoot Pass, Dyea, and salt water; and that led north seventy miles to Dawson, and still on to the north a thousand miles to Nulato, and finally to St. Michael on Bering Sea, a thousand miles and half a thousand more.

But all this—the mysterious, far-reaching hair-line trail, the absence of sun from the sky, the tremendous cold, and the strangeness and weirdness of it all—made no impression on the man. It was not because he was long used to it. He was a newcomer in the land, a *chechaquo,* and this was his first winter. The trouble with him was that he was without imagination. He was quick and alert in the things of life, but only in the things, and not in the significances. Fifty degrees below zero meant eighty-odd degrees of frost. Such fact impressed him as being cold and uncomfortable, and that was all. It did not lead him to meditate upon his frailty as a creature of temperature, and upon man's frailty in general, able only to live within certain narrow limits of heat and cold; and from there on it did not lead him to the conjectural field of immortality and man's place in the universe. Fifty degrees below zero stood for a bite of frost that hurt and that must be guarded against by the use of mittens, ear-flaps, warm moccasins, and thick socks. Fifty degrees below zero was to him just precisely fifty degrees below zero. That there should be anything more to it than that was a thought that never entered his head.

As he turned to go on, he spat speculatively. There was a sharp, explosive crackle that startled him. He spat again. And again, in the air, before it could fall to the snow, the spittle crackled. He knew that at fifty below spittle crackled on the snow, but this spittle had crackled in the air. Undoubtedly it was colder than fifty below— how much colder he did not know. But the temperature did not matter. He was bound for the old claim on the left fork of Henderson Creek, where the boys were already. They had come over across the divide from the Indian Creek country, while he had come the roundabout way to take a look at the possibilities of getting out logs in the spring from the islands in the Yukon. He would be in to camp by six o'clock; a bit after dark, it was true, but the boys would be there, a fire would be going, and a hot supper would be ready. As for lunch, he pressed his hand against the protruding bundle under his jacket. It was also under his shirt, wrapped up in a handkerchief and lying against the naked skin. It was the only way to keep the biscuits from freezing. He smiled agreeably to himself as he thought of those biscuits, each cut open and sopped in bacon grease, and each enclosing a generous slice of fried bacon.

He plunged in among the big spruce trees. The trail was faint. A foot of snow had fallen since the last sled had passed over, and he was glad he was without a sled, travelling light. In fact, he carried nothing but the lunch wrapped in the handkerchief. He was surprised, however, at the cold. It certainly was cold, he concluded, as he rubbed his numb nose and cheek-bones with his mittened hand. He was a warm-whiskered man, but the hair on his face did not protect the high cheek-bones and the eager nose that thrust itself aggressively into the frosty air.

At the man's heels trotted a dog, a big native husky, the proper wolfdog, gray-coated and without any visible or temperamental difference from its brother, the wild wolf. The animal was depressed by the tremendous cold. It knew that it was no time for travelling. Its instinct told it a truer tale than was told to the man by the man's judgment. In reality, it was not merely colder than fifty below zero; it was colder than sixty below, than seventy below. It was seventy-five below zero. Since the freezing-point is thirty-two above zero, it meant that one hundred and seven degrees of frost obtained. The dog did not know anything about thermometers. Possibly in its brain there was no sharp consciousness of a condition of very cold such as was in the man's brain. But the brute had its instinct. It experienced a vague but menacing apprehension that subdued it and made it slink along at the man's heels, and that made it question eagerly every unwonted movement of the man as if expecting him to go into camp or to seek shelter somewhere and build a fire. The dog had learned fire, and it wanted fire, or else to burrow under the snow and cuddle its warmth away from the air.

The frozen moisture of its breathing had settled on its fur in a fine powder of frost, and especially were its jowls, muzzle, and eye-lashes whitened by its crystalled breath. The man's red beard and mus-tache were likewise frosted, but more solidly, the deposit taking the form of ice and increasing with every warm, moist breath he exhaled. Also, the man was chewing tobacco, and the muzzle of ice held his lips so rigidly that he was unable to clear his chin when he expelled the juice. The result was that a crystal beard of the color and solidity of amber was increasing its length on his chin. If he fell down it would shatter itself, like glass, into brittle fragments. But he did not mind the appendage. It was the penalty all tobacco-chewers paid in that coun-try, and he had been out before in two cold snaps. They had not been so cold as this, he knew, but by the spirit thermometer at Sixty Mile he knew they had been registered at fifty below and at fifty-five.

He held on through the level stretch of woods for several miles, crossed a wide flat of niggerheads, and dropped down a bank to the frozen bed of a small stream. This was Henderson Creek, and he knew he was ten miles from the forks. He looked at his watch. It was ten o'clock. He was making four miles an hour, and he calculated that he would arrive at the forks at half-past twelve. He decided to celebrate that event by eating his lunch there.

The dog dropped in again at his heels, with a tail drooping discouragement, as the man swung along the creek-bed. The furrow of the old sled-trail was plainly visible, but a dozen inches of snow covered the marks of the last runners. In a month no man had come up or down that silent creek. The man held steadily on. He was not much given to thinking, and just then particularly he had nothing to think about save that he would eat lunch at the forks and that at six o'clock he would be in camp with the boys. There was nobody to talk to; and, had there been, speech would have been impossible because of the ice-muzzle on his mouth. So he continued monotonously to chew tobacco and to increase the length of his amber beard.

Once in a while the thought reiterated itself that it was very cold and that he had never experienced such cold. As he walked along he rubbed his cheek-bones and nose with the back of his mittened hand. He did this automatically, now and again changing hands. But rub as he would, the instant he stopped his cheek-bones went numb, and the following instant the end of his nose went numb. He was sure to frost his cheeks; he knew that, and experienced a pang of regret that he had not devised a nose-strap of the sort Bud wore in cold snaps. Such a strap passed across the cheeks, as well, and saved them. But it didn't matter much, after all. What were frosted cheeks? A bit painful, that was all; they were never serious.

Empty as the man's mind was of thoughts, he was keenly observant, and he noticed the changes in the creek, the curves and bends and timber-jams, and always he sharply noted where he placed his feet. Once, coming around a bend, he shied abruptly, like a startled horse curved away from the place where he had been walking, and retreated several paces back along the trail. The creek he knew was frozen clear to the bottom,—no creek could contain water in that arctic winter,—but he knew also that there were springs that bubbled out from the hillsides and ran along under the snow and on top the ice of the creek. He knew that the coldest snaps never froze these springs, and he knew likewise their danger. They were traps. They hid pools of water under the snow that might be three inches deep, or three feet.

Sometimes a skin of ice half an inch thick covered them, and in turn was covered by the snow. Sometimes there were alternate layers of water and iceskin, so that when one broke through he kept on breaking through for a while, sometimes wetting himself to the waist.

That was why he had shied in such panic. He had felt the give under his feet and heard the crackle of a snow-hidden ice-skin. And to get his feet wet in such a temperature meant trouble and danger. At the very least it meant delay, for he would be forced to stop and build a fire, and under its protection to bare his feet while he dried his socks and moccasins. He stood and studied the creek-bed and its banks, and decided that the flow of water came from the right. He reflected awhile, rubbing his nose and cheeks, then skirted to the left, stepping gingerly and testing the footing for each step. Once clear of the danger, he took a fresh chew of tobacco and swung along at his four-mile gait.

In the course of the next two hours he came upon several similar traps. Usually the snow above the hidden pools had a sunken, candied appearance that advertised the danger. Once again, however, he had a close call; and once, suspecting danger, he compelled the dog to go on in front. The dog did not want to go. It hung back until the man shoved it forward, and then it went quickly across the white, unbroken surface. Suddenly it broke through, floundered to one side, and got away to firmer footing. It had wet its forefeet and legs, and almost immediately the water that clung to it turned to ice. It made quick efforts to lick the ice off its legs, then dropped down in the snow and began to bite out the ice that had formed between the toes. This was a matter of instinct. To permit the ice to remain would mean sore feet. It did not know this. It merely obeyed the mysterious prompting that arose from the deep crypts of its being. But the man knew, having achieved a judgment on the subject, and he removed the mitten from his right hand and helped tear out the ice-particles. He did not expose his fingers more than a minute, and was astonished at the swift numbness that smote them. It certainly was cold. He pulled on the mitten hastily, and beat the hand savagely across his chest.

At twelve o'clock the day was at its brightest. Yet the sun was too far south on its winter journey to clear the horizon. The bulge of the earth intervened between it and Henderson Creek, where the man walked under a clear sky at noon and cast no shadow. At half-past twelve, to the minute, he arrived at the forks of the creek. He was pleased at the speed he had made. If he kept it up, he would certainly be with the boys by six. He unbuttoned his jacket and shirt and drew forth his lunch. The action consumed no more than a quarter of a minute, yet in that brief moment the numbness laid hold of the exposed fingers. He did not put the mitten on, but, instead, struck the fingers a dozen sharp smashes against his leg. Then he sat down on a snow-covered log to eat. The sting that followed upon the striking of his fingers against his leg ceased so quickly that he was startled. He had had no chance to take a bite of biscuit. He struck the fingers repeatedly and returned them to the mitten, baring the other hand for the purpose of eating. He tried to take a mouthful, but the ice-muzzle prevented. He had forgotten to build a fire and thaw out. He chuckled at his foolishness, and as he chuckled he noted the numbness creeping into the exposed fingers. Also, he noted that the stinging which had first come to his toes when he sat down was already passing away. He wondered whether the toes were warm or numb. He moved them inside the moccasins and decided that they were numb.

He pulled the mitten on hurriedly and stood up. He was a bit frightened. He stamped up and down until the stinging returned into the feet. It certainly was cold, was his thought. That man from Sulphur Creek had spoken the truth when telling how cold it sometimes got in the country. And he had laughed at him at the time! That showed one must not be too sure of things. There was no mistake about it, it *was* cold. He strode up and down, stamping his feet and threshing his arms, until reassured by the returning warmth. Then he got out matches and proceeded to make a fire. From the undergrowth, where high water of the previous spring had lodged a supply of seasoned twigs, he got his fire-wood. Working carefully from a small beginning, he soon had a roaring fire, over which he thawed the ice from his face and in the protection of which he ate his biscuits. For the moment the cold of space was outwitted. The dog took satisfaction in the fire, stretching out close enough for warmth and far enough away to escape being singed.

When the man had finished, he filled his pipe and took his comfortable time over a smoke. Then he pulled on his mittens, settled the ear-flaps of his cap firmly about his ears, and took the creek trail up the left fork. The dog was disappointed and yearned back toward the fire. This man did not know cold. Possibly all the generations of his ancestry had been ignorant of cold, of real cold, of cold one hundred and seven degrees below freezing-point. But the dog knew; all its ancestry knew, and it had inherited the knowledge. And it knew that it was not good to walk abroad in such fearful cold. It was the time to lie snug in a hole in the snow and wait for a curtain of cloud to be drawn across the face of outer space whence this cold came. On the other hand, there was no keen intimacy between the dog and the man. The one was the toilslave of the other, and the only caresses it had ever received were the caresses of the whip-lash and of harsh and menacing throat-sounds that threatened the whip-lash. So the dog made no effort to communicate its apprehension to the man. It was not concerned in the welfare of the man; it was for its own sake that it yearned back toward the fire. But the man whistled, and spoke to it with the sound of whip-lashes, and the dog swung in at the man's heels and followed after.

The man took a chew of tobacco and proceeded to start a new amber beard. Also, his moist breath quickly powdered with white his mustache, eyebrows, and lashes. There did not seem to be so many springs on the left fork of the Henderson, and for half an hour the man saw no signs of any. And then it happened. At a place where there were no signs, where the soft, unbroken snow seemed to advertise solidity beneath, the man broke through. It was not deep. He wet himself halfway to the knees before he floundered out to the firm crust.

He was angry, and cursed his luck aloud. He had hoped to get into camp with the boys at six o'clock, and this would delay him an hour, for he would have to build a fire and dry out his foot-gear. This was imperative at that low temperature—he knew that much; and he turned aside to the bank, which he climbed. On top, tangled in the underbrush about the trunks of several small spruce trees, was a high-water deposit of dry fire-wood—sticks and twigs, principally, but also larger portions of seasoned branches and fine, dry, last-year's grasses. He threw down several large pieces on top of the snow. This served for a foundation and prevented the young flame from drowning itself in the snow it otherwise would melt. The flame he got by touching a match to a small shred of birch-bark that he took from his pocket. This burned even more readily than paper. Placing it on the foundation, he fed the young flame with wisps of dry grass and with the tiniest dry twigs.

He worked slowly and carefully, keenly aware of his danger. Gradually, as the flame grew stronger, he increased the size of the twigs with which he fed it. He squatted in the snow, pulling the twigs out from their entanglement in the brush and feeding directly to the flame. He knew there must be no failure. When it is seventy-five below zero, a man must not fail in his first attempt to build a fire—that is, if his feet are wet. If his feet are dry, and he fails, he can run along the trail for half a mile and restore his circulation. But the circulation of wet and freezing feet cannot be restored by running when it is seventy-five below. No matter how fast he runs, the wet feet will freeze the harder.

All this the man knew. The old-timer on Sulphur Creek had told him about it the previous fall, and now he was appreciating the advice. Already all sensation had gone out of his feet. To build the fire he had been forced to remove his mittens, and the fingers had quickly gone numb. His pace of four miles an hour had kept his heart pumping blood to the surface of his body and to all the extremities. But the instant he stopped, the action of the pump eased down. The cold of space smote the unprotected tip of the planet, and he, being on that unprotected tip, received the full force of the blow. The blood of his body recoiled before it. The blood was alive, like the dog, and like the dog it wanted to hide away and cover itself up from the fearful cold. So long as he walked four miles an hour, he pumped that blood, willy-nilly, to the surface; but now it ebbed away and sank down into the recesses of his body. The extremities were the first to feel its absence. His wet feet froze the faster, and his exposed fingers numbed the faster, though they had not yet begun to freeze. Nose and cheeks were already freezing, while the skin of all his body chilled as it lost its blood.

But he was safe. Toes and nose and cheeks would be only touched by the frost, for the fire was beginning to burn with strength. He was feeding it with twigs the size of his finger. In another minute he would be able to feed it with branches the size of his wrist, and then he could remove his wet foot-gear, and, while it dried, he could keep his naked feet warm by the fire, rubbing them at first, of course, with snow. The fire was a success. He was safe. He remembered the advice of the old-timer on Sulphur Creek, and smiled. The old-timer had been very serious in laying down the law that no man must travel alone in the Klondike after fifty below. Well, here he was; he had had the accident; he was alone; and he had saved himself. Those old-timers were rather womanish, some of them, he thought. All a man had to do was to keep his head, and he was all right. Any man who was a man could travel alone. But it was surprising, the rapidity with which his cheeks and nose were freezing. And he had not thought his fingers could go lifeless in so short a time. Lifeless they were, for he could scarcely make them move together to grip a twig, and they seemed remote from his body and from him. When he touched a twig, he had to look and see whether or not he had hold of it. The wires were pretty well down between him and his finger-ends.

All of which counted for little. There was the fire, snapping and crackling and promising life with every dancing flame. He started to untie his moccasins. They were coated with ice; the thick German socks were like sheaths of iron halfway to the knees; and the moccasin strings were like rods of steel all twisted and knotted as by some conflagration. For a moment he tugged with his numb fingers, then, realizing the folly of it, he drew his sheath-knife.

But before he could cut the strings, it happened. It was his own fault or, rather, his mistake. He should not have built the fire under the spruce tree. He should have built it in the open. But it had been easier to pull the twigs from the brush and drop them directly on the fire. Now the tree under which he had done this carried a weight of snow on its boughs. No wind had blown for weeks, and each bough was fully freighted. Each time he had pulled a twig he had communicated a slight agitation to the tree—an imperceptible agitation, so far as he was concerned, but an agitation sufficient to bring about the disaster. High up in the tree one bough capsized its load of snow. This fell on the boughs beneath, capsizing them. This process continued, spreading out and involving the whole tree. It grew like an avalanche, and it descended without warning upon the man and the fire, and the fire was blotted out! Where it had burned was a mantle of fresh and disordered snow.

The man was shocked. It was as though he had just heard his own sentence of death. For a moment he sat and stared at the spot where the fire had been. Then he grew very calm. Perhaps the old-timer on Sulphur Creek was right. If he had only had a trail-mate he would have been in no danger now. The trail-mate could have built the fire. Well, it was up to him to build the fire over again, and this second time there must be no failure. Even if he succeeded, he would most likely lose some toes. His feet must be badly frozen by now, and there would be some time before the second fire was ready.

Such were his thoughts, but he did not sit and think them. He was busy all the time they were passing through his mind. He made a new foundation for a fire, this time in the open, where no treacherous tree could blot it out. Next, he gathered dry grasses and tiny twigs from the high-water flotsam. He could not bring his fingers together to pull them out, but he was able to gather them by the handful. In this way he got many rotten twigs and bits of green moss that were undesirable, but it was the best he could do. He worked methodically, even collecting an armful of the larger branches to be used later when the fire gathered strength. And all the while the dog sat and watched him, a certain yearning wistfulness in its eyes, for it looked upon him as the fire-provider, and the fire was slow in coming.

When all was ready, the man reached in his pocket for a second piece of birch-bark. He knew the bark was there, and, though he could not feel it with his fingers, he could hear its crisp rustling as he fumbled for it. Try as he would, he could not clutch hold of it. And all the time, in his consciousness, was the knowledge that each instant his feet were freezing. This thought tended to put him in a panic, but he fought against it and kept calm. He pulled on his mittens with his teeth, and threshed his arms back and forth, beating his hands with all his might against his sides. He did this sitting down, and he stood up to do it; and all the while the dog sat in the snow, its wolf-brush of a tail curled around warmly over its forefeet, its sharp wolf-ears pricked forward intently as it watched the man. And the man, as he beat and threshed with his arms and hands, felt a great surge of envy as he regarded the creature that was warm and secure in its natural covering.

After a time he was aware of the first far-away signals of sensation in his beaten fingers. The faint tingling grew stronger till it evolved into a stinging ache that was excruciating, but which the man hailed with satisfaction. He stripped the mitten from his right hand and fetched forth the birch-bark. The exposed fingers were quickly going numb again. Next he brought out his bunch of sulphur matches. But the tremendous cold had already driven the life out of his fingers. In his effort to separate one match from the others, the whole bunch fell in the snow. He tried to pick it out of the snow, but failed. The dead fingers could neither touch nor clutch. He was very careful. He drove the thought of his freezing feet, and nose, and cheeks, out of his mind, devoting his whole soul to the matches. He watched, using the sense of vision in place of that of touch, and when he saw his fingers on each side the bunch, he closed them—that is, he willed to close them, for the wires were down, and the fingers did not obey. He pulled the mitten on the right hand, and beat it fiercely against his knee. Then, with both mittened hands, he scooped the bunch of matches, along with much snow, into his lap. Yet he was no better off.

After some manipulation he managed to get the bunch between the heels of his mittened hands. In this fashion he carried it to his mouth. The ice crackled and snapped when by a violent effort he opened his mouth. He drew the lower jaw in, curled the upper lip out of the way, and scraped the bunch with his upper teeth in order to separate a match. He succeeded in getting one, which he dropped on his lap. He was no better off. He could not pick it up. Then he devised a way. He picked it up in his teeth and scratched it on his leg. Twenty times he scratched before he succeeded in lighting it. As it flamed he held it with his teeth to the birch-bark. But the burning brimstone went up his nostrils and into his lungs, causing him to cough spasmodically. The match fell into the snow and went out.

The old-timer on Sulphur Creek was right, he thought in the moment of controlled despair that ensued: after fifty below, a man should travel with a partner. He beat his hands, but failed in exciting any sensation. Suddenly he bared both hands, removing the mittens with his teeth. He caught the whole bunch between the heels of his hands. His arm-muscles not being frozen enabled him to press the hand-heels tightly against the matches. Then he scratched the bunch along his leg. It flared into flame, seventy sulphur matches at once! There was no wind to blow them out. He kept his head to one side to escape the strangling fumes, and held the blazing bunch to the birch-bark. As he so held it, he became aware of sensation in his hand. His flesh was burning. He could smell it. Deep down below the surface he could feel it. The sensation developed into pain that grew acute. And still he endured it, holding the flame of the matches clumsily to the bark that would not light readily because his own burning hands were in the way, absorbing most of the flame.

At last, when he could endure no more, he jerked his hands apart. The blazing matches fell sizzling into the snow, but the birch-bark was alight. He began laying dry grasses and the tiniest twigs on the flame. He could not pick and choose, for he had to lift the fuel between the heels of his hands. Small pieces of rotten wood and green moss clung to the twigs, and he bit them off as well as he could with his teeth. He cherished the flame carefully and awkwardly. It meant life, and it must not perish. The withdrawal of blood from the surface of his body now made him begin to shiver, and he grew more awkward. A large piece of green moss fell squarely on the little fire. He tried to poke it out with his fingers, but his shivering frame made him poke too far, and he disrupted the nucleus of the little fire, the burning grasses and tiny twigs separating and scattering. He tried to poke them together again, but in spite of the tenseness of the effort, his shivering got away with him, and the twigs were hopelessly scattered. Each twig gushed a puff of smoke and went out. The fire-provider had failed. As he looked apathetically about him, his eyes chanced on the dog, sitting across the ruins of the fire from him, in the snow, making restless, hunching movements, slightly lifting one forefoot and then the other, shifting its weight back and forth on them with wistful eagerness.

The sight of the dog put a wild idea into his head. He remembered the tale of the man, caught in a blizzard, who killed a steer and crawled inside the carcass, and so was saved. He would kill the dog and bury his hands in the warm body until the numbness went out of them. Then he could build another fire. He spoke to the dog, calling it to him; but in his voice was a strange note of fear that frightened the animal, who had never known the man to speak in such way before. Something was the matter, and its suspicious nature sensed danger—it knew not what danger, but somewhere, somehow, in its brain arose an apprehension of the man. It flattened its ears down at the sound of the man's voice, and its restless, hunching movements and the liftings and shiftings of its forefeet became more pronounced; but it would not come to the man. He got on his hands and knees and crawled toward the dog. This unusual posture again excited suspicion, and the animal sidled mincingly away.

The man sat up in the snow for a moment and struggled for calmness. Then he pulled on his mittens, by means of his teeth, and got upon his feet. He glanced down at first in order to assure himself that he was really standing up, for the absence of sensation in his feet left him unrelated to the earth. His erect position in itself started to drive the webs of suspicion from the dog's mind; and when he spoke peremptorily, with the sound of whip-lashes in his voice, the dog rendered its customary allegiance and came to him. As it came within reaching distance, the man lost his control. His arms flashed out to the dog, and he experienced genuine surprise when he discovered that his hands could not clutch, that there was neither bend nor feeling in the fingers. He had forgotten for the moment that they were frozen and that they were freezing more and more. All this happened quickly, and before the animal could get away, he encircled its body with his arms. He sat down in the snow, and in this fashion held the dog, while it snarled and whined and struggled.

But it was all he could do, hold its body encircled in his arms and sit there. He realized that he could not kill the dog. There was no way to do it. With his helpless hands he could neither draw nor hold his sheathknife nor throttle the animal. He released it, and it plunged wildly away, with tail between its legs, and still snarling. It halted forty feet away and surveyed him curiously, with ears sharply pricked forward. The man looked down at his hands in order to locate them, and found them hanging on the ends of his arms. It struck him as curious that one should have to use his eyes in order to find out where his hands were. He began threshing his arms back and forth, beating the mittened hands against his sides. He did this for five minutes, violently, and his heart pumped enough blood up to the surface to put a stop to his shivering. But no sensation was aroused in the hands. He had an impression that they hung like weights on the ends of his arms, but when he tried to run the impression down, he could not find it.

A certain fear of death, dull and oppressive, came to him. This fear quickly became poignant as he realized that it was no longer a mere matter of freezing his fingers and toes, or of losing his hands and feet, but that it was a matter of life and death with the chances against him. This threw him into a panic, and he turned and ran up the creek-bed along the old, dim trail. The dog joined in behind and kept up with him. He ran blindly, without intention, in fear such as he had never known in his life. Slowly, as he ploughed and floundered through the snow, he began to see things again,—the banks of the creek, the old timber-jams, the leafless aspens, and the sky. The running made him feel better. He did not shiver. Maybe, if he ran on, his feet would thaw out; and, anyway, if he ran far enough, he would reach camp and the boys. Without doubt he would lose some fingers and toes and some of his face; but the boys would take care of him, and save the rest of him when he got there. And at the same time there was another thought in his mind that said he would never get to the camp and the boys; that it was too many miles away, that the freezing had too great a start on him, and that he would soon be stiff and dead.

This thought he kept in the background and refused to consider. Sometimes it pushed itself forward and demanded to be heard, but he thrust it back and strove to think of other things.

It struck him as curious that he could run at all on feet so frozen that he could not feel them when they struck the earth and took the weight of his body. He seemed to himself to skim along above the surface, and to have no connection with the earth. Somewhere he had once seen a winged Mercury, and he wondered if Mercury felt as he felt when skimming over the earth.

His theory of running until he reached camp and the boys had one flaw in it: he lacked the endurance. Several times he stumbled, and finally he tottered, crumpled up, and fell. When he tried to rise, he failed. He must sit and rest, he decided, and next time he would merely walk and keep on going. As he sat and regained his breath, he noted that he was feeling quite warm and comfortable. He was not shivering, and it even seemed that a warm glow had come to his chest and trunk. And yet, when he touched his nose or cheeks, there was no sensation. Running would not thaw them out. Nor would it thaw out his hands and feet. Then the thought came to him that the frozen portions of his body must be extending. He tried to keep this thought down, to forget it, to think of something else; he was aware of the panicky feeling that it caused, and he was afraid of the panic. But the thought asserted itself, and persisted, until it produced a vision of his body totally frozen. This was too much, and he made another wild run along the trail. Once he slowed down to a walk, but the thought of the freezing extending itself made him run again.

And all the time the dog ran with him, at his heels. When he fell down a second time, it curled its tail over its forefeet and sat in front of him, facing him, curiously eager and intent. The warmth and security of the animal angered him, and he cursed it till it flattened down its ears appeasingly. This time the shivering came more quickly upon the man. He was losing in his battle with the frost. It was creeping into his body from all sides. The thought of it drove him on, but he ran no more than a hundred feet, when he staggered and pitched headlong. It was his last panic. When he had recovered his breath and control, he sat up and entertained in his mind the conception of meeting death with dignity. However, the conception did not come to him in such terms. His idea of it was that he had been making a fool of himself, running around like a chicken with its head cut off—such was the simile that occurred to him. Well, he was bound to freeze anyway, and he might as well take it decently. With this new-found peace of mind came the first glimmerings of drowsiness. A good idea, he thought, to sleep off to death. It was like taking an anaesthetic. Freezing was not so bad as people thought. There were lots worse ways to die.

He pictured the boys finding his body next day. Suddenly he found himself with them, coming along the trail and looking for himself. And, still with them, he came around a turn in the trail and found himself lying in the snow. He did not belong with himself any more, for even then he was out of himself, standing with the boys and looking at himself in the snow. It certainly was cold, was his thought. When he got back to the States he could tell the folks what real cold was. He drifted on from this to a vision of the old-timer on Sulphur Creek. He could see him quite clearly, warm and comfortable, and smoking a pipe.

"You were right, old hoss; you were right," the man mumbled to the old-timer of Sulphur Creek.

Then the man drowsed off into what seemed to him the most comfortable and satisfying sleep he had ever known. The dog sat facing him and waiting. The brief day drew to a close in a long, slow twilight. There were no signs of a fire to be made, and, besides, never in the dog's experience had it known a man to sit like that in the snow and make no fire. As the twilight drew on, its eager yearning for the fire mastered it, and with a great lifting and shifting of forefeet, it whined softly, then flattened its ears down in anticipation of being chidden by the man. But the man remained silent. Later, the dog whined loudly. And still later it crept close to the man and caught the scent of death. This made the animal bristle and back away. A little longer it delayed, howling under the stars that leaped and danced and shone brightly in the cold sky. Then it turned and trotted up the trail in the direction of the camp it knew, where were the other food-providers and fire-providers.

1907

In a Far Country

BY JACK LONDON

WHEN A MAN JOURNEYS into a far country, he must be prepared to forget many of the things he has learned, and to acquire such customs as are inherent with existence in the new land; he must abandon the old ideals and the old gods, and oftentimes he must reverse the very codes by which his conduct has hitherto been shaped. To those who have the protean faculty of adaptability, the novelty of such change may even be a source of pleasure; but to those who happen to be hardened to the ruts in which they were created, the pressure of the altered environment is unbearable, and they chafe in body and in spirit under the new restrictions which they do not understand. This chafing is bound to act and react, producing divers evils and leading to various misfortunes. It were better for the man who cannot fit himself to the new groove to return to his own country; if he delay too long, he will surely die.

The man who turns his back upon the comforts of an elder civilization, to face the savage youth, the primordial simplicity of the North, may estimate success at an inverse ratio to the quantity and quality of his hopelessly fixed habits. He will soon discover, if he be a fit candidate, that the material habits are the less important. The exchange of such things as a dainty menu for rough fare, of the stiff leather shoe for the soft, shapeless moccasin, of the feather bed for a couch in the snow, is after all a very easy matter. But his pinch will come in learning properly to shape his mind's attitude toward all things, and especially toward his fellow man. For the courtesies of ordinary life, he must substitute unselfishness, forbearance, and tolerance. Thus, and thus only, can he gain that pearl of great price,—true comradeship. He must not say "Thank you"; he must mean it without opening his mouth, and prove it by responding in kind. In short, he must substitute the deed for the word, the spirit for the letter.

When the world rang with the tale of Arctic gold, and the lure of the North gripped the heartstrings of men, Carter Weatherbee threw up his snug clerkship, turned the half of his savings over to his wife, and with the remainder bought an outfit. There was no romance in his nature,—the bondage of commerce had crushed all that; he was simply tired of the ceaseless grind, and wished to risk great hazards in view of corresponding returns. Like many another fool, disdaining the old trails used by the Northland pioneers for a score of years, he hurried to Edmonton in the spring of the year; and there, unluckily for his soul's welfare, he allied himself with a party of men.

There was nothing unusual about this party, except its plans. Even its goal, like that of all other parties, was the Klondike. But the route it had mapped out to attain that goal took away the breath of the hardiest native, born and bred to the vicissitudes of the Northwest. Even Jacques Baptiste, born of a Chippewa woman and a renegade *voyageur* (having raised his first whimpers in a deerskin lodge north of sixty-fifth parallel, and had the same hushed by blissful sucks of raw tallow), was surprised. Though he sold his services to them and agreed to travel even to the never-opening ice, he shook his head ominously whenever his advice was asked.

Percy Cuthfert's evil star must have been in the ascendant, for he, too, joined this company of argonauts. He was an ordinary man, with a bank account as deep as his culture, which is saying a good deal. He had no reason to embark on such a venture,—no reason in the world, save that he suffered from an abnormal development of sentimentality. He mistook this for the true spirit of romance and adventure. Many another man has done the like, and made as fatal a mistake.

The first break-up of spring found the party following the ice-run of Elk River. It was an imposing fleet, for the outfit was large, and they were accompanied by a disreputable contingent of half-breed *voyageurs* with their women and children. Day in and day out, they labored with the bateaux and canoes, fought mosquitoes and other kindred pests, or sweated and swore at the portages. Severe toil like this lays a man naked to the very roots of his soul, and ere Lake Athabasca was lost in the south, each member of the party had hoisted his true colors.

The two shirks and chronic grumblers were Carter Weather-bee and Percy Cuthfert. The whole party complained less of its aches and pains than did either of them. Not once did they volunteer for the thousand and one petty duties of the camp. A bucket of water to be brought, an extra armful of wood to be chopped, the dishes to be washed and wiped, a search to be made through the outfit for some suddenly indispensable article,—and these two effete scions of civi-lization discovered sprains or blisters requiring instant attention. They were the first to turn in at night, with a score of tasks yet undone; the last to turn out in the morning, when the start should be in readiness before the breakfast was begun. They were the first to fall to at meal-time, the last to have a hand in the cooking; the first to dive for a slim delicacy, the last to discover they had added to their own another man's share. If they toiled at the oars, they slyly cut the water at each stroke and allowed the boat's momentum to float up the blade. They thought nobody noticed; but their comrades swore under their breaths and grew to hate them, while Jacques Baptiste sneered openly and damned them from morning till night. But Jacques Baptiste was no gentleman.

At the Great Slave, Hudson Bay dogs were purchased, and the fleet sank to the guards with its added burden of dried fish and pemmican. Then canoe and bateau answered to the swift current of the Mackenzie, and they plunged into the Great Barren Ground. Every likely-looking "feeder" was prospected, but the elusive "pay-dirt" danced ever to the north. At the Great Bear, overcome by the common dread of the Unknown Lands, their *voyageurs* began to desert, and Fort of Good Hope saw the last and bravest bending to the tow-lines as they bucked the current down which they had so treach-erously glided. Jacques Baptiste alone remained. Had he not sworn to travel even to the never-opening ice?

The lying charts, compiled in main from hearsay, were now constantly consulted. And they felt the need of hurry, for the sun had already passed its northern solstice and was leading the winter south again. Skirting the shores of the bay, where the Mackenzie disem-bogues into the Arctic Ocean, they entered the mouth of the Little Peel River. Then began the arduous up-stream toil, and the two Inca-pables fared worse than ever. Tow-line and pole, paddle and tump-line, rapids and portages,—such tortures served to give the one a deep disgust for great hazards, and printed for the other a fiery text on the true romance of adventure. One day they waxed mutinous, and being vilely cursed by Jacques Baptiste, turned, as worms sometimes will. But the half-breed thrashed the twain, and sent them, bruised and bleeding, about their work. It was the first time either had been man-handled.

Abandoning their river craft at the headwaters of the Little Peel, they consumed the rest of the summer in the great portage over the Mackenzie watershed to the West Rat. This little stream fed the Porcupine, which in turn joined the Yukon where that mighty highway of the North countermarches on the Arctic Circle. But they had lost in the race with winter, and one day they tied their rafts to the thick eddy-ice and hurried their goods ashore. That night the river jammed and broke several times; the following morning it had fallen asleep for good.

"We can't be more 'n four hundred miles from the Yukon," concluded Sloper, multiplying his thumb nails by the scale of the map. The council, in which the two Incapables had whined to excellent disadvantage, was drawing to a close.

"Hudson Bay Post, long time ago. No use um now." Jacques Baptiste's father had made the trip for the Fur Company in the old days, incidentally marking the trail with a couple of frozen toes.

"Sufferin' cracky!" cried another of the party. "No whites?"

"Nary white," Sloper sententiously affirmed; "but it's only five hundred more up the Yukon to Dawson. Call it a rough thousand from here."

Weatherbee and Cuthfert groaned in chorus.

"How long'll that take, Baptiste?"

The half-breed figured for a moment. "Workum like hell, no man play out, ten—twenty—forty—fifty days. Um babies come" (designating the Incapables), "no can tell. Mebbe when hell freeze over; mebbe not then."

The manufacture of snowshoes and moccasins ceased. Somebody called the name of an absent member, who came out of an ancient cabin at the edge of the camp-fire and joined them. The cabin was one of the many mysteries which lurk in the vast recesses of the North. Built when and by whom, no man could tell. Two graves in the open, piled high with stones, perhaps contained the secret of those early wanderers. But whose hand had piled the stones?

The moment had come. Jacques Baptiste paused in the fitting of a harness and pinned the struggling dog in the snow. The cook made mute protest for delay, threw a handful of bacon into a noisy pot of beans, then came to attention. Sloper rose to his feet. His body was a ludicrous contrast to the healthy physiques of the Incapables. Yellow and weak, fleeing from a South American fever-hole, he had not broken his flight across the zones, and was still able to toil with men.

His weight was probably ninety pounds, with the heavy hunting-knife thrown in, and his grizzled hair told of a prime which had ceased to be. The fresh young muscles of either Weatherbee or Cuthfert were equal to ten times the endeavor of his; yet he could walk them into the earth in a day's journey. And all this day he had whipped his stronger comrades into venturing a thousand miles of the stiffest hardship man can conceive. He was the incarnation of the unrest of his race, and the old Teutonic stubbornness, dashed with the quick grasp and action of the Yankee, held the flesh in the bondage of the spirit.

"All those in favor of going on with the dogs as soon as the ice sets, say ay."

"Ay!" rang out eight voices,—voices destined to string a trail of oaths along many a hundred miles of pain.

"Contrary minded?"

"No!" For the first time the Incapables were united without some compromise of personal interests.

"And what are you going to do about it?" Weatherbee added belligerently.

"Majority rule! Majority rule!" clamored the rest of the party.

"I know the expedition is liable to fall through if you don't come," Sloper replied sweetly; "but I guess, if we try real hard, we can manage to do without you. What do you say, boys?"

The sentiment was cheered to the echo.

"But I say, you know," Cuthfert ventured apprehensively; "what's a chap like me to do?"

"Ain't you coming with us?"

"No-o."

"Then do as you damn well please. We won't have nothing to say."

"Kind o' calkilate yuh might settle it with that canoodlin' pardner of yourn," suggested a heavy-going Westerner from the Dakotas, at the same time pointing out Weatherbee. "He'll be shore to ask yuh what yur a-goin' to do when it comes to cookin' an' gatherin' the wood."

"Then we'll consider it all arranged," concluded Sloper. "We'll pull out to-morrow, if we camp within five miles,—just to get everything in running order and remember if we've forgotten anything."

The sleds groaned by on their steel-shod runners, and the dogs strained low in the harnesses in which they were born to die. Jacques Baptiste paused by the side of Sloper to get a last glimpse of the cabin. The smoke curled up pathetically from the Yukon stovepipe. The two Incapables were watching them from the doorway.

Sloper laid his hand on the other's shoulder.

"Jacques Baptiste, did you ever hear of the Kilkenny cats?"

The half-breed shook his head.

"Well, my friend and good comrade, the Kilkenny cats fought till neither hide, nor hair, nor yowl, was left. You understand?—till nothing was left. Very good. Now, these two men don't like work. They won't work. We know that. They'll be alone in that cabin all winter,—a mighty long, dark winter. Kilkenny cats,—well?"

The Frenchman in Baptiste shrugged his shoulders, but the Indian in him was silent. Nevertheless, it was an eloquent shrug, pregnant with prophecy.

Things prospered in the little cabin at first. The rough badinage of their comrades had made Weatherbee and Cuthfert conscious of the mutual responsibility which had devolved upon them; besides, there was not so much work after all for two healthy men. And the removal of the cruel whip-hand, or in other words the bulldozing half-breed, had brought with it a joyous reaction. At first, each strove to outdo the other, and they performed petty tasks with an unction which would have opened the eyes of their comrades who were now wearing out bodies and souls on the Long Trail.

All care was banished. The forest, which shouldered in upon them from three sides, was an inexhaustible woodyard. A few yards from their door slept the Porcupine, and a hole through its winter robe formed a bubbling spring of water, crystal clear and painfully cold. But they soon grew to find fault with even that. The hole would persist in freezing up, and thus gave them many a miserable hour of ice-chopping. The unknown builders of the cabin had extended the side-logs so as to support a cache at the rear. In this was stored the bulk of the party's provisions. Food there was, without stint, for three times the men who were fated to live upon it. But the most of it was of the kind which built up brawn and sinew, but did not tickle the palate. True, there was sugar in plenty for two ordinary men; but these two were little else than children. They early discovered the virtues of hot water judiciously saturated with sugar, and they prodigally swam their flapjacks and soaked their crusts in the rich, white syrup. Then coffee and tea, and especially the dried fruits, made disastrous inroads upon it. The first words they had were over the sugar question. And it is a really serious thing when two men, wholly dependent upon each other for company, begin to quarrel.

Weatherbee loved to discourse blatantly on politics, while Cuthfert, who had been prone to clip his coupons and let the commonwealth jog on as best it might, either ignored the subject or delivered himself of startling epigrams. But the clerk was too obtuse to appreciate the clever shaping of thought, and this waste of ammunition irritated Cuthfert. He had been used to blinding people by his brilliancy, and it worked him quite a hardship, this loss of an audience. He felt personally aggrieved and unconsciously held his mutton-head companion responsible for it.

Save existence, they had nothing in common,—came in touch on no single point. Weatherbee was a clerk who had known naught but clerking all his life; Cuthfert was a master of arts, a dabbler in oils, and had written not a little. The one was a lower-class man who considered himself a gentleman, and the other was a gentleman who knew himself to be such. From this it may be remarked that a man can be a gentleman without possessing the first instinct of true comradeship. The clerk was as sensuous as the other was aesthetic, and his love adventures, told at great length and chiefly coined from his imagination, affected the supersensitive master of arts in the same way as so many whiffs of sewer gas. He deemed the clerk a filthy, uncultured brute, whose place was in the muck with the swine, and told him so; and he was reciprocally informed that he was a milk-and-water sissy and a cad. Weatherbee could not have defined "cad" for his life; but it satisfied its purpose, which after all seems the main point in life.

Weatherbee flatted every third note and sang such songs as "The Boston Burglar" and "The Handsome Cabin Boy," for hours at a time, while Cuthfert wept with rage, till he could stand it no longer and fled into the outer cold. But there was no escape. The intense frost could not be endured for long at a time, and the little cabin crowded them—beds, stove, table, and all—into a space of ten by twelve. The very presence of either became a personal affront to the other, and they lapsed into sullen silences which increased in length and strength as the days went by. Occasionally, the flash of an eye or the curl of a lip got the better of them, though they strove to wholly ignore each other during these mute periods. And a great wonder sprang up in the breast of each, as to how God had ever come to create the other.

With little to do, time became an intolerable burden to them. This naturally made them still lazier. They sank into a physical lethargy which there was no escaping, and which made them rebel at the performance of the smallest chore. One morning when it was his turn to cook the common breakfast, Weatherbee rolled out of his blankets, and to the snoring of his companion, lighted first the slush-lamp and then the fire. The kettles were frozen hard, and there was no water in the cabin with which to wash. But he did not mind that. Waiting for it to thaw, he sliced the bacon and plunged into the hateful task of breadmaking. Cuthfert had been slyly watching through his half-closed lids. Consequently there was a scene, in which they fervently blessed each other, and agreed, thenceforth, that each do his own cooking. A week later, Cuthfert neglected his morning ablutions, but none the less complacently ate the meal which he had cooked. Weatherbee grinned. After that the foolish custom of washing passed out of their lives.

As the sugar-pile and other little luxuries dwindled, they began to be afraid they were not getting their proper shares, and in order that they might not be robbed, they fell to gorging themselves. The luxuries suffered in this gluttonous contest, as did also the men. In the absence of fresh vegetables and exercise, their blood became impoverished, and a loathsome, purplish rash crept over their bodies. Yet they refused to heed the warning. Next, their muscles and joints began to swell, the flesh turning black, while their mouths, gums, and lips took on the color of rich cream. Instead of being drawn together by their misery, each gloated over the other's symptoms as the scurvy took its course.

They lost all regard for personal appearance, and for that matter, common decency. The cabin became a pigpen, and never once were the beds made or fresh pine boughs laid underneath. Yet they could not keep to their blankets, as they would have wished; for the frost was inexorable, and the fire box consumed much fuel. The hair of their heads and faces grew long and shaggy, while their garments would have disgusted a ragpicker. But they did not care. They were sick, and there was no one to see; besides, it was very painful to move about.

To all this was added a new trouble,—the Fear of the North. This Fear was the joint child of the Great Cold and the Great Silence, and was born in the darkness of December, when the sun dipped below the southern horizon for good. It affected them according to their natures. Weatherbee fell prey to the grosser superstitions, and did his best to resurrect the spirits which slept in the forgotten graves. It was a fascinating thing, and in his dreams they came to him from out of the cold, and snuggled into his blankets, and told him of their toils and troubles ere they died. He shrank away from the clammy contact as they drew closer and twined their frozen limbs about him, and when they whispered in his ear of things to come, the cabin rang with his frightened shrieks. Cuthfert did not understand,—for they no longer spoke,—and when thus awakened he invariably grabbed for his revolver. Then he would sit up in bed, shivering nervously, with the weapon trained on the unconscious dreamer. Cuthfert deemed the man going mad, and so came to fear for his life.

His own malady assumed a less concrete form. The mysterious artisan who had laid the cabin, log by log, had pegged a wind-vane to the ridge-pole. Cuthfert noticed it always pointed south, and one day, irritated by its steadfastness of purpose, he turned it toward the east. He watched eagerly, but never a breath came by to disturb it. Then he turned the vane to the north, swearing never again to touch it till the wind did blow. But the air frightened him with its unearthly calm, and he often rose in the middle of the night to see if the vane had veered,—ten degrees would have satisfied him. But no, it poised above him as unchangeable as fate. His imagination ran riot, till it became to him a fetich. Sometimes he followed the path it pointed across the dismal dominions, and allowed his soul to become saturated with the Fear. He dwelt upon the unseen and the unknown till the burden of eternity appeared to be crushing him. Everything in the Northland had that crushing effect,—the absence of life and motion; the darkness; the infinite peace of the brooding land; the ghastly silence, which made the echo of each heart-beat a sacrilege; the solemn forest which seemed to guard an awful, inexpressible something, which neither word nor thought could compass.

The world he had so recently left, with its busy nations and great enterprises, seemed very far away. Recollections occasionally obtruded,—recollections of marts and galleries and crowded thoroughfares, of evening dress and social functions, of good men and dear women he had known,—but they were dim memories of a life he had lived long centuries agone, on some other planet. This phantasm was the Reality. Standing beneath the wind-vane, his eyes fixed on the polar skies, he could not bring himself to realize that the Southland really existed, that at that very moment it was a-roar with life and action. There was no Southland, no men being born of women, no giving and taking in marriage. Beyond his bleak sky-line there stretched vast solitudes, and beyond these still vaster solitudes. There were no lands of sunshine, heavy with the perfume of flowers. Such things were only old dreams of paradise. The sunlands of the West and the spicelands of the East, the smiling Arcadias and blissful Islands of the Blest,—ha! ha! His laughter split the void and shocked him with its unwonted sound. There was no sun. This was the Universe, dead and cold and dark, and he its only citizen. Weatherbee? At such moments Weatherbee did not count. He was a Caliban, a monstrous phantom, fettered to him for untold ages, the penalty of some forgotten crime.

He lived with Death among the dead, emasculated by the sense of his own insignificance, crushed by the passive mastery of the slumbering ages. The magnitude of all things appalled him. Everything partook of the superlative save himself,—the perfect cessation of wind and motion, the immensity of the snow-covered wilderness, the height of the sky and the depth of the silence. That wind-vane,—if it would only move. If a thunderbolt would fall, or the forest flare up in flame. The rolling up of the heavens as a scroll, the crash of Doom—anything, anything! But no, nothing moved; the Silence crowded in, and the Fear of the North laid icy fingers on his heart.

Once, like another Crusoe, by the edge of the river he came upon a track,—the faint tracery of a snowshoe rabbit on the delicate snowcrust. It was a revelation. There was life in the Northland. He would follow it, look upon it, gloat over it. He forgot his swollen muscles, plunging through the deep snow in an ecstasy of anticipation. The forest swallowed him up, and the brief midday twilight vanished; but he pursued his quest till exhausted nature asserted itself and laid him helpless in the snow. There he groaned and cursed his folly, and knew the track to be the fancy of his brain; and late that night he dragged himself into the cabin on hands and knees, his cheeks frozen and a strange numbness about his feet. Weatherbee grinned malevolently, but made no offer to help him. He thrust needles into his toes and thawed them out by the stove. A week later mortification set in.

But the clerk had his own troubles. The dead men came out of their graves more frequently now, and rarely left him, waking or sleeping. He grew to wait and dread their coming, never passing the twin cairns without a shudder. One night they came to him in his sleep and led him forth to an appointed task. Frightened into inarticulate horror, he awoke between the heaps of stones and fled wildly to the cabin. But he had lain there for some time, for his feet and cheeks were also frozen.

Sometimes he became frantic at their insistent presence, and danced about the cabin, cutting the empty air with an axe, and smashing everything within reach. During these ghostly encounters, Cuthfert huddled into his blankets and followed the madman about with a cocked revolver, ready to shoot him if he came too near. But, recovering from one of these spells, the clerk noticed the weapon trained upon him. His suspicions were aroused, and thenceforth he, too, lived in fear of his life. They watched each other closely after that, and faced about in startled fright whenever either passed behind the other's back. This apprehensiveness became a mania which controlled them even in their sleep. Through mutual fear they tacitly let the slush-lamp burn all night, and saw to a plentiful supply of bacon-grease before retiring. The slightest movement on the part of one was sufficient to arouse the other, and many a still watch their gazes countered as they shook beneath their blankets with fingers on the trigger-guards.

What with the Fear of the North, the mental strain, and the ravages of the disease, they lost all semblance of humanity, taking on the appearance of wild beasts, hunted and desperate. Their cheeks and noses, as an aftermath of the freezing, had turned black. Their frozen toes had begun to drop away at the first and second joints. Every movement brought pain, but the fire box was insatiable, wringing a ransom of torture from their miserable bodies. Day in, day out, it demanded its food, —a veritable pound of flesh,—and they dragged themselves into the forest to chop wood on their knees. Once, crawling thus in search of dry sticks, unknown to each other they entered a thicket from opposite sides. Suddenly, without warning, two peering death's-heads confronted each other. Suffering had so transformed them that recognition was impossible. They sprang to their feet, shrieking with terror, and dashed away on their mangled stumps; and falling at the cabin door, they clawed and scratched like demons till they discovered their mistake.

Occasionally they lapsed normal, and during one of these sane intervals, the chief bone of contention, the sugar, had been divided equally between them. They guarded their separate sacks, stored up in the cache, with jealous eyes; for there were but a few cupfuls left, and they were totally devoid of faith in each other. But one day Cuthfert made a mistake. Hardly able to move, sick with pain, with his head swimming and eyes blinded, he crept into the cache, sugar canister in hand, and mistook Weatherbee's sack for his own.

January had been born but a few days when this occurred. The sun had some time since passed its lowest southern declination, and at meridian now threw flaunting streaks of yellow light upon the northern sky. On the day following his mistake with the sugarbag, Cuthfert found himself feeling better, both in body and in spirit. As noontime drew near and the day brightened, he dragged himself outside to feast on the evanescent glow, which was to him an earnest of the sun's future intentions. Weatherbee was also feeling somewhat better, and crawled out beside him. They propped themselves in the snow beneath the moveless wind-vane, and waited.

The stillness of death was about them. In other climes, when nature falls into such moods, there is a subdued air of expectancy, a waiting for some small voice to take up the broken strain. Not so in the North. The two men had lived seeming æons in this ghostly peace. They could remember no song of the past; they could conjure no song of the future. This unearthly calm had always been,—the tranquil silence of eternity.

Their eyes were fixed upon the north. Unseen, behind their backs, behind the towering mountains to the south, the sun swept toward the zenith of another sky than theirs. Sole spectators of the mighty canvas, they watched the false dawn slowly grow. A faint flame began to glow and smoulder. It deepened in intensity, ringing the changes of reddish-yellow, purple, and saffron. So bright did it become that Cuthfert thought the sun must surely be behind it,—a miracle, the sun rising in the north! Suddenly, without warning and without fading, the canvas was swept clean. There was no color in the sky. The light had gone out of the day. They caught their breaths in half-sobs. But lo! the air was a-glint with particles of scintillating frost, and there, to the north, the wind-vane lay in vague outline on the snow. A shadow! A shadow! It was exactly midday. They jerked their heads hurriedly to the south. A golden rim peeped over the mountain's snowy shoulder, smiled upon them an instant, then dipped from sight again.

There were tears in their eyes as they sought each other. A strange softening came over them. They felt irresistibly drawn toward each other. The sun was coming back again. It would be with them tomorrow, and the next day, and the next. And it would stay longer every visit, and a time would come when it would ride their heaven day and night, never once dropping below the sky-line. There would be no night. The ice-locked winter would be broken; the winds would blow and the forests answer; the land would bathe in the blessed sunshine, and life renew. Hand in hand, they would quit this horrid dream and journey back to the Southland. They lurched blindly forward, and their hands met,—their poor maimed hands, swollen and distorted beneath their mittens.

But the promise was destined to remain unfulfilled. The Northland is the Northland, and men work out their souls by strange rules, which other men, who have not journeyed into far countries, cannot come to understand.

An hour later, Cuthfert put a pan of bread into the oven, and fell to speculating on what the surgeons could do with his feet when he got back. Home did not seem so very far away now. Weatherbee was rummaging in the cache. Of a sudden, he raised a whirlwind of blasphemy, which in turn ceased with startling abruptness. The other man had robbed his sugar-sack. Still, things might have happened differently, had not the two dead men come out from under the stones and hushed the hot words in his throat. They led him quite gently from the cache, which he forgot to close. That consummation was reached; that something they had whispered to him in his dreams was about to happen. They guided him gently, very gently, to the woodpile, where they put the axe in his hands. Then they helped him shove open the cabin door, and he felt sure they shut it after him,—at least he heard it slam and the latch fall sharply into place. And he knew they were waiting just without, waiting for him to do his task.

"Carter! I say, Carter!"

Percy Cuthfert was frightened at the look on the clerk's face, and he made haste to put the table between them.

Carter Weatherbee followed, without haste and without enthusiasm. There was neither pity nor passion in his face, but rather the patient, stolid look of one who has certain work to do and goes about it methodically.

"I say, what's the matter?"

The clerk dodged back, cutting off his retreat to the door, but never opening his mouth.

"I say, Carter, I say; let's talk. There's a good chap."

The master of arts was thinking rapidly, now, shaping a skillful flank movement on the bed where his Smith & Wesson lay. Keeping his eyes on the madman, he rolled backward on the bunk, at the same time clutching the pistol.

"Carter!"

The powder flashed full in Weatherbee's face, but he swung his weapon and leaped forward. The axe bit deeply at the base of the spine, and Percy Cuthfert felt all consciousness of his lower limbs leave him. Then the clerk fell heavily upon him, clutching him by the throat with feeble fingers. The sharp bite of the axe had caused Cuthfert to drop the pistol, and as his lungs panted for release, he fumbled aimlessly for it among the blankets. Then he remembered. He slid a hand up the clerk's belt to the sheathknife; and they drew very close to each other in that last clinch.

Percy Cuthfert felt his strength leave him. The lower portion of his body was useless. The inert weight of Weatherbee crushed him,—crushed him and pinned him there like a bear under a trap. The cabin became filled with a familiar odor, and he knew the bread to be burning. Yet what did it matter? He would never need it. And there were all of six cupfuls of sugar in the cache,—if he had foreseen this he would not have been so saving the last several days. Would the wind-vane ever move? It might even be veering now. Why not? Had he not seen the sun to-day? He would go and see. No; it was impossible to move. He had not thought the clerk so heavy a man.

How quickly the cabin cooled! The fire must be out. The cold was forcing in. It must be below zero already, and the ice creeping up the inside of the door. He could not see it, but his past experience enabled him to gauge its progress by the cabin's temperature. The lower hinge must be white ere now. Would the tale of this ever reach the world? How would his friends take it? They would read it over their coffee, most likely, and talk it over at the clubs. He could see them very clearly. "Poor Old Cuthfert," they murmured; "not such a bad sort of a chap, after all." He smiled at their eulogies, and passed on in search of a Turkish bath. It was the same old crowd upon the streets. Strange, they did not notice his moosehide moccasins and tattered German socks! He would take a cab. And after the bath a shave would not be bad. No; he would eat first. Steak, and potatoes, and green things,—how fresh it all was! And what was that? Squares of honey, streaming liquid amber! But why did they bring so much? Ha! ha! he could never eat it all. Shine! Why certainly! He put his foot on the box. The bootblack looked curiously up at him, and he remembered his moosehide moccasins and went away hastily.

Hark! The wind-vane must be surely spinning. No; a mere singing in his ears. That was all,—a mere singing. The ice must have passed the latch by now. More likely the upper hinge was covered. Between the moss-chinked roof-poles, little points of frost began to appear. How slowly they grew! No; not so slowly. There was a new one, and there another. Two—three—four; they were coming too fast to count. There were two growing together. And there, a third had joined them. Why, there were no more spots. They had run together and formed a sheet.

Well, he would have company. If Gabriel ever broke the silence of the North, they would stand together, hand in hand, before the great White Throne. And God would judge them, God would judge them!

Then Percy Cuthfert closed his eyes and dropped off to sleep.

1899

The Shooting of Dan McGrew

BY ROBERT SERVICE

A BUNCH OF THE BOYS WERE WHOOPING IT UP IN THE
    Malamute saloon;
The kid that handles the music-box was hitting a jagtime
    tune;
Back of the bar, in a solo game, sat Dangerous Dan
    McGrew,
And watching his luck was his light-o'-love, the lady that's
    known as Lou.

When out of the night, which was fifty below, and into the
    din and the glare,
There stumbled a miner fresh from the creeks, dogdirty,
    and loaded for bear.
He looked like a man with a foot in the grave, and scarcely
    the strength of a louse,
Yet he tilted a poke of dust on the bar, and he called for
    drinks for the house.
There was none could place the stranger's face, though we
    searched ourselves for a clue;
But we drank his health, and the last to drink was
    Dangerous Dan McGrew.

There's men that somehow just grip your eyes, and hold
      them hard like a spell;
And such was he, and he looked to me like a man who had
      lived in hell;
With a face most hair, and the dreary stare of a dog whose
      day is done,
As he watered the green stuff in his glass, and the drops fell
      one by one.
Then I got to figgering who he was, and wondering what
      he'd do,
And I turned my head—and there watching him was the
      lady that's known as Lou.

His eyes went rubbering round the room, and he seemed
      in a kind of daze,
Till at last that old piano fell in the way of his wandering
      gaze.
The rag-time kid was having a drink; there was no one else
      on the stool,
So the stranger stumbles across the room, and flops down
      there like a fool.
In a buckskin shirt that was glazed with dirt he sat, and I
      saw him sway;
Then he clutched the keys with his talon hands—my God!
      but that man could play!

Were you ever out in the Great Alone, when the moon was
      awful clear,
And the icy mountains hemmed you in with a silence you
      most could *hear;*
With only the howl of a timber wolf, and you camped
      there in the cold,
A half-dead thing in a stark, dead world, clean mad for the
      muck called gold;
While high overhead, green, yellow and red, the North
      Lights swept in bars—
Then you've a haunch what the music meant . . . hunger
      and night and the stars.

And hunger not of the belly kind, that's banished with
    bacon and beans;
But the gnawing hunger of lonely men for a home and all
    that it means;
For a fireside far from the cares that are, four walls and a
    roof above;
But oh! so cramful of cosy joy, and crowned with a
    woman's love;
A woman dearer than all the world, and true as Heaven is
    true—
(God! how ghastly she looks through her rouge,—the lady
    that's known as Lou).

Then on a sudden the music changed, so soft that you
    scarce could hear;
But you felt that your life had been looted clean of all that
    it once held dear;
That someone had stolen the woman you loved; that her
    love was a devil's lie;
That your guts were gone, and the best for you was to
    crawl away and die.
'Twas the crowning cry of a heart's despair, and it thrilled
    you through and through—
"I guess I'll make it a spread misere," said Dangerous Dan
    McGrew.

The music almost died away . . . then it burst like a pent-
    up flood;
And it seemed to say, "Repay, repay," and my eyes were
    blind with blood.
The thought came back of an ancient wrong, and it stung
    like a frozen lash,
And the lust awoke to kill, to kill . . . then the music
    stopped with a crash,

And the stranger turned, and his eyes they burned in a
    most peculiar way;
In a buckskin shirt that was glazed with dirt he sat, and I
    saw him sway;

Then his lips went in in a kind of grin, and he spoke, and
     his voice was calm;
And, "Boys," says he, "you don't know me, and none of
     you care a damn;
But I want to state, and my words are straight, and I'll bet
     my poke they're true,
That one of you is a hound of hell . . . and that one is Dan
     McGrew."

Then I ducked my head, and the lights went out, and two
     guns blazed in the dark;
And a woman screamed, and the lights went up, and two
     men lay stiff and stark;
Pitched on his head, and pumped full of lead, was Danger-
     ous Dan McGrew,
While the man from the creeks lay clutched to the breast of
     the lady that's known as Lou.

These are the simple facts of the case, and I guess I ought
     to know;
They say that the stranger was crazed with "hooch," and
     I'm not denying it's so.
I'm not so wise as the lawyer guys, but strictly between us
     two—
The woman that kissed him and—pinched his poke—was
     the lady that's known as Lou.

In a Klondike Cabin

What a lone man thinks about

BY JOAQUIN MILLER

AND YOU WONDER WHAT A lone man in a Klondike cabin does and thinks about, with nothing at all to read? Would it bore you if I took you into my confidence and told you, frankly and truly, what a live man really does besides hawling wood with a dull old meat ax and carrying water from the Bonanza in a gunny bag? What if I should tell you, heart to heart, soul to soul, what a thinking man thinks about where there are no books, no friends at hand?

It never crossed my mind before, but now in this dead calm that has followed a month of stormy stampedes and excitements I have a mind to risk the pride's displeasure and be a bit boyish—even childish. I have not plucked any roses for a long time; nor eat in the sunlight for months and months. I have only seen a single gleam of sunlight for a few minutes up at the mouth of El Dorado on a high hill-top opposite and run the very breath out of me to try and photograph it and keep it with me. But the sun is getting in his wedge of gold now a bit, just a little bit further in between those black blocks of night every day. To my boundless delight, the sun at 12:00 A.M. to-day felt like a halo on the head of a great mountain peak across the Klondike, and, forgive my folly, I started to try and reach it. Silly? Of course; that is conceded. But, frankly, I would have gone through fire, floods, anything that man might pass, at almost any price, to feel, to touch, to make familiar with once more a little bit of real, solid sunlight.

It was a half mile hard run down the sled trail to the Klondike—then not any trail at all, only the icy river, with its great uplands of blocks and dips and spurs and angles of broken ice. The lion was asleep, so fast asleep! This stormy and swift little river that has shaken the whole world for a year, as the roar of a lion might startle the Arabs of the desert, was as utterly dead as if this snow to your waist was its shroud and the granite walls of the cañon its coffin. Not a ripple of water in the ice, under, the ice, or anywhere. These strange rivers freeze from the bottom, not from the top, like other well-regulated rivers. They freeze first at the mouth, gorge and block up there first, not at the source, as other rivers. This is because the whole under world here is solid ice all summer and all winter—all the year.

I climbed from ice-point to ice-point. The winds had blown the highest here. In some places the snow was solid as a floor; in others, soft and dusty, up to the waist. But it was great fun to wallow through this from point to point till the further shores of this dead river in its shroud and coffin was reached, and the climb! (The Klondike is wide but not deep. I waded it in topboots, dry footed, many times last summer.) The snowshoes had not been thought of this winter day. What could anybody think of but the new-born baby sunlight and the hope of standing once more with the un on the mountain top! The climb was hard and steep and hazardous I made my way up from one clump of trees to another. The snow is not deep under the trees. I took off my fur coat, unbottoned my skin vest, tightened my belt, and at last, breathless, wet all over, I stood—stood where the sun had been. Away over yonder, down the Yukon, the topmost peak of a far out-reaching spur of the Rocky Mountain, where the snow is always there my great golden eagle rested. His plumes were folded, fading, and he was gone in a sudden swoop before the pursuing night.

Ever thus! This is the story of life. We may climb from peak to peak and still the golden sunlight goes ever on before a pillar of the fire that we may never lay hands upon. And who would have it otherwise? A savage, a dog, may await for the sun to come to him, and bask in it but he will still be a savage, a dog. It is the endeavor, the aspiration, that makes manhood. Better to be beaten in any battle of life than never to have lifted your face to combat at all. Ay, ever have I dared do just such foolish ventures, if you choose to call them foolish, looking for the light, the high, bright light above, rather than the blackness below. And this has kept me young and strong and exultant. And my mother even stronger than I at this hour, has ever looked and is still up with the morning, lifting, her face to the peaks for the first sunlight; and after her day in the garden looking for the last ray of fading sunlight above and about her while the world below is drowsily waiting for the gathering darkness. May it ever be so with us both to the end! May she, especially, be ever to the end a lover of the light on the mountain top, ever climbing to attain it! For it seems to me the final step may not be far for such a soul from the peak in its halo of gold to some sweet star outheld to her in the hollow of His hand.

Thus much for the day, one day, at least, when a man is all alone in a Klondike cabin. Ah, but you would have gone and got down in a hole and looked for gold there? Perhaps not. Six months of that sort of work makes you want a change. Five months of candlelight and camplight, and you want a little sunlight. I find others here, strong, good, gold-heaping fellows, so much like myself in these things that they surprise me; only they are not confiding enough, afraid you will laugh at them, to tell you what they really do and want to do and what they think about these long, long nights. You think you would go out and look up at the great, big, buxom moon, in her white evening dress as she walks around and around in low neck all the long night over your head? No! you would like the rest of us, get very tired of her constant familiarity, and almost despire here. The Northern Lights? I had thirty-five days, or rather nights, of flitting, floating, cold and ghostly light as if from some fearful graveyard. Grateful I am for having seen the sudden changes, the floods of light that might fill a world, the blackness, the amber, the gold, the ruby, the great cathedral state of gold, the jasper walls about and the seas of blood above, where the vast white moon waded through; but I could never see these things any more as I saw them those unutterable days of storms and counter elements, those thirty-five nights with scarce a wedge of sunlight driven between the color, the polished light, the awe of it all. I shall never look to these again, for never again might they be seen so divinely terrible.

But what do we think about? I said to Adney, of the London Graphic, a little time ago, at midnight, "You are thinking of the gold, moon, stars, North Pole, Polar bears—or what, these long long, black nights?"

He smiled pleasantly, and at last said, "No; I think most about the birds along the St. Lawrence—the birds, and some pretty little Indian children that I used to play with when a lad."

"What was her name, Adney?"

He drew back a little, looked me in the face and said, "You tell me what you think about first, and what your first little sweetheart's name was, and then maybe I will tell you. But I am not thinking all the time about birds and a little brown sweetheart. I am thinking a great deal about building a home far away where there is no snow. I thought of California first, but now I have got far on down the line, to Nicaragua, for I hear you have snow sometimes in California."

And that is about all the heart I could, without being too familiar, dig out of this very thoughtful and earnest man of art and letters. But it is enough. We are none of us thinking, these long nights, of the gold underfoot, or the moon overhead, or the North Pole at our backs, but sweethearts, birds and kindly climes—all things of life and love and beauty, far, far away.

A gentle, good man whom the world knows and respects, said to me, a month ago, "I think of things at night when alone that I have not thought of for forty years. The other night I got to thinking and thinking, and that night I dreamed of my first school. I had utterly forgotten all about that first time I went to school; yet now I can call the names of at least a dozen of my little schoolmates."

"Tell me the name of the one particular one."

"Her name is sacred, sir; and all the sweet little story of her is sacred. Besides, these things would be nothing to you. Almost anybody would laugh at me for telling any of it, but it is all very dear to me, and I will never forget one hour of it any more."

Now this man thinks he is alone in his pilgrimage back to the buried past. He is, so far as I can find out, no better, nor worse, than the rest of us. And let it not be said of us, in the language of Holy Writ, "The eyes of the fool are in the end of the earth." I have never seen such home-sickness as here. It is more than home-sickness; it is heart-sickness. It is a sighing for and crying crying out for sunlight, warmth, birds, children, one touch of a woman's hand, the sound of a human-woman's voice. Little wonder we go away back in our dreams and look up our lost and long forgotten little sweethearts of the time when we first began to learn the alphabet.

May I diverge here to note three little signs of life that have in the last hour broken the monotony of night? In the first place, a midge, or gnat, tried to crawl across my paper, till he drowned from the ink— and the mercury at 51° below outside! Then, a few minutes later, I heard a buzz in a big block of wood—a log that stood at my side, by the stove, to rest the bread-pan on while the yeast was raising—and soon a big bluebottle fly crawled out of a hole in the log. Now we know where these ugly flies hide and hibernate. And now, mice! First a noiseless little thing, no bigger than a big cricket came timidly out from among the meal bags under the bunks; then another, then another, all white, very small and timid. I think they have pink eyes but am not certain. They all got under cover as I moved to try and find out. In line with this I may mention that we have a little bird here, about the size of the robin, that chirps very like a robin, only not so cheerfully, at night. It is colored a little like the wood dove, and is very tame, and is omnivores. I took one in my hand—one that has been about the door all along—and it readily ate whatever I gave it. The Indians call it the moose bird. The miners call these birds camp robbers. I have seen them in Canadian logging camps, where they are called whiskey jacks. They are always in pairs, like doves, and if one is killed the other is soon found dead near the spot. This makes them more or less sacred, and their rare loyalty keeps them untouched. That, maybe, is why they are so tame. And this little round of insect and animal life is all the showing that this vast, lone land has to offer. Little wonder that, wearying of gold, and cold, and snow, and these endless rounds of the moon, the mind of the exile, when alone in his cabin, will go back—far back—even to babyhood. We have absolutely next to no diversion at all. Yet I should add that we did have three pretty little brown hillside Douglass squirrels, that used to chatter and cheer us from under their tossing tails up in the tree tops; but they suddenly disappeared, hibernating like bears, we hope. When the sun comes this way once more, and reaches out his sword of gold to strike us on the shoulder, and knight us and ennoble us for the battle of life, let us hope the little squirrels will rise up, knighted and ennobled also. A big raven still bowns over us regularly each morning on his way to Dawson, and each evening he drops the same deep, dolorous and cold croak—so cold and hard and heavy that you can almost hear it fall on the cabin roof as he passes. And that is all—quite all of life, action, utterance, that a lone man sees, hears or hears of in any way in a Klondike cabin for more than half the year.

As I write, a young poet of New York City, Howard Hall, drops in to warm his fingers. A heavy pack is on his shoulders; he is on his way, at night, to "stake" on Dominion—a bold thing for a comparative boy, this fronting of a sixty mile tramp through the snow to his hips, and over mountain peaks that companion with the stars! And he knows it, and is, of course, serious as a man who goes into battle knowing the burden of it.

"What do you find to think about, Howard, with no mail, and few congenial men to talk with?"

"Home—home and early childhood. It seems to me that this is a good thing in here to develop and refine the affections. This is a hard venture in here, but I shall be the better for it. I am remembering little things of my early life that I had forgotten long ago. There is, or was, a little girl—she is an old woman now, almost—that I am going to remember in a substantial way if I ever get back with gold enough."

He said much more in his good, sweet way, of home, heart, sweet remembrances of child life, and of later life, too; but perhaps that is all I should print of a man with his future not behind him, as mine is mainly. But the man who is most responsible for his sketch lives in Dawson, is rich, rugged, and has lived—a man of the world, and who is most widely known. He houses alone, but has a sharer in a "roustabout," who goes from cabin to cabin, makes fires, brings water, sweeps floors and sees to the wood pile.

"How long do you sleep, colonel?"

"'Bout seven hours, but stay in bed sixteen or twenty; for wood is forty dollars a cord, and candles cost just about their weight in silver, and as there is nothing to read, why, I just lie in bed and think."

"Now, man to man," and I laid a hand forth on his as we sat sipping his fragrant coffee with a dash of brandy in it, "would you mind telling me, fair, square and fully, what you find to think about?"

He pushed out both feet under the table till they touched mine; he threw back his big bushy iron-gray head, laid his arms out right and left along the edge of the table and laughed—laughed like a giant. He protested. I would put it in the papers? Yes; but not his name, and not her name. Here he laughed and laughed again.

"Not her name? No, I should think not. Her name would fill a bigger paper than yours. But that's just what I think about, old boy, and I am glad I have been driven to it—glad there is no mail, no telegraph, telephone, nothing, not even a dog-fight in Dawson to keep one from remembering the good and the bad. Lots of bad, old boy, but that's past praying for now. I shall be a different man when I get out of this. And let me tell you something right here. These daily papers, hourly telegrams, and five minute telephones are going to take us right to the dogs. We can't keep up this speed. We are going to explode or go to Gehanna. A man don't have time to think of a thing. His childhood is lost to him; his own mother and her sweet lessons are lost; his manhood is lost to him, and an old drivel like myself remembers only the battle and bother of the day before, and at the midnight club dinner is sad because he knows that he can't eat and frolic and flirt as he used to and that at best the most of tomorrow will taste of tonight."

"But tell me about her, if only just one of her."

"Ha, ha, ha, ha! Let me see—how many rooms has the Vatican? Fifteen hundred or fifteen thousand? Well, no matter, my Vatican, in the corner of my own dead and buried old Rome is full—full from cellar to dome. And I go through it every night, a sort of mental Turk; it is my spiritual harem, and it is a great thing, keeps me out of mischief. Why, these poor, skimpy, gold-hunting harpies come here and I give them coffee; and I would give them gold, too, if I had it to throw at birds. Yes, I have money to throw at birds, but not at that sort of birds. I can only pity them. I think, maybe, my dead people, my poor little dead playmates, keep me all right. You see, there was one of them in our miserable, poverty-stricken neck of the woods who was lame. I used to pack her on my back to school. Once I took her some ginger cake; told mother I was sick and couldn't eat it. She cried as she ate it—cried for joy, but ate it through her tears, for she was hungry. She was not pretty, except her great, sad eyes. She was a hunchback, and died before I left there; fell away to be only skin and bone. But do you know who is the queen of my immense harem? That little lame girl of the backwoods. And I had almost forgotten her—in fact, quite forgotten her for more than forty years; but now, every night, she is the first one I call upon. I enter my harem by her door, and I sometimes sit with her a whole hour. I was not very good to anybody after her, as a rule, except to myself, but I believe, as firmly as I believe I am looking you in the face, that she is good to me now. And oh yes, you want to see the beauties, eh? Well, there is one who loves sandal wood, silks, satins, carpets that seem to be pillows. Like all most beautiful women she could not talk very well, and unlike nearly all most beautiful women, had the good sense to be very quiet. And because she is quiet, I like to sit down there a little time now and then. But, as a rule, I run through the whole harem in a short time, and then get back to my childhood of poverty, mother and my little cripple. I go to school, swinging my little dinner basket, looking back at mother on the porch, and remembering each name now."

Of course, the colonel said ever so much more, but not right to the purpose, as this I have here set down almost exactly as it fell from his lips. Dear, honest, frank old scamp and scapegrace of the world! he has no idea that he is only one of a thousand, of five thousand, of us in here.

And now, shall I tell you of my own sweetheart? Well, there was a little girl—all our old sweethearts were little, or should have been—by the name of Harriet Jacobs. Her father had a mill on the waters of the Wabash, and she was with mother much to help along with us three little boys. Papa was the squire, and used to marry people, and perhaps that is what first put it into my mind to marry Harriet Jacobs. She was small and sickly, always shaking with the ague. I was seven years old. "Seven years old, a-goin' on eight," is the way they used to put it in dear old Indiana, and in fact, do still, as I observed when there a few years ago. She was perhaps twenty. Maybe she was twenty, a-goin' on twenty-one. But if anybody had told me I should not marry Harriet Jacobs it would have broken my heart of hearts. Mother says that I was always doing foolish things. I was, in my boyhood, a very gushing, awkward and ungainly lad, with bristling yellow hair that looked like a little brush heap on fire when I was excited; and I remember now, here on the Klondike, although I had forgotten, that I used to comb and comb at that hair, but the more I combed the worse it got. One day, having seen how the lather made papa's beard and hair stick to his face and temples, I stole his cake of castile soap from his shaving box and went to the branch and pasted my hair all down solid. Then I ran to the house and showed it to Harriet. Mother got sight of it, then she took down the stick, a little tough hickory which she always kept for me, and I was made a wailing threshing floor. For I had also lost papa's soap in the branch. The next day that hair was worse than ever, and I went to the wagon wheels and got tar. Tar held it down all right, but when mother tucked us three little boys down in the trundle bed and put her face down she drew it back from me; and then I heard her tell papa she was going to whip me if I didn't stop playing about that old wagon.

Three days I stood the agony of that tar on my head, and then I went to mother, laid my head in her lap and made a howling confession. It was pulling my very boots off by the hair of my aching head. She did not whip me half to death, as I expected, but almost laughed at me, for she knew all about it. And now, after these more than forty years, I can see that my dear older brother, whom I had taken tearfully into my confidence, had told mother and had her promise not to whip me. I was turned over to Harriet Jacobs and sent down to the branch where some Indians were camped and catching fish. On the way, and while she gently cut away the hair and dug at the tar while the Indians looked on, she told me that my hair was very pretty, if I would only let it alone; that it made a sort of halo in the sun, and was not red, but had a sort of Titian and old-gold tint. Harriet had helped papa at his school, and that evening when papa went to feed the hogs I asked him about Titian tints, and he was greatly pleased and told me all about the old Venetian painter who had come down from the Alps to be the lion of Venice. And now I was more certain than ever I should marry poor, sickly little Harriet Jacobs.

A few days later my elder brother and she sat together on the shady side of a big walnut stump that stood in the garden before the door. Now, I was not jealous. To this day, I hardly know what jealousy is except from books, and then I loved my gentle, manly little brother dearly. But I saw some big, yellow ripe cucumbers lying on that stump, and I thought to slip up from the other side and push one of them down on their heads and scare them. But after I crept up there I found these were rotten, and so I thought instead to push off a stone that papa had laid there when planting the garden. I could not see where it would fall, but I was so full of laugh at what I was doing that I gave it a shove, and then ran away with a shout. Mother heard me and came to the door. Then she ran to Harriet, and she and my brother helped her into the house and to bed, and tied up her head in vinegar. Goodness gracious! How all these things come back to me now, as distinctly as if yesterday! Mother took me behind the smoke-house. She had her right hand behind her till she got out of Harriet's hearing, then out came the hand and the hickory. There was a blotch of blood on my little homemade shirt when I got to the branch and jerked it and my other things off to drown myself. Oh, I was going to die right there. I had nearly killed Harriet and she never, never would marry me now, anyhow. And then, that thrashing! That thrashing was really terrible, and was all wrong, too. I can say this truly, after all these years, that this ungainly gosling of mother's got thrashed when he did not deserve it many times when he was little. But on the other hand, let it be as frankly admitted that he deserved many a thrashing when he got big that he did not get. So the thing is about even. Anyhow, mother did what she thought was her duty, and she always told me that the whipping hurt her more than it did me. And after all these years, as I sit here by the frozen Klondike bank, I know it was true, but I didn't believe a word of it then.

I rushed out to the willows where the Indians camped and was going to throw myself into the water far out, in a most dramatic fashion, after my last words of farewell to Harriet and mother, which I hoped the Indians would hear and take to them along with my clothes and my dead and dripping body. But I fell in over my head before I got to my last words, and an Indian mother swam in, laughing gleefully, and took me down to where her children were at play in the water. The naked, brown children laughed and played and tried to make me swim. But I was so shy and naked that I had only one use for my two hands. Then a pretty little girl pulled me into the water with her and almost drowned me till I had to swim. And then, what fun! We swam, we dived, we laughed, we flirted. I forgot Harriet. I was in love, my second love, in less than an hour. The little black-eyed Indian girl was really very, very pretty. She is at this hour the queen of my early memories. I was so happy I pulled some wild flowers for mother on my way to the house, and she took my head in her lap with the flowers and we kissed and made up. I was never—as I remember it now—I have never been so happy as I was that day when I rolled a big stone down from the stump on the head of my first love. I wanted to tell mother all about the Indian girl, but I was afraid she would tell Harriet, and that she might be jealous and miserable, and also try to drown herself.

I was often and often in the water with the Indian children after that and so became a famous swimmer and lover of streams. Some days I went in quite another direction and got wild flowers and fruit for mother, fearing she might follow me and find out about my sweetheart, with whom I was determined to elope and marry and die. And this it was that got me to loving the woods, wild flowers, birds, solitude, song. But the Indians folded their tents at last and suddenly went. I never knew where.

Would it seem silly if I should write it down here on the Klondike banks as a cold, frozen truth that the unkind and thoughtless rolling of that stone made me to love the wilderness, solitude, savages and savage life—made me, good or bad, what I am? Why, but for that, I should have gone to town as other boys, stood on street corners, talked politics, attended conventions, kept with the crowd, made speeches, kept on and on in my low ways, getting lower and lower, till at last, possibly, I should have found myself in the lower House of Congress.

The Test

BY REX BEACH

PIERRE "FEROCE" SHOWED disapproval in his every attitude as plainly as disgust peered from the seams in his dark face; it lurked in his scowl and in the curl of his long rawhide that bit among the sled dogs. So at least thought Willard, as he clung to the swinging sledge.

They were skirting the coast, keeping to the glare ice, windswept and clean, that lay outside the jumbled shore pack. The team ran silently in the free gait of the gray wolf, romping in harness from pure joy of motion and the intoxication of perfect life, making the sled runners whine like the song of a cutlass.

This route is dangerous, of course, from hidden cracks in the floes, and most travelers hug the bluffs, but he who rides with Pierre "Feroce" takes chances. It was this that had won him the name of "Wild" Pierre—the most reckless, tireless man of the trails, a scoffer at peril, bolting through danger with rush and frenzy, overcoming sheerly by vigor those obstacles which destroy strong men in the North.

The power that pulsed within him gleamed from his eyes, rang in his song, showed in the aggressive thrust of his sensual face.

This particular morning, however, Pierre's distemper had crystallized into a great contempt for his companion. Of all trails, the most detestable is to hit the trail with half a man, a pale, anemic weakling like this stranger.

Though modest in the extent of his learning, Pierre gloated in a freedom of speech, the which no man dared deny him. He turned to eye his companion cynically for a second time, and contempt was patent in his gaze. Willard appeared slender and pallid in his furs, though his clear-cut features spoke a certain strength and much refinement.

"Bah! I t'ink you dam poor feller," he said finally. "Ow'ye goin' stan' thees trip, eh? She's need beeg mans not leetle runt like you?"

Amusement at this frankness glimmered in Willard's eyes.

"You're like all ignorant people. You think in order to stand hardship a man should be able to toss a sack of flour in his teeth or juggle a cask of salt-horse."

"Sure t'ing," grinned Pierre. "That's right. Look at me. Mebbe you hear 'bout Pierre 'Feroce' sometime, eh?"

"Oh, yes; everybody knows you; knows you're a big bully. I've seen you drink a quart of this wood alcohol they call whiskey up here, and then jump the bar from a stand, but you're all animal—you haven't the refinement and the culture that makes real strength. It's the mind that makes us stand punishment."

"Ha! ha! ha!" laughed the Canadian. "W'at a fonny talk. She'll take the heducate man for stan' the col', eh? Mon Dieu!" He roared again till the sled dogs turned fearful glances backward and bushy tails dropped under the weight of their fright. Great noise came oftenest with great rage from Pierre, and they had too frequently felt the both to forget.

"Yes, you haven't the mentality. Sometime you'll use up your physical resources and go to pieces like a burned wick."

Pierre was greatly amused. His yellow teeth shone, and he gave vent to violent mirth as, following the thought, he pictured a naked mind wandering over the hills with the quicksilver at sixty degrees.

"Did you ever see a six-day race? Of course not; you barbarians haven't sunk to the level of our dissolute East, where we joy in Roman spectacles, but if you had you'd see it's will that wins; it's the man that eats his soul by inches. The educated soldier stands the campaign best. You run too much to muscle—you're not balanced."

"I t'ink mebbe you'll 'ave chance for show 'im, thees stout will of yours. She's goin' be long 'mush' troo the mountains, plentee snow, plentee cold."

Although Pierre's ridicule was galling, Willard felt the charm of the morning too strongly to admit of anger or to argue his pet theory.

The sun, brilliant and cold, lent a paradoxical cheerfulness to the desolation, and, though never a sign of life broke the stillness around them, the beauty of the scintillant, gleaming mountains, distinct as cameos, that guarded the bay, appealed to him with the strange attraction of the Arctics; that attraction that calls and calls insistently, till men forsake God's country for its mystery.

He breathed the biting air cleaned by leagues of lifeless barrens and voids of crackling frost till he ached with the exhilaration of a perfect morning on the Circle.

Also before him undulated the grandest string of dogs the Coast had known. Seven there were, tall and gray, with tails like plumes, whom none but Pierre could lay hand upon, fierce and fearless as their master. He drove with the killing cruelty of a stampeder, and they loved him.

"You say you have grub cachèd at the old Indian hut on the Good Hope?" questioned Willard.

"Sure! five poun' bacon, leetle flour and rice. I cachè one gum-boot too, ha! Good thing for make fire queeck, eh?"

"You bet; an old rubber boot comes handy when it's too cold to make shavings."

Leaving the coast, they ascended a deep and tortuous river where the snow lay deep and soft. One man on snow-shoes broke trail for the dogs till they reached the foothills. It was hard work, but infinitely preferable to that which followed, for now they came into a dangerous stretch of overflows. The stream, frozen to its bed, clogged the passage of the spring water beneath, forcing it up through cracks till it spread over the solid ice, forming pools and sheets covered with treacherous ice-skins. Wet feet are fatal to man and beast, and they made laborious detours, wallowing trails through tangled willows waist deep in the snow smother, or clinging precariously to the over-hanging bluffs. As they reached the river's source the sky blackened suddenly, and great clouds of snow rushed over the bleak hills, boiling down into the valley with a furious draught. They flung up their flimsy tent, only to have it flattened by the force of the gale that cut like well-honed steel. Frozen spots leaped out white on their faces, while their hands stiffened ere they could fasten the guy strings.

Finally, having lashed the tent bottom to the protruding willow tops, by grace of heavy lifting they strained their flapping shelter up sufficiently to crawl within.

"By Gar! She's blow hup ver' queek," yelled Pierre, as he set the ten-pound sheet-iron stove, its pipe swaying drunkenly with the heaving tent.

"Good t'ing she hit us in the brush." He spoke as calmly as though danger was distant and a moment later the little box was roaring with its oil-soaked kindlings.

"Will this stove burn green willow tops?" cried Willard.

"Sure! She's good stove. She'll burn hicicles eef you get 'im start one times. See 'im get red!"

They rubbed the stiff spots from their cheeks, then, seizing the axe, Willard crawled forth into the storm and dug at the base of the gnarled bushes. Occasionally a shrub assumed the proportions of a man's wrist—but rarely. Gathering an armful, he bore them inside and twisting the tips into withes, he fed the fire. The frozen twigs sizzled and snapped, threatening to fail utterly, but with much blowing he sustained a blaze sufficient to melt a pot of snow. Boiling was out of the question, but the tea leaves became soaked and the bacon cauterized.

Pierre freed and fed the dogs. Each gulped its dried salmon, and, curling in the lee of the tent, was quickly drifted over. Next he cut blocks from the solid bottom snow and built a barricade to windward. Then he accumulated a mow of willow tops without the tent-fly. All the time the wind drew down the valley like the breath of a giant bellows.

"Supper," shouted Willard, and as Pierre crawled into the candle-light he found him squatted, fur-bundled, over the stove, which settled steadily into the snow, melting its way downward toward a firmer foundation.

The heat was insufficient to thaw the frozen sweat in his clothes; his eyes were bleary and wet from smoke, and his nose needed continuous blowing, but he spoke pleasantly, a fact which Pierre noted with approval.

"We'll need a habeas corpus for this stove if you don't get something to hold her up, and I might state, if it's worthy of mention, that your nose is frozen again."

Pierre brought an armful of stones from the creek edge, distributing them beneath the stove on a bed of twisted willows; then swallowing their scanty, half-cooked food, they crawled, shivering, into the deerskin sleeping bags, that animal heat might dry their clammy garments.

Four days the wind roared and the ice filings poured over their shelter while they huddled beneath. When one travels on rations delay is dangerous. Each morning, dragging themselves out into the maelstrom, they took sticks and poked into the drifts for dogs. Each animal as found was exhumed, given a fish, and became straightway reburied in the whirling white that seethed down from the mountains.

On the fifth, without warning, the storm died, and the air stilled to a perfect silence.

"These dog bad froze," said Pierre, swearing earnestly as he harnessed. "I don't like eet much. They goin' play hout I'm 'fraid." He knelt and chewed from between their toes the ice pellets that had accumulated. A malamoot is hard pressed to let his feet mass, and this added to the men's uneasiness.

As they mounted the great divide, mountains rolled away on every hand, barren, desolate, marble-white; always the whiteness; always the listening silence that oppressed like weight. Myriads of creek valleys radiated below in a bewildering maze of twisting seams.

"Those are the Ass's Ears, I suppose," said Willard, gazing at two great fangs that bit deep into the sky-line. "Is it true that no man has ever reached them?"

"Yes. The hinjun say that's w'ere hall the storm come from, biccause w'en the win' blow troo the Ass's Ear, look out! Somebody goin' ketch 'ell."

Dogs' feet wear quickly after freezing, for crusted snow cuts like a knife. Spots of blood showed in their tracks, growing more plentiful till every print was a crimson stain. They limped pitifully on their raw pads, and occasionally one whined. At every stop they sank in the track, licking their lacerated paws, rising only at the cost of much whipping.

On the second night, faint and starved, they reached the hut. Digging away the drifts, they crawled inside to find it half full of snow —snow which had sifted through the crevices. Pierre groped among the shadows and swore excitedly.

"What's up?" said Willard.

Vocal effort of the simplest is exhausting when spent with hunger, and these were the first words he had spoken for hours.

"By Gar! she's gone. Somebody stole my grub!"

Willard felt a terrible sinking, and his stomach cried for food.

"How far is it to the Crooked River Road House?"

"One long day drive—forty mile."

"We must make it to-morrow or go hungry, eh? Well, this isn't the first dog fish I ever ate." Both men gnawed a moldy dried salmon from their precious store.

As Willard removed his footgear, he groaned.

"W'at's the mattaire?"

"I froze my foot two days ago—snowshoe strap too tight." He exhibited a heel, from which, in removing his inner sock, the flesh and skin had come away.

"That's all right," grinned Pierre. "You got the beeg will lef' yet. It take the heducate man for stan' the col', you know."

Willard gritted his teeth.

They awoke to the whine of a gray windstorm that swept the cutting snow in swirling clouds and made travel a madness. The next day was worse.

Two days of hunger weigh heavy when the cold weakens, and they grew gaunt and fell away in their features.

"I'm glad we've got another feed for the dogs," remarked Willard. "We can't let *them* run hungry, even if *we* do."

"I t'ink she's be hall right to-mor'," ventured Pierre. "Thees ain't snow—jus' win'; bimeby all blow hout. Sacré! I'll can eat 'nuff for 'ole harmy."

For days both men had been cold, and the sensation of complete warmth had come to seem strange and unreal, while their faces cracked where the spots had been.

Willard felt himself on the verge of collapse. He recalled his words about strong men gazing the while at Pierre. The Canadian evinced suffering only in the haggard droop of eye and mouth; otherwise he looked strong and dogged.

Willard felt his own features had shrunk to a mask of loose-jawed suffering, and he set his mental sinews, muttering to himself.

He was dizzy and faint as he stretched himself in the still morning air upon waking, and hobbled painfully, but as his companion emerged from the darkened shelter into the crystalize brightness he forgot his own misery at sight of him. The big man reeled as though struck when the dazzle from the hills reached him, and he moaned, shielding his sight. Snow blindness had found him in a night.

Slowly they plodded out of the valley, for hunger gnawed acutely, and they left a trail of blood tracks from the dogs. It took the combined efforts of both men to lash them to foot after each pause. Thus progress was slow and fraught with agony.

As they rose near the pass, miles of Arctic wastes bared themselves. All about towered bald domes, while everywhere stretched the monotonous white, the endless snow unbroken by tree or shrub, pallid and menacing, maddening to the eye.

"Thank God, the worst's over," sighed Willard, flinging himself onto the sled. "We'll make it to the summit next time; then she's down hill all the way to the road house."

Pierre said nothing.

Away to the northward glimmered the Ass's Ears, and as the speaker eyed them carelessly he noted gauzy shreds and streamers veiling their tops. The phenomena interested him, for he knew that here must be wind—wind, the terror of the bleak tundra; the hopeless, merciless master of the barrens! However the distant range beneath the twin peaks, showed clear-cut and distinct against the sky, and he did not mention the occurrence to the guide, although he recalled the words of the Indians: "Beware of the wind through the Ass's Ears."

Again they labored up the steep slope, wallowing in the sliding snow, straining silently at the load; again they threw themselves, exhausted, upon it. Now, as he eyed the panorama below, it seemed to have suffered a subtle change, indefinable and odd. Although but a few minutes had elapsed, the coast mountains no longer loomed clear against the horizon, and his visual range appeared foreshortened, as though the utter distances had lengthened, bringing closer the edge of things. The twin peaks seemed endlessly distant and hazy, while the air had thickened as though congested with possibilities, lending a remoteness to the landscape.

"If it blows up on us here, we're gone," he thought, "for it's miles to shelter, and we're right in the saddle of the hills."

Pierre, half blinded as he was, arose uneasily and cast the air like a wild beast, his great head thrown back, his nostrils quivering.

"I smell the win'," he cried. "Mon Dieu! She's goin' blow!"

A volatile pennant floated out from a near-by peak hanging about its crest like faint smoke. Then along the brow of the pass writhed a wisp of drifting, twisting flaklets, idling hither and yon, astatic and aimless, settling in a hollow. They sensed a thrill and rustle to the air, though never a breath had touched them; then, as they mounted higher, a draught fanned them, icy as interstellar space. The view from the summit was grotesquely distorted, and glancing upward they found the guardian peaks had gone asmoke with clouds of snow that whirled confusedly, while an increasing breath sucked over the summit, stronger each second. Dry snow began to rustle slothfully about their feet. So swiftly were the changes wrought, that before the mind had grasped their import the storm was on them, roaring down from every side, swooping out of the boiling sky, a raging blast from the voids of sunless space.

Pierre's shouts as he slashed at the sled lashings were snatched from his lips in scattered scraps. He dragged forth the whipping tent and threw himself upon it with the sleeping bags. Having cut loose the dogs, Willard crawled within his sack and they drew the flapping canvas over them. The air was twilight and heavy with efflorescent granules that hurtled past in a drone.

They removed their outer garments that the fur might fold closer against them, and lay exposed to the full hate of the gale. They hoped to be drifted over, but no snow could lodge in this hurricane, and it sifted past, dry and sharp, eddying out a bare place wherein they lay. Thus the wind drove the chill to their bones bitterly.

An unnourished human body responds but weakly, so, vitiated by their fast and labors, their suffering smote them with tenfold cruelty.

All night the north wind shouted, and, as the next day waned with its violence undiminished, the frost crept in upon them till they rolled and tossed, shivering. Twice they essayed to crawl out, but were driven back to cover for endless, hopeless hours.

It is in such black, aimless times that thought becomes distorted. Willard felt his mind wandering through bleak dreams and tortured fancies, always to find himself harping on his early argument with Pierre: "It's the mind that counts." Later he roused to the fact that his knees, where they pressed against the bag, were frozen; also his feet were numb and senseless. In his acquired consciousness he knew that along the course of his previous mental vagary lay madness, and the need of action bore upon him imperatively.

He shouted to his mate, but "Wild" Pierre seemed strangely apathetic.

"We've got to run for it at daylight. We're freezing. Here! Hold on! What are you doing? Wait for daylight!" Pierre had scrambled stiffly out of his cover and his gabblings reached Willard. He raised a clenched fist into the darkness of the streaming night, cursing horribly with words that appalled the other.

"Man! man! don't curse your God. This is bad enough as it is. Cover up. Quick!"

Although apparently unmindful of his presence, the other crawled back muttering.

As the dim morning grayed the smother they rose and fought their way downward toward the valley. Long since they had lost their griping hunger, and now held only an apathetic indifference to food, with a cringing dread of the cold and a stubborn sense of their extreme necessity.

They fell many times, but gradually drew themselves more under control, the exercise suscitating them, as they staggered downward, blinded and buffeted, their only hope the road house.

Willard marveled dully at the change in Pierre. His great face had shriveled to blackened freezes stretched upon a bony substructure, and lighted by feverish, glittering, black, black eyes. It seemed to him that his own lagging body had long since failed, and that his aching, naked soul wandered stiffly through the endless day. As night approached Pierre stopped frequently, propping himself with legs far apart; sometimes he laughed. Invariably this horrible sound shocked Willard into a keener sense of the surroundings, and it grew to irritate him, for the Frenchman's mental wanderings increased with the darkness. What made him rouse one with his awful laughter? These spells of walking insensibility were pleasanter far. At last the big man fell. To Willard's mechanical endeavors to help he spoke sleepily, but with the sanity of a man under great stress.

"Dat, no god. I'm goin' freeze right 'ere—freeze stiff as 'ell. Au revoir."

"Get up!" Willard kicked him weakly, then sat upon the prostrate man as his own faculties went wandering.

Eventually he roused, and digging into the snow burned the other, first covering his face with the ample parka hood. Then he struck down the valley. In one lucid spell he found he had followed a sled trail, which was blown clear and distinct by the wind that had now almost died away.

Occasionally his mind grew clear, and his pains beat in upon him till he grew furious at the life in him which refused to end, which forced him ever through his gauntlet of misery. Most often he was conscious only of a vague and terrible extremity outside of himself that goaded him forever forward. Anon he strained to recollect his destination. His features had set in an implacable grimace of physical torture—like a runner in the fury of a finish—till the frost hardened them so. At times he fell heavily, face downward; and at length upon the trail, lying so till that omnipresent coercion that had frozen in his brain drove him forward.

He heard his own voice maundering through lifeless lips like that of a stranger: "The man that can eat his soul will win, Pierre."

Sometimes he cried like a child and slaver ran from his open mouth, freezing at his breast. One of his hands was going dead. He stripped the left mitten off and drew it laboriously over the right. One he would save at least, even though he lost the other. He looked at the bare member dully, and he could not tell that the cold had eased till the bitterness was nearly out of the air. He labored with the fitful spurts of a machine run down.

Ten men and many dogs lay together in the Crooked River Road House through the storm. At late bedtime of the last night came a scratching on the door.

"Somebody's left a dog outside," said a teamster, and rose to let him in. He opened the door only to retreat affrightedly.

"My God!" he said. "My God!" and the miners crowded forward.

A figure tottered over the portal, swaying drunkenly. They shuddered at the sight of its face as it crossed toward the fire. It did not walk; it shuffled, haltingly, with flexed knees and hanging shoulders, the strides measuring inches only—a grisly burlesque upon senility.

Pausing in the circle, it mumbled thickly, with great effort, as though gleaning words from infinite distance.

"Wild Pierre—frozen—buried—in—snow—hurry!" then he straightened and spoke strongly, his voice flooding the room:

"It's the mind, Pierre. Ha! ha! ha! The mind."

He cackled hideously, and plunged forward into a miner's arms.

It was many days before his delirium broke. Gradually he felt the pressure of many bandages upon him, and the hunger of convalescence. As he lay in his bunk the past came to him hazy and horrible; then the hum of voices, one loud, insistent, and familiar.

He turned weakly, to behold Pierre propped in a chair by the stove, frost-scarred and pale, but aggressive even in recuperation. He gesticulated fiercely with a bandaged hand, hot in controversy with some big-limbed, bearded strangers.

"Bah! You fellers no good—too beeg in the ches', too leetle in the forehead. She'll tak' the heducate mans for stan' the 'ard-sheep—lak' me an' Meestaire Weelard."

The Weight of Obligation

BY REX BEACH

THIS IS THE STORY OF A burden, the tale of a load that irked a strong man's shoulders. To those who do not know the North it may seem strange, but to those who understand the humors of men in solitude, and the extravagant vagaries that steal in upon their minds, as fog drifts with the night, it will not appear unusual. There are spirits in the wilderness, eerie forces which play pranks; some droll or whimsical, others grim.

Johnny Cantwell and Mortimer Grant were partners, trailmates, brothers in soul if not in blood. The ebb and flow of frontier life had brought them together, its hardships had united them until they were as one. They were something of a mystery to each other, neither having surrendered all his confidence, and because of this they retained their mutual attraction. Had they known each other fully, had they thoroughly sounded each other's depths, they would have lost interest, just like husbands and wives who give themselves too freely and reserve nothing.

They had met by accident, but they remained together by desire, and so satisfactory was the union that not even the jealousy of women had come between them. There had been women, of course, just as there had been adventures of other sorts, but the love of the partners was larger and finer than anything else they had experienced. It was so true and fine and unselfish, in fact, that either would have smilingly relinquished the woman of his desires had the other wished to possess her. They were young, strong men, and the world was full of sweethearts, but where was there a partnership like theirs, they asked themselves.

The spirit of adventure bubbled merrily within them, too, and it led them into curious byways. It was this which sent them northward from the States in the dead of winter, on the heels of the Stony River strike; it was this which induced them to land at Katmai instead of Illiamna, whither their land journey should have commenced.

"There are two routes over the coast range," the captain of the *Dora* told them, "and only two. Illiamna Pass is low and easy, but the distance is longer than by way of Katmai. I can land you at either place."

"Katmai is pretty tough, isn't it?" Grant inquired.

"We've understood it's the worst pass in Alaska." Cantwell's eyes were eager.

"It's a heller! Nobody travels it except natives, and they don't like it. Now, Illiamna—"

"We'll try Katmai. Eh, Mort?"

"Sure! They don't come hard enough for us, Cap. We'll see if it's as bad as it's painted."

So, one gray January morning they were landed on a frozen beach, their outfit was flung ashore through the surf, the life-boat pulled away, and the *Dora* disappeared after a farewell toot of her whistle. Their last glimpse of her showed the captain waving good-by and the purser flapping a red table-cloth at them from the after-deck.

"Cheerful place, this," Grant remarked, as he noted the desolate surroundings of dune and hillside.

The beach itself was black and raw where the surf washed it, but elsewhere all was white, save for the thickets of alder and willow which protruded nakedly. The bay was little more than a hollow scooped out of the Alaskan range; along the foot-hills behind there was a belt of spruce and cottonwood and birch. It was a lonely and apparently unpeopled wilderness in which they had been set down.

"Seems good to be back in the North again, doesn't it?" said Cantwell, cheerily. "I'm tired of the booze, and the street-cars, and the dames, and all that civilized stuff. I'd rather be broke in Alaska—with you—than a banker's son, back home."

Soon a globular Russian half-breed, the Katmai trader, appeared among the dunes, and with him were some native villagers. That night the partners slept in a snug log cabin, the roof of which was chained down with old ships' cables. Petellin, the fat little trader, explained that roofs in Katmai had a way of sailing off to seaward when the wind blew. He listened to their plan of crossing the divide and nodded.

It could be done, of course, he agreed, but they were foolish to try it, when the Illiamna route was open. Still, now that they were here, he would find dogs for them, and a guide. The village hunters were out after meat, however, and until they returned the white men would need to wait in patience.

There followed several days of idleness, during which Cantwell and Grant amused themselves around the village, teasing the squaws, playing games with the boys, and flirting harmlessly with the girls, one of whom, in particular, was not unattractive. She was perhaps three-quarters Aleut, the other quarter being plain coquette, and, having been educated at the town of Kodiak, she knew the ways and the wiles of the white man.

Cantwell approached her, and she met his extravagant advances more than half-way. They were getting along nicely together when Grant, in a spirit of fun, entered the game and won her fickle smiles for himself. He joked his partner unmercifully, and Johnny accepted defeat gracefully, never giving the matter a second thought.

When the hunters returned, dogs were bought, a guide was hired, and, a week after landing, the friends were camped at timberline awaiting a favorable moment for their dash across the range. Above them white hillsides rose in irregular leaps to the gash in the saw-toothed barrier which formed the pass; below them a short valley led down to Katmai and the sea. The day was bright, the air clear, nevertheless after the guide had stared up at the peaks for a time he shook his head, then re-entered the tent and lay down. The mountains were "smoking"; from their tops streamed a gossamer veil which the travellers knew to be drifting snow clouds carried by the wind. It meant delay, but they were patient.

They were up and going on the following morning, however, with the Indian in the lead. There was no trail; the hills were steep; in places they were forced to unload the sled and hoist their outfit by means of ropes, and as they mounted higher the snow deepened. It lay like loose sand, only lighter; it shoved ahead of the sled in a feathery mass; the dogs wallowed in it and were unable to pull, hence the greater part of the work devolved upon the men. Once above the foothills and into the range proper, the going became more level, but the snow remained knee-deep.

The Indian broke trail stolidly; the partners strained at the sled, which hung back like a leaden thing. By afternoon the dogs had become disheartened and refused to heed the whip. There was neither fuel nor running water, and therefore the party did not pause for luncheon. The men were sweating profusely from their exertions and had long since become parched with thirst, but the dry snow was like chalk and scoured their throats.

Cantwell was the first to show the effects of his unusual exertions, for not only had he assumed a lion's share of the work, but the last few months of easy living had softened his muscles, and in consequence his vitality was quickly spent. His undergarments were drenched; he was fearfully dry inside; a terrible thirst seemed to penetrate his whole body; he was forced to rest frequently.

Grant eyed him with some concern, finally inquiring, "Feel bad, Johnny?"

Cantwell nodded. Their fatigue made both men economical of language.

"What's the matter?"

"Thirsty!" The former could barely speak.

"There won't be any water till we get across. You'll have to stand it."

They resumed their duties; the Indian "swish-swished" ahead, as if wading through a sea of swan's-down; the dogs followed listlessly; the partners leaned against the stubborn load.

A faint breath finally came out of the north, causing Grant and the guide to study the sky anxiously. Cantwell was too weary to heed the increasing cold. The snow on the slopes above began to move; here and there, on exposed ridges, it rose in clouds and puffs; the cleancut outlines of the hills became obscured as by a fog; the languid wind bit cruelly.

After a time Johnny fell back upon the sled and exclaimed: "I'm—all in, Mort. Don't seem to have the—guts." He was pale, his eyes were tortured. He scooped a mitten full of snow and raised it to his lips, then spat it out, still dry.

"Here! Brace up!" In a panic of apprehension at this collapse Grant shook him; he had never known Johnny to fail like this. "Take a drink of booze; it'll do you good." He drew a bottle of brandy from one of the dunnage bags and Cantwell seized it avidly. It was wet; it would quench his thirst, he thought. Before Mort could check him he had drunk a third of the contents.

The effect was almost instantaneous, for Cantwell's stomach was empty and his tissues seemed to absorb the liquor like a dry sponge; his fatigue fell away, he became suddenly strong and vigorous again. But before he had gone a hundred yards the reaction followed. First his mind grew thick, then his limbs became unmanageable and his muscles flabby. He was drunk. Yet it was a strange and dangerous intoxication, against which he struggled desperately. He fought it for perhaps a quarter of a mile before it mastered him; then he gave up.

Both men knew that stimulants are never taken on the trail, but they had never stopped to reason why, and even now they did not attribute Johnny's breakdown to the brandy. After a while he stumbled and fell, then, the cool snow being grateful to his face, he sprawled there motionless until Mort dragged him to the sled. He stared at his partner in perplexity and laughed foolishly. The wind was increasing, darkness was near, they had not yet reached the Bering slope.

Something in the drunken man's face frightened Grant and, extracting a ship's biscuit from the grub-box, he said, hurriedly: "Here, Johnny. Get something under your belt, quick."

Cantwell obediently munched the hard cracker, but there was no moisture on his tongue; his throat was paralyzed; the crumbs crowded themselves from the corners of his lips. He tried with limber fingers to stuff them down, or to assist the muscular action of swallowing, but finally expelled them in a cloud. Mort drew the parka hood over his partner's head, for the wind cut like a scythe and the dogs were turning tail to it, digging holes in the snow for protection. The air about them was like yeast; the light was fading.

The Indian snow-shoed his way back, advising a quick camp until the storm abated, but to this suggestion Grant refused to listen, knowing only too well the peril of such a course. Nor did he dare take Johnny on the sled, since the fellow was half asleep already, but instead whipped up the dogs and urged his companion to follow as best he could.

When Cantwell fell, for a second time, he returned, dragged him forward, and tied his wrists firmly, yet loosely, to the load.

The storm was pouring over them now, like water out of a spout; it seared and blinded them; its touch was like that of a flame. Nevertheless they struggled on into the smother, making what headway they could. The Indian led, pulling at the end of a rope; Grant strained at the sled and hoarsely encouraged the dogs; Cantwell stumbled and lurched in the rear like an unwilling prisoner. When he fell his companion lifted him, then beat him, cursed him, tried in every way to rouse him from his lethargy.

After an interminable time they found they were descending and this gave them heart to plunge ahead more rapidly. The dogs began to trot as the sled overran them; they rushed blindly into gullies, fetching up at the bottom in a tangle, and Johnny followed in a nerveless, stupefied condition. He was dragged like a sack of flour, for his legs were limp and he lacked muscular control, but every dash, every fall, every quick descent drove the sluggish blood through his veins and cleared his brain momentarily. Such moments were fleeting, however; much of the time his mind was a blank, and it was only by a mechanical effort that he fought off unconsciousness.

He had vague memories of many beatings at Mort's hands, of the slippery clean-swept ice of a stream over which he limply skidded, of being carried into a tent where a candle flickered and a stove roared. Grant was holding something hot to his lips, and then—

It was morning. He was weak and sick; he felt as if he had awakened from a hideous dream. "I played out, didn't I?" he queried, wonderingly.

"You sure did," Grant laughed. "It was a tight squeak, old boy. I never thought I'd get you through."

"Played out! I can't understand it." Cantwell prided himself on his strength and stamina, therefore the truth was unbelievable. He and Mort had long been partners, they had given and taken much at each other's hands, but this was something altogether different. Grant had saved his life, at risk of his own; the older man's endurance had been the greater and he had used it to good advantage. It embarrassed Johnny tremendously to realize that he had proven unequal to his share of the work, for he had never before experienced such an obligation. He apologized repeatedly during the few days he lay sick, and meanwhile Mort waited upon him like a mother.

Cantwell was relieved when at last they had abandoned camp, changed guides at the next village, and were on their way along the coast, for somehow he felt very sensitive about his collapse. He was, in fact, extremely ashamed of himself.

Once he had fully recovered he had no further trouble, but soon rounded into fit condition and showed no effects of his ordeal. Day after day he and Mort travelled through the solitudes, their isolation broken only by occasional glimpses of native villages, where they rested briefly and renewed their supply of dog-feed.

But although the younger man was now as well and strong as

ever, he was uncomfortably conscious that his trail-mate regarded him as the weaker of the two and shielded him in many ways. Grant performed most of the unpleasant tasks, and occasionally cautioned Johnny about overdoing. This protective attitude at first amused, then offended Cantwell; it galled him until he was upon the point of voicing his resentment, but reflected that he had no right to object, for, judging by past performances, he had proved his inferiority. This uncomfortable realization forever arose to prevent open rebellion, but he asserted himself secretly by robbing Grant of his self-appointed tasks. He rose first in the mornings, he did the cooking, he lengthened his turns ahead of the dogs, he mended harness after the day's hike had ended. Of course the older man objected, and for a time they had a good-natured rivalry as to who should work and who should rest—only it was not quite so good-natured on Cantwell's part as he made it appear.

Mort broke out in friendly irritation one day: "Don't try to do everything, Johnny. Remember I'm no cripple."

"Humph! You proved that. I guess it's up to me to do your work."

"Oh, forget that day on the pass, can't you?"

Johnny grunted a second time, and from his tone it was evident that he would never forget, unpleasant though the memory remained. Sensing his sullen resentment, the other tried to rally him, but made a bad job of it. The humor of men in the open is not delicate; their wit and their words become coarsened in direct proportion as they revert to the primitive; it is one effect of the solitudes.

Grant spoke extravagantly, mockingly, of his own superiority in a way which ordinarily would have brought a smile to Cantwell's lips, but the latter did not smile. He taunted Johnny humorously on his lack of physical prowess, his lack of good looks and manly qualities—something which had never failed to result in a friendly exchange of badinage; he even teased him about his defeat with the Katmai girl.

Cantwell did respond finally, but afterward he found himself wondering if Mort could have been in earnest. He dismissed the thought with some impatience. But men on the trail have too much time for their thoughts; there is nothing in the monotonous routine of the day's work to distract them, so the partner who had played out dwelt more and more upon his debt and upon his friend's easy assumption of pre-eminence. The weight of obligation began to chafe him, lightly at first, but with ever-increasing discomfort. He began to think that Grant honestly considered himself the better man, merely because chance had played into his hands.

It was silly, even childish, to dwell on the subject, he reflected, and yet he could not banish it from his mind. It was always before him, in one form or another. He felt the strength in his lean muscles, and sneered at the thought that Mort should be deceived. If it came to a physical test he felt sure he could break his slighter partner with his bare hands, and as for endurance—well, he was hungry for a chance to demonstrate it.

They talked little; men seldom converse in the wastes, for there is something about the silence of the wilderness which discourages speech. And no land is so grimly silent, so hushed and soundless, as the frozen North. For days they marched through desolation, without glimpse of human habitation, without sight of track or trail, without sound of a human voice to break the monotony. There was no game in the country, with the exception of an occasional bird or rabbit, nothing but the white hills, the fringe of aldertops along the watercourses, and the thickets of gnarled, unhealthy spruce in the smothered valleys.

Their destination was a mysterious stream at the headwaters of the unmapped Kuskokwim, where rumor said there was gold, and whither they feared other men were hastening from the mining country far to the north.

Now it is a penalty of the White Country that men shall think of women. The open life brings health and vigor, strength and animal vitality, and these clamor for play. The cold of the still, clear days is no more biting than the fierce memories and appetites which charge through the brain at night. Passions intensify with imprisonment, recollections come to life, longings grow vivid and wild. Thoughts change to realities, the past creeps close, and dream figures are filled with blood and fire. One remembers pleasures and excesses, women's smiles, women's kisses, the invitation of outstretched arms. Wasted opportunities mock at one.

Cantwell began to brood upon the Katmai girl, for she was the last; her eyes were haunting and distance had worked its usual enchantment. He reflected that Mort had shouldered him aside and won her favor, then boasted of it. Johnny awoke one night with a dream of her, and lay quivering.

Grant lay beside him, snoring; the heat of their bodies inter-mingled. The waking man tried to compose himself, but his partner's stertorous breathing irritated him beyond measure; for a long time he remained motionless, staring into the gray blur of the tent-top. He had played out. He owed his life to the man who had cheated him of the Katmai girl, and that man knew it. He had become a weak, help-less thing, dependent upon another's strength, and that other now accepted his superiority as a matter of course. The obligation was insufferable, and—it was unjust. The North had played him a devil-ish trick, it had betrayed him, it had bound him to his benefactor with chains of gratitude which were irksome. Had they been real chains they could have galled him no more than at this moment.

As time passed the men spoke less frequently to each other. Grant joshed his mate roughly, once or twice, masking beneath an assumption of jocularity his own vague irritation at the change that had come over them. It was as if he had probed at an open wound with clumsy fingers.

Cantwell had by this time assumed most of those petty camp tasks which provoke tired trailers, those humdrum duties which are so trying to exhausted nerves, and of course they wore upon him as they wear upon every man. But, once he had taken them over, he began to resent Grant's easy relinquishment; it rankled him to realize how willingly the other allowed him to do the cook-ing, the dish-washing, the fire-building, the bed-making. Little monotonies of this kind form the hardest part of winter travel, they are the rocks upon which friendships founder and partnerships are wrecked. Out on the trail, nature equalizes the work to a great extent, and no man can shirk unduly, but in camp, inside the cramped confines of a tent pitched on boughs laid over the snow, it is very different. There one must busy himself while the other rests and keeps his legs out of the way if possible. One man sits on the bedding at the rear of the shelter, and shivers, while the other squats over a tantalizing fire of green wood, blistering his face and parboil-ing his limbs inside his sweaty clothing. Dishes must be passed, food divided, and it is poor food, poorly prepared at best. Sometimes men criticize and voice longings for better grub and better cooking. Remarks of this kind have been known to result in tragedies, bitter words and flaming curses—then, perhaps, wild actions, memories of which the later years can never erase.

It is but one prank of the wilderness, one grim manifestation of its silent forces.

Had Grant been unable to do his part Cantwell would have willingly accepted the added burden, but Mort was able, he was nimble and "handy," he was the better cook of the two; in fact, he was the better man in every way—or so he believed. Cantwell sneered at the last thought, and the memory of his debt was like bitter medicine.

His resentment—in reality nothing more than a phase of insanity begot of isolation and silence—could not help but communicate itself to his companion, and there resulted a mutual antagonism, which grew into a dislike, then festered into something more, something strange, reasonless, yet terribly vivid and amazingly potent for evil. Neither man ever mentioned it—their tongues were clenched between their teeth and they held themselves in check with harsh hands—but it was constantly in their minds, nevertheless. No man who has not suffered the manifold irritations of such an intimate association can appreciate the gnawing canker of animosity like this. It was dangerous because there was no relief from it: the two were bound together as by gyves; they shared each other's every action and every plan; they trod in each other's tracks, slept in the same bed, ate from the same plate. They were like prisoners ironed to the same staple.

Each fought the obsession in his own way, but it is hard to fight the impalpable, hence their sick fancies grew in spite of themselves. Their minds needed food to prey upon, but found none. Each began to criticize the other silently, to sneer at his weaknesses, to meditate derisively upon his peculiarities. After a time they no longer resisted the advance of these poisonous thoughts, but welcomed it.

On more than one occasion the embers of their wrath were upon the point of bursting into flame, but each realized that the first ill-considered word would serve to slip the leash from those demons that were straining to go free, and so managed to restrain himself.

The crisis came one crisp morning when a dog-team whirled around a bend in the river and a white man hailed them. He was the mail-carrier, on his way out from Nome, and he brought news of the "inside."

"Where are you boys bound for?" he inquired when greetings were over and gossip of the trail had passed.

"We're going to the Stony River strike," Grant told him.

"Stony River? Up the Kuskokwim?"

"Yes!"

The mail-man laughed. "Can you beat that? Ain't you heard about Stony River?"

"No!"

"Why, it's a fake—no such place."

There was a silence; the partners avoided each other's eyes.

"MacDonald, the fellow that started it, is on his way to Dawson. There's a gang after him, too, and if he's caught it'll go hard with him. He wrote the letters—to himself—and spread the news just to raise a grub-stake. He cleaned up big before they got onto him. He peddled his tips for real money."

"Yes!" Grant spoke quietly. "Johnny bought one. That's what brought us from Seattle. We went out on the last boat and figured we'd come in from this side before the break-up. So—fake! By God!"

"Gee! You fellers bit good." The mail-carrier shook his head. "Well! You'd better keep going now; you'll get to Nome before the season opens. Better take dog-fish from Bethel—it's four bits a pound on the Yukon. Sorry I didn't hit your camp last night; we'd 'a' had a visit. Tell the gang that you saw me." He shook hands ceremoniously, yelled at his panting dogs, and went swiftly on his way, waving a mitten on high as he vanished around the next bend.

The partners watched him go, then Grant turned to Johnny, and repeated: "Fake! By God! MacDonald stung you."

Cantwell's face went as white as the snow behind him, his eyes blazed. "Why did you tell him I bit?" he demanded, harshly.

"Hunh! *Didn't* you bite? Two thousand miles afoot; three months of hell; for nothing. That's biting some."

"Well!" The speaker's face was convulsed, and Grant's flamed with an answering anger. They glared at each other for a moment. "Don't blame me. You fell for it, too."

"I—" Mort checked his rushing words.

"Yes, *you!* Now, what are you going to do about it? Welch?"

"I'm going through to Nome." The sight of his partner's rage had set Mort to shaking with a furious desire to fly at his throat, but, fortunately, he retained a spark of sanity.

"Then shut up, and quit chewing the rag. You—talk too damned much."

Mort's eyes were bloodshot; they fell upon the carbine under the sled lashings, and lingered there, then wavered. He opened his lips, reconsidered, spoke softly to the team, then lifted the heavy dog-whip and smote the malamutes with all his strength.

The men resumed their journey without further words, but each was cursing inwardly.

"So! I talk too much," Grant thought. The accusation stuck in his mind and he determined to speak no more.

"He blames me," Cantwell reflected, bitterly. "I'm in wrong again and he couldn't keep his mouth shut. A hell of a partner, he is!"

All day they plodded on, neither trusting himself to speak. They ate their evening meal like mutes; they avoided each other's eyes. Even the guide noticed the change and looked on curiously.

There were two robes and these the partners shared nightly, but their hatred had grown so during the past few hours that the thought of lying side by side, limb to limb, was distasteful. Yet neither dared suggest a division of the bedding, for that would have brought further words and resulted in the crash which they longed for, but feared. They stripped off their furs, and lay down beside each other with the same repugnance they would have felt had there been a serpent in the couch.

This unending malevolent silence became terrible. The strain of it increased, for each man now had something definite to cherish in the words and the looks that had passed. They divided the camp work with scrupulous nicety, each man waited upon himself and asked no favors. The knowledge of his debt forever chafed Cantwell; Grant resented his companion's lack of gratitude.

Of course they spoke occasionally—it was beyond human endurance to remain entirely dumb—but they conversed in monosyllables, about trivial things, and their voices were throaty, as if the effort choked them. Meanwhile they continued to glow inwardly at a white heat.

Cantwell no longer felt the desire to merely match his strength against Grant's; the estrangement had become too wide for that; a physical victory would have been flat and tasteless; he craved some deeper satisfaction. He began to think of the ax—just how or when or why he never knew. It was a thin-bladed, polished thing of frosty steel, and the more he thought of it the stronger grew his impulse to rid himself once for all of that presence which exasperated him. It would be very easy, he reasoned; a sudden blow, with the weight of his shoulders behind it—he fancied he could feel the bit sink into Grant's flesh, cleaving bone and cartilage in its course—a slanting downward stroke, aimed at the neck where it joined the body, and he would be forever satisfied. It would be ridiculously simple. He practiced in the gloom of evening as he felled spruce-trees for fire-wood; he guarded the ax religiously; it became a living thing which urged him on to violence. He saw it standing by the tent-fly when he closed his eyes to sleep; he dreamed of it; he sought it out with his eyes when he first awoke. He slid it loosely under the sled lashings every morning, thinking that its use could not long be delayed.

As for Grant, the carbine dwelt forever in his mind, and his fingers itched for it. He secretly slipped a cartridge into the chamber, and when an occasional ptarmigan offered itself for a target he saw the white spot on the breast of Johnny's reindeer parka, dancing ahead of the Lyman bead.

The solitude had done its work; the North had played its grim comedy to the final curtain, making sport of men's affections and turning love to rankling hate. But into the mind of each man crept a certain craftiness. Each longed to strike, but feared to face the conse-quences. It was lonesome, here among the white hills and the deathly silences, yet they reflected that it would be still more lonesome if they were left to keep step with nothing more substantial than a memory. They determined, therefore, to wait until civilization was nearer, meanwhile rehearsing the moment they knew was inevitable. Over and over in their thoughts each of them enacted the scene, ending it always with the picture of a prostrate man in a patch of trampled snow which grew crimson as the other gloated.

They paused at Bethel Mission long enough to load with dried salmon, then made the ninety-mile portage over lake and tundra to the Yukon. There they got their first touch of the "inside" world. They camped in a barabara where white men had slept a few nights before, and heard their own language spoken by native tongues. The time was growing short now, and they purposely dismissed their guide, knowing that the trail was plain from there on. When they hitched up, on the next morning, Cantwell placed the ax, bit down, between the tarpaulin and the sled rail, leaving the helve projecting where his hand could reach it. Grant thrust the barrel of the rifle beneath a lashing, with the butt close by the handle-bars, and it was loaded.

A mile from the village they were overtaken by an Indian and his squaw, travelling light behind hungry dogs. The natives attached themselves to the white men and hung stubbornly to their heels, taking advantage of their tracks. When night came they camped alongside, in the hope of food. They announced that they were bound for St. Michaels, and in spite of every effort to shake them off they remained close behind the partners until that point was reached.

At St. Michaels there were white men, practically the first Johnny and Mort had encountered since landing at Katmai, and for a day at least they were sane. But there were still three hundred miles to be travelled, three hundred miles of solitude and haunting thoughts. Just as they were about to start, Cantwell came upon Grant and the A. C. agent, and heard his name pronounced, also the word "Katmai." He noted that Mort fell silent at his approach, and instantly his anger blazed afresh. He decided that the latter had been telling the story of their experience on the pass and boasting of his service. So much the better, he thought, in a blind rage; that which he planned doing would appear all the more like an accident, for who would dream that a man could kill the person to whom he owed his life?

That night he waited for a chance.

They were camped in a dismal hut on a wind-swept shore; they were alone. But Grant was waiting also, it seemed. They lay down beside each other, ostensibly to sleep; their limbs touched; the warmth from their bodies intermingled, but they did not close their eyes.

They were up and away early, with Nome drawing rapidly nearer. They had skirted an ocean, foot by foot; Bering Sea lay behind them, now, and its northern shore swung westward to their goal. For two months they had lived in silent animosity, feeding on bitter food while their elbows rubbed.

Noon found them floundering through one of those unheralded storms which make coast travel so hazardous. The morning had turned off gray, the sky was of a leaden hue which blended perfectly with the snow underfoot, there was no horizon, it was impossible to see more than a few yards in any direction. The trail soon became obliterated and their eyes began to play tricks. For all they could distinguish, they might have been suspended in space; they seemed to be treading the measures of an endless dance in the center of a whirling cloud. Of course it was cold, for the wind off the open sea was damp, but they were not men to turn back.

They soon discovered that their difficulty lay not in facing the storm, but in holding to the trail. That narrow, two-foot causeway, packed by a winter's travel and frozen into a ribbon of ice by a winter's frosts, afforded their only avenue of progress, for the moment they left it the sled plowed into the loose snow, well-nigh disappearing and bringing the dogs to a standstill. It was the duty of the driver, in such case, to wallow forward, right the load if necessary, and lift it back into place. These mishaps were forever occurring, for it was impossible to distinguish the trail beneath its soft covering. However, if the driver's task was hard it was no more trying than that of the man ahead, who was compelled to feel out and explore the ridge of hardened snow and ice with his feet, after the fashion of a man walking a plank in the dark. Frequently he lunged into the drifts with one foot, or both; his glazed mukluk soles slid about, causing him to bestride the invisible hogback, or again his legs crossed awkwardly, throwing him off his balance. At times he wandered away from the path entirely and had to search it out again. These exertions were very wearing and they were dangerous, also, for joints are easily dislocated, muscles twisted, and tendons strained.

Hour after hour the march continued, unrelieved by any change, unbroken by any speck or spot of color. The nerves of their eyes, wearied by constant near-sighted peering at the snow, began to jump so that vision became untrustworthy. Both travellers appreciated the necessity of clinging to the trail, for, once they lost it, they knew they might wander about indefinitely until they chanced to regain it or found their way to the shore, while always to seaward was the menace of open water, of air-holes, or cracks which might gape beneath their feet like jaws. Immersion in this temperature, no matter how brief, meant death.

The monotony of progress through this unreal, leaden world became almost unbearable. The repeated strainings and twistings they suffered in walking the slippery ridge reduced the men to weariness; their legs grew clumsy and their feet uncertain. Had they found a camping-place they would have stopped, but they dared not forsake the thin thread that linked them with safety to go and look for one, not knowing where the shore lay. In storms of this kind men have lain in their sleeping-bags for days within a stone's throw of a road-house or village. Bodies had been found within a hundred yards of shelter after blizzards have abated.

Cantwell and Grant had no choice, therefore, except to bore into the welter of drifting flakes.

It was late in the afternoon when the latter met with an accident. Johnny, who had taken a spell at the rear, heard him cry out, saw him stagger, struggle to hold his footing, then sink into the snow. The dogs paused instantly, lay down, and began to strip the ice pellets from between their toes.

Cantwell spoke harshly, leaning upon the handle-bars: "Well! What's the idea?"

It was the longest sentence of the day.

"I've—hurt myself." Mort's voice was thin and strange; he raised himself to a sitting posture, and reached beneath his parka, then lay back weakly. He writhed, his face was twisted with pain. He continued to lie there, doubled into a knot of suffering. A groan was wrenched from between his teeth.

"Hurt? How?" Johnny inquired, dully.

It seemed very ridiculous to see that strong man kicking around in the snow.

"I've ripped something loose—here." Mort's palms were pressed in upon his groin, his fingers were clutching something. "Ruptured—I guess." He tried again to rise, but sank back. His cap had fallen off and his forehead glistened with sweat.

Cantwell went forward and lifted him. It was the first time in many days that their hands had touched, and the sensation affected him strangely. He struggled to repress a devilish mirth at the thought that Grant had played out—it amounted to that and nothing less; the trail had delivered him into his enemy's hands, his hour had struck. Johnny determined to square the debt now, once for all, and wipe his own mind clean of that poison which corroded it. His muscles were strong, his brain clear, he had never felt his strength so irresistible as at this moment, while Mort, for all his boasted superiority, was nothing but a nerveless thing hanging limp against his breast. Providence had arranged it all. The younger man was impelled to give raucous voice to his glee, and yet—his helpless burden exerted an odd effect upon him.

He deposited his foe upon the sled and stared at the face he had not met for many days. He saw how white it was, how wet and cold, how weak and dazed, then as he looked he cursed inwardly, for the triumph of his moment was spoiled.

The ax was there, its polished bit showed like a piece of ice, its helve protruded handily, but there was no need of it now; his fingers were all the weapons Johnny needed; they were more than sufficient, in fact, for Mort was like a child.

Cantwell was a strong man, and, although the North had coarsened him, yet underneath the surface was a chivalrous regard for all things weak, and this the trail-madness had not affected. He had longed for this instant, but now that it had come he felt no enjoyment, since he could not harm a sick man and waged no war on cripples. Perhaps, when Mort had rested, they could settle their quarrel; this was as good a place as any. The storm hid them, they would leave no traces, there could be no interruption.

But Mort did not rest. He could not walk; movement brought excruciating pain.

Finally Cantwell heard himself saying: "Better wrap up and lie still for a while. I'll get the dogs under way." His words amazed him dully. They were not at all what he had intended to say.

The injured man demurred, but the other insisted gruffly, then brought him his mittens and cap, slapping the snow out of them before rousing the team to motion. The load was very heavy now, the dogs had no footprints to guide them, and it required all of Cantwell's efforts to prevent capsizing. Night approached swiftly, the whirling snow particles continued to flow past upon the wind, shrouding the earth in an impenetrable pall.

The journey soon became a terrible ordeal, a slow, halting progress that led nowhere and was accomplished at the cost of tremendous exertion. Time after time Johnny broke trail, then returned and urged the huskies forward to the end of his tracks. When he lost the path he sought it out, laboriously hoisted the sledge back into place, and coaxed his four-footed helpers to renewed effort. He was drenched with perspiration, his inner garments were steaming, his outer ones were frozen into a coat of armor; when he paused he chilled rapidly. His vision was untrustworthy, also, and he felt snow-blindness coming on. Grant begged him more than once to unroll the bedding and prepare to sleep out the storm; he even urged Johnny to leave him and make a dash for his own safety, but at this the younger man cursed and bade him hold his tongue.

Night found the lone driver slipping, plunging, lurching ahead of the dogs, or shoving at the handle-bars and shouting at the dogs. Finally during a pause for rest he heard a sound which roused him. Out of the gloom to the right came the faint, complaining howl of a malamute; it was answered by his own dogs, and the next moment they had caught a scent which swerved them shoreward and led them scrambling through the drifts. Two hundred yards, and a steep bank loomed above, up and over which they rushed, with Cantwell yelling encouragement; then a light showed, and they were in the lee of a low-roofed hut.

A sick native, huddled over a Yukon stove, made them welcome to his mean abode, explaining that his wife and son had gone to Unalaklik for supplies.

Johnny carried his partner to the one unoccupied bunk and stripped his clothes from him. With his own hands he rubbed the warmth back into Mortimer's limbs, then swiftly prepared hot food, and, holding him in the hollow of his aching arm, fed him, a little at a time. He was like to drop from exhaustion, but he made no complaint. With one folded robe he made the hard boards comfortable, then spread the other as a covering. For himself he sat beside the fire and fought his weariness. When he dozed off and the cold awakened him, he renewed the fire; he heated beef-tea, and, rousing Mort, fed it to him with a teaspoon. All night long, at intervals, he tended the sick man, and Grant's eyes followed him with an expression that brought a fierce pain to Cantwell's throat.

"You're mighty good—after the rotten way I acted," the former whispered once.

And Johnny's big hand trembled so that he spilled the broth.

His voice was low and tender as he inquired, "Are you resting easier now?"

The other nodded.

"Maybe you're not hurt badly, after—all. God! That would be awful—" Cantwell choked, turned away, and, raising his arms against the log wall, buried his face in them.

The morning broke clear; Grant was sleeping. As Johnny stiffly mounted the creek bank with a bucket of water he heard a jingle of sleigh-bells and saw a sled with two white men swing in toward the cabin.

"Hello!" he called, then heard his own name pronounced.

"Johnny Cantwell, by all that's holy!"

The next moment he was shaking hands vigorously with two old friends from Nome.

"Martin and me are bound for Saint Mike's," one of them explained. "Where the deuce did you come from, Johnny?"

"The 'outside,' started for Stony River, but—"

"Stony River!" The newcomers began to laugh loudly and Cantwell joined them. It was the first time he had laughed for weeks. He realized the fact with a start, then recollected also his sleeping partner, and said, "Sh-h! Mort's inside, asleep!"

During the night everything had changed for Johnny Cantwell; his mental attitude, his hatred, his whole reasonless insanity. Everything was different now, even his debt was cancelled, the weight of obligation was removed, and his diseased fancies were completely cured.

"Yes! Stony River," he repeated, grinning broadly. "I bit!"

Martin burst forth gleefully, "They caught MacDonald at Holy Cross and ran him out on a limb. He'll never start another stampede. Old Man Baker gun-branded him."

"What's the matter with Mort?" inquired the second traveller.

"He's resting up. Yesterday, during the storm, he—" Johnny was upon the point of saying "played out," but changed it to "had an accident. We thought it was serious, but a few days' rest'll bring him around all right. He saved me at Katmai, coming in. I petered out and threw up my tail, but he got me through. Come inside and tell him the news."

"Sure thing."

"Well, well!" Martin said. "So you and Mort are still partners, eh?"

"*Still* partners!" Johnny took up the pail of water. "Well, rather! We'll always be partners." His voice was young and full and hearty as he continued: "Why, Mort's the best damned fellow in the world. I'd lay down my life for him."

For the Under Dog

BY RILEY H. ALLEN

IT WAS IN DECEMBER, '97 that a half-dead Tahkheena River Indian, his frozen feet showing through worn caribou-skin moccasins, came into the Police Post at Lake Linderman with a letter for the captain. It said:

Chambers has turned up here and there'll be the deuce to pay. For Heaven's sake, send McWilliams.
—Powell, Tahkheena Road House

The captain swore and called McWilliams. To the latter he said: "I want you to go to Powell's Roadhouse. Chambers is there. When can you start?"

"An hour," said McWilliams, and an hour later he was *mushing* his dog-team toward the Tahkheena River, two hundred miles away across the frozen snow-fields.

McWilliams was a sergeant in the Canadian Mounted Police, a dour old Scotchman, with a pair of steady gray eyes and a big chin under his close-cropped, grizzly beard; six foot one of bone and sinew on his moose-hide snow-shoes—and the silence of Alaskan snow-fields clothed him like a mantle. He had been in the service of the Queen for twenty years, and they said of him in the North that he had never failed to get his man, dead or alive. It was McWilliams that faced three hundred raging miners at Miles Canyon and saved the horse thief, Dixon, from hanging to the nearest mountain pine. It was McWilliams who brought "Nigger" Sloan back to Haines Mission on a dog sled, after a running fight of twenty miles. It was McWilliams who was known from Skagway to Dawson as the grimmest machine of a man that ever carried justice into a lawless country.

McWilliams traveled light, for he had to go far and fast. An average Eskimo "husky" can cover fifty miles a day on good going, and McWilliams's dogs were malamoots—great, savage brutes, thin and hungry, but trained like race-horses. On the sled were twelve days' provisions, a coffee-pot, and a sleeping bag. There was also a bundle of wood, chopped fine, and dry as three months' seasoning under shelter could make it, for in winter the Yukon mercury crawls down to forty or fifty below and ten feet of ice grips the rivers. Then the sled driver is glad of a tiny, chip-fed fire to thaw his freezing fingers, and sleeps on hard snow six inches from the glowing embers.

The low-running dogs headed up the ice-packed trail toward the Tahkheena River, and McWilliams smiled grimly under his gray-shot beard when he thought of Chambers.

Chambers! Outlaw and thief, gambler and murderer; under sentence of death three times and each time escaping: "Badman" Chambers—sworn to kill McWilliams on sight and to die rather than be taken; and yet in his desperate heart a fierce pride of manhood that made him scorn to strike the under dog. McWilliams smiled grimly that night as he *cached* two days' provisions at Lake Argell, sixty miles out from Linderman, for use on his return trip with Chambers; and after he had fed the dogs on dried salmon, he threw the empty paper sack into the air and drew a revolver. There were three quick reports and the sack fell to the ground with three holes neatly drilled within the round of a dollar. The revolver was not a dainty pearl-handled one such as ladies use. The barrels were of blued-steel and the caliber was forty-four. And as McWilliams crawled into his sleeping-bag he smiled, and smiled grimly as he slept, with the dogs howling about him.

McWilliams bent forward a little and looked into the window of Powell's Roadhouse, blinking as the light fell upon his eyes. Back on the trail stood the dogteam, a patch of gray against the star-lit snow.

The room was full of men, gambling and drinking—great, rough, heavy-bearded fellows and boisterous with whisky. Behind the bar stood Powell; his ruddy face was troubled and his eyes glanced continually toward a table near the door.

There were three men at the table, playing poker. One of the men was a dark-browned miner, his companion a tenderfoot—a mere boy—and both were excited. The third man lolled back in his chair with easy grace, dealing the cards with swift, sure flips of his wrist and white fingers. His eyes were slow and languid, but there was alertness in the poise of his blond head and audacity in his clean-cut features.

When he moved, the muscles flowed under his skin like those of a panther. Altogether, a handsome, mocking devil, and a slow smile touched his face as he added the miner's chips to the stack before him.

McWilliams knew enough about poker to see that the miner and the boy were losing heavily. The third man played carelessly and smiled at the flushed faces and trembling hands of his companions. He reached for a stack of chips and, as he did so, from the sleeve of his woolen jacket a card dropped and lay face upward on the table.

There was a loud oath from the miner and the tenderfoot sprang to his feet, his hands clenched. The slow smile deepened on the gambler's face and, with an easy, almost a careless motion, he drew his revolver. McWilliams turned from the window and flung himself into the room.

Yet in that time many things had happened. On the floor, beside the overturned table, lay the tenderfoot—shot through the head, and blood spurted over a scattered stack of poker chips just in front of his face. The miner lay in a shapeless heap, all knees and elbows; his limbs jerked spasmodically, and then stiffened. Back to the wall, the third man covered the room with his revolver. Powder smoke, biting and pungent, eddied out the open door.

McWilliams stepped forward and his voice stung the silence like the lash of a whip. "Chambers, drop that gun!"

Chambers whirled. "McWilliams!" he said; both revolvers spoke, and the crowd of miners surged forward with a yell. The light went out with a crash of broken glass, and the room was filled with human tigers.

Out of the thick of it staggered McWilliams, his right arm limp and twisted, but with him came Chambers, handcuffed, and the sergeant's steel fingers were sunk deep in his shoulder.

McWilliams knew the Alaska miner when his blood is up as a child knows its book. He turned to the trail, flung Chambers upon the ten-foot sled, and called to the dogs. There was a tightening of leather traces, a leap against collar, and the malamoots settled into their stride—the stride that eats up the miles like fire. The roadhouse sank behind them and they headed for Lake Argell.

"I sure reckon," said Chambers, "there'd been some fun if you hadn't got me. Guess I'd been there yet."

"Aye," grunted McWilliams, and he lashed Chambers more securely—a slow proceeding with a broken arm; but it was done at last, and Chambers lay helpless on the sled and cursed McWilliams reprovingly.

That night, twenty miles out, the gambler slept in the wadded canvas bag, while McWilliams, among the dogs for warmth, kept back the groans when his crushed arm bit and tortured. His face was hard the next morning after breakfast, as he motioned Chambers to the sled. The gambler threw back his head and laughed.

"Curse you, McWilliams," he said pleasantly; "can't you talk once in a while?"

There was a sudden flush in the sergeant's gray eyes, and with one sound arm he threw Chambers across the sled. And still Chambers laughed.

So into the south McWilliams drove the malamoots. By day the air glistened with millions of diamond atoms, and great orange sun-dogs flashed and played around them. The cold drove straight to the heart like a pang, and the reflection of sunlight across miles of snow was blinding. Sometimes a puff of wind spat the powdered ice of the trail against their faces lightly, yet with the cut of steel. At night the strange northern fires flickered redly on the far horizon, streaming across the sky in ribbons of crimson and the stars were cold and merciless.

McWilliams never spoke save to the dogs, but the man going to his death down at Linderman hummed airily the songs of Klondike dance-halls, or sometimes broke into oaths and beat his steel wrist-bands against the sled till the sergeant would raise his revolver with a look in his steady eyes that killed the words of Chambers's lips.

Two days of watchfulness and pain for McWilliams and latter-ly a weariness of body and mind that was worse than pain. And on the third-night the gaunt dog-team stopped in front of the cabin on frozen Argell where McWilliams had *cached* provisions on the way out.

The sergeant staggered as he unbound the rope from Chambers's feet and built a fire on the cabin floor. There were two rude bunks and a table, and to one of these bunks McWilliams fastened the gambler with buckskin thongs from the sled harness. The wolf-dogs howled outside, and the northern lights wavered on the far horizon, while within the sergeant turned restlessly on his narrow bed of pine boards, muttering brokenly. The gambler, tied to his bunk, looked on and hummed a gay little song under his breath.

In the early morning light the sergeant's gray eyes were set in deep, dusky circles, but they looked steadily out from a resolute white face and the fever was quite gone. Chambers, lashed to his bunk, smiled at the trembling fingers of the other and his smile was not good to see.

McWilliams crossed the room and unfastened the ropes around the gambler's feet—it was a long job, for the fingers continued to tremble, but it was finished. The he slipped a hand underneath his deerskin *parka* and brought forth a small key. There was no comprehension in Chambers's eyes, but he smiled lightly. McWilliams fitted the key to the gambler's handcuffs and turned the lock. Chambers shook off the manacles. The sergeant sank back upon the bunk, panting and white.

Chambers rose to his feet and stretched himself, just as a wintry sun shot redly through a chink in the wall. He threw open the door, and the sunlight, straight over a thousand miles of virgin snow, leaped into the room and filled it with a merry gleam. Outside the lean wolf-dogs were stretching themselves, and they crowded around him for the breakfast of dried salmon.

Far to the southeast the trail ran, till it dwindled to a darker streak on the snow and disappeared. Straight down to Linderman; of, if you choose, swing to the left at Tornado Creek and on to Skayway, then—

Chambers turned back into the cabin and seated himself on the table; he looked at McWilliams, lying white and weak in the bunk, at the sergeant's shattered arm and at the handcuffs on the floor with the key still in the lock, at the buckskin thongs inside them.

There were four days provisions in the cabin; outside stood a sled, and even now a ring of impatient, wistful canine faces filled the doorway. Turn off at Tornado Creek, and on to Skagway and the States. This man—who would know? A lonely trail—perhaps in the spring—surely not for weeks. By that time—the fight at Powell's Roadhouse? Well, he could have got out without McWilliams's help— at least, he could have made it hot for those devils. After all, what would it matter, back in the States, with gold, plenty of gold, and no one need know—could know. Ten days to Seattle—he was safe there—ten days. And at Linderman? What chance of escape there? Linderman, sixty miles away, and McWilliams, dying from exposure, had saved his life. McWilliams had got him out the roadhouse— McWilliams—with one arm broken; right arm, too. Tornado Creek at noon, four days to Skagway—Seattle—

McWilliams watched the murderer's pale face without a word, but in his eyes was the look of a trapped wildcat as he dies unconquered. Then Chambers's head went up, inch by inch; on his lower lip burned a red line, but his eyes were glad.

McWilliams turned his face away to hide its emotion.

"Curse you, McWilliams," said Chambers; "I sure reckon I've got to take you down to Linderman."

The Ice Goes Out

BY ELIZABETH ROBINS

'I am a part of all that I have seen'

IT HAD BEEN THAWING AND freezing, freezing and thawing, for so long that men lost account of the advance of a summer coming, with such balked, uncertain steps. Indeed, the weather variations had for several weeks been so great that no journey, not the smallest, could be calculated with any assurance. The last men to reach Minóok were two who had made a hunting and prospecting trip to an outlying district. They had gone there in six days, and were nineteen in returning.

The slush was waist-deep in the gulches. On the benches, in the snow, holes appeared, as though red-hot stones had been thrown upon the surface. The little settlement by the mouth of the Minóok sat insecurely on the boggy hillside, and its inhabitants waded knee-deep in soaking tundra moss and mire.

And now, down on the Never-Know-What, water was beginning to run on the marginal ice. Up on the mountains the drifted snow was honey-combed. Whole fields of it gave way and sunk a foot under any adventurous shoe. But although these changes had been wrought slowly, with backsets of bitter nights, when everything was frozen hard as flint, the illusion was general that summer came in with a bound. On the 9th of May, Minóok went to bed in winter, and woke to find the snow almost gone under the last nineteen hours of hot, unwinking sunshine, and the first geese winging their way up the valley—sight to stir men's hearts. Stranger still, the eight months' Arctic silence broken suddenly by a thousand voices. Under every snow-bank a summer murmur, very faint at first, but hourly louder— the sound of falling water softly singing over all the land.

As silence had been the distinguishing feature of the winter, so was the noise the sign of spring. No ear so dull but now was full of it. All the brooks on all the hills, tinkling, babbling of some great and universal joy, all the streams of all the glutches joining with every little rill to find the old way, or to carve a new, back to the Father of Waters.

And a strange thing had happened on the Yukon. The shore-edges of the ice seemed sunken, and the water ran yet deeper there. But of a certainty the middle part had risen! The cheechalkos thought it an optical illusion. But old Brandt from Forty-Mile had seen the ice go out for two-and-twenty years, and he said it went out always so— 'humps his back, an' gits up gits, and when he's a gitten', jest look out!' Those who, in spite of warning, ventured in hip-boots down on the Never-Know-What, found that, in places, the under side of the ice was worn nearly through. If you bent your head and listened, you could plainly hear that greater music of the river running underneath, low as yet, but deep, and strangely stirring—dominating in the hearer's ears all the clear, high clamour from gulch and hill.

In some men's hearts the ice 'went out' at the sound, and the melting welled up in their eyes. Summer and liberty were very near.

'Oh, hurry, Yukon Inua; let the ice go out and let the boats come in.'

But the next few days hung heavily. The river-ice humped its back still higher, but showed no disposition to 'git.' The wonder was it did not crack under the strain; but Northern ice has the air of being strangely flexile. Several feet in depth, the water ran now along the margin.

More geese and ducks appeared, and flocks of little birds— Canada jays, robins, joined the swelling chorus of the waters.

Oh, hurry, hurry Inua, and open the great highway! Not at Minóok alone: at every wood camp, mining town and mission, at every white post and Indian village, all along the Yukon, groups were gathered waiting the great moment of the year.

No one had ever heard of the ice breaking up before the 11th of May or later than the 28th. And yet men had begun to keep a hopeful eye on the river from the 10th of April, when a white ptarmigan was reported wearing a collar of dark-brown feathers, and his wings tipped brown. That was a month ago, and the great moment could not possibly be far now.

The first thing everybody did on getting up, and the last thing everybody did on going to bed, was to look at the river. It was not easy to go to bed; and even if you got so far it was not easy to sleep. The sun poured into the cabins by night as well as by day, and there was nothing to divide one part of the twenty-four hours from another. You slept when you were too tired to watch the river. You breakfasted, like as not, at six in the evening; you dined at midnight. Through all your waking hours you kept an eye on the window overlooking the river. In your bed you listened for that ancient Yukon cry, 'The ice is going out!'

For ages it had meant to the timid: Beware the fury of the shattered ice-fields; beware the caprice of the flood. Watch! lest many lives go out with the ice as aforetime. And for ages to the stout-hearted it had meant: Make ready the kyaks and the birch canoes; see that tackle and traps are strong—for plenty or famine wait upon the hour. As the white men waited for boats to-day, the men of the older time had waited for the salmon—for those first impatient adventurers that would force their way under the very ice-jam, tenderest and best of all the season's catch, as eager to prosecute that journey from the ocean to the Klondyke as if they had been men marching after the gold boom.

No one could settle to anything. It was by fits and starts that the steadier hands indulged even in target practice, with a feverish subconsciousness that events were on the way that might make it inconvenient to have lost the art of sending a bullet straight. After a diminutive tin can, hung on a tree, had been made to jump at a hundred paces, the marksman would glance at the river and forget to fire. It was by fits and starts that they even drank deeper or played for higher stakes.

The Wheel of Fortune, in the Gold Nugget, was in special demand. It was a means of trying your luck with satisfactory despatch 'between drinks' or between long bouts of staring at the river. Men stood in shirt-sleeves at their cabin doors in the unwinking sunshine, looking up the valley or down, betting that the 'first boat in' would be one of those nearest neighbours, *May West* or *Muckluck,* coming up from Woodworth; others as ready to back heavily their opinion that the first blast of the steam whistle would come down on the flood from Circle or from Dawson.

The Colonel had bought and donned a new suit of 'store clothes,' and urged on his companion the necessity of at least a whole pair of breeches in honour of his entrance into the Klondyke. But the Boy's funds were low and his vanity chastened. Besides, he had other business on his mind.

After sending several requests for the immediate return of his dog, requests that received no attention, the Boy went out to the gulch to recover him. Nig's new master paid up all arrears of wages readily enough, but declined to surrender the dog. 'Oh no, the ice wasn't thinkin' o' goin' out yit.'

'I want my dog.'

'You'll git him sure.'

'I'm glad you understand that much.'

'I'll bring him up to Rampart in time for the first boat.'

'Where's my dog?'

No answer. The Boy whistled. No Nig. Dread masked itself in choler. He jumped on the fellow, forced him down, and hammered him till he cried for mercy.

'Where's my dog, then?'

'He—he's up to Idyho Bar,' whimpered the prostrate one. And there the Boy found him, staggering under a pair of saddle-bags, hired out to Mike O'Reilly for a dollar and a half a day. Together they returned to Rampart to watch for the boat.

Certainly the ice was very late in breaking up this year. The men of Rampart stood about in groups in the small hours of the morning of the 16th of May; as usual, smoking, yarning, speculating, inventing elaborate joshes. Somebody remembered that certain cheechalkos had gone to bed at midnight. Now this was unprecedented, even impertinent. If the river is not open by the middle of May, your Sour-dough may go to bed—only he doesn't. Still, he may do as he lists. But your cheechako—why, this is the hour of his initiation. It was as if a man should yawn at his marriage or refuse to sleep at his funeral. The offenders were some of those Woodworth fellows, who, with a dozen or so others, had built shacks below 'the street,' yet well above the river. At two in the morning Sour-dough Saunders knocked them up.

The ice is goin' out!

In a flash the sleepers stood at the door.

'Only a josh.' One showed fight.

'Well, it's true what I'm tellin' yer,' persisted Saunders seriously: 'the ice *is* goin' out, and it's goin' soon, and when you're washed out o' yer bunks ye needn't blame me, fur I warned yer.'

'You don't mean the flood'll come up *here?*'

'Mebbe you've arranged so she won't *this* year.'

The cheechalkos consulted. In the end, four of them occupied the next two hours (to the infinite but masked amusement of the town) in floundering about in the mud, setting up tents in the boggy wood above the settlement, and with much pains transporting thither as many of their possessions as they did not lose in the bottomless pit of the mire.

When the business was ended, Minóok's self-control gave way. The cheechalkos found themselves the laughing-stock of the town. The others, who hadn't dared to build down on the bank, but who 'hadn't scared worth a cent,' sauntered up to the Gold Nugget to enjoy the increased esteem of the Sour-doughs, and the humiliation of the men who had thought 'the Yukon was goin' over the Ramparts this year—haw, haw!'

It surprises the average mind to discover that one of civilization's most delicate weapons is in such use and is so potently dreaded among the roughest frontier spirits. No fine gentleman in a drawing room, no sensitive girl, shrinks more from what Meredith calls 'the comic laugh,' none feels irony more keenly than yo· r ordinary American pioneer. The men who had moved up into the soaking wood saw they had run a risk as great to them as the fabled danger of the river— the risk of the josher's irony, the dire humiliation of the laugh. If a man up here does you an injury, and you kill him, you haven't after all taken the ultimate revenge. You might have 'got the laugh on him,' and let him live to hear it.

While all Minóok was 'jollying' the Woodworth men, Maudie made one of her sudden raids out of the Gold Nugget. She stood nearly up to the knees of her high rubber boots in the bog of 'Main Street,' talking earnestly with the Colonel. Keith and the Boy, sitting on a store box outside of the saloon, had looked on at the fun over the timid cheechakos, and looked on now at Maudie and the Colonel. It crossed the Boy's mind that they'd be putting up a josh on his pardner pretty soon, and at the thought he frowned.

Keith had been saying that the old miners had nearly all got 'squawed.' He had spoken almost superstitiously of the queer, lasting effect of the supposedly temporary arrangement.

'No, they don't leave their wives as often as you'd expect, but in most cases it seems to kill the pride of the man. He gives up all idea of ever going home, and even if he makes a fortune, they say, he stays on here. And year by year he sinks lower and lower, till he's farther down in the scale of things human than his savage wife.

'Yes, it's awful to think how the life up here can take the stiffening out of a fella.'

He looked darkly at the two out there in the mud. Keith nodded.

'Strong men have lain down on the trail this winter and cried.' But it wasn't that sort of thing the other meant.

Keith followed his friend's glowering looks.

'Yes. That's just the kind of man that gets taken in.'

'What?' said the Boy brusquely.

'Just the sort that goes and marries some flighty creature.'

'Well,' said his pardner haughtily, *'he* could afford to marry a "flighty creature." *The Colonel's got both feet on the ground.'*

And Keith felt properly snubbed. But what Maudie was saying to the Colonel was:

'You're goin' up in the first boat, I s'pose?'

'Yes.'

'Looks like I'll be the only person left in Minóok.'

'I don't imagine you'll be quite alone.'

'No? Why, there's only between five and six hundred expectin' to board a boat that'll be crowded before she gets here.'

'Does everybody want to go to Dawson?'

'Everybody except a few boomers who mean to stay long enough to play off their misery on someone else before they move on.'

The Colonel looked a trifle anxious.

'I hadn't thought of that. I suppose there *will* be a race for the boat.'

'There'll be a race all the way up the river for all the early boats. Ain't half enough to carry the people. But you look to me like you'll stand as good a chance as most, and anyhow, you're the one man I know, I'll trust my dough to.'

The Colonel stared.

'You see, I want to get some money to my kiddie, an' besides, I got m'self kind o' scared about keepin' dust in my cabin. I want it in a bank, so's if I should kick the bucket (there'll be some pretty high rollin' here when there's been a few boats in, and my life's no better than any other feller's), I'd feel a lot easier if I knew the kiddie'd have six thousand clear, even if I *did* turn up my toes. See?'

'A—yes—I see. But—'

The door of the cabin next the saloon opened suddenly. A graybeard with a young face came out rubbing the sleep from his eyes.

He stared interrogatively at the river, and then to the world in general:

'What time is it?'

'Half-past four.'

'Mornin' or evenin'?' and no one thought the question strange.

Maudie lowered her voice.

'No need to mention it to pardners and people. You don't want every feller to know you're goin' about loaded; but will you take my dust up to Dawson and get it sent to 'Frisco on the first boat?'

"The ice! the ice! It's moving!"

The ice is going out!'

'Look! the ice!'

From end to end of the settlement the cry was taken up. People darted out of cabins like beavers out of their burrows. Three little half-breed Indian boys, yelling with excitement, tore past the Gold Nugget, crying now in their mother's Minóok, now in their father's English, 'The ice is going out!' From the depths of the store-box whereon his master had sat, Nig darted, howling excitedly and waving a muddy tail like a draggled banner, saying in Mahlemeut: 'The ice is going out! The fish are coming in.' All the other dogs waked and gave tongue, running in and out among the huddled rows of people gathered on the Ramparts.

Every ear full of the rubbing, grinding noise that came up out of the Yukon—noise not loud, but deep—an undercurrent of heavy sound. As they stood there, wide-eyed, gaping, their solid winter world began to move. A compact mass of ice, three quarters of a mile wide and four miles long, with a great grinding and crushing went down the valley. Some distance below the town it jammed, building with incredible quickness a barrier twenty feet high.

The people waited breathless. Again the ice-mass trembled. But the watchers lifted their eyes to the heights above. Was that thunder in the hills? No, the ice again; again crushing, grinding, to the low accompaniment of thunder that seemed to come from far away.

Sections a mile long and a half a mile wide were forced up, carried over the first ice-pack, and summarily stopped below the barrier. Huge pieces, broken off from the sides, came crunching their way angrily up the bank, as if acting on some independent impulse. There they sat, great fragments, glistening in the sunlight, as big as cabins. It was something to see them come walking up the shelving bank! The cheechalkos who laughed before are contented now with running, leaving their goods behind. Sour-dough Saunders himself never dreamed the ice would push its way so far.

In mid-channel a still unbroken sheet is bent yet more in the centre. Every now and then a wide crack opens near the margin, and the water rushes out with a roar. Once more the mass is nearly still, and now all's silent. Not till the water, dammed and thrown back by the ice, not until it rises many feet and comes down with a volume and momentum irresistible, will the final conflict come.

Hour after hour the people stand there on the bank, waiting to see the barrier go down. Unwillingly, as the time goes on, this one, that one, hurries away for a few minutes to prepare and devour a meal, back again, breathless, upon rumour of that preparatory trembling, that strange thrilling of the ice. The grinding and the crushing had begun again.

The long tension, the mysterious sounds, the sense of some great unbridled power at work, wrought on the steadiest nerves. People did the oddest things. Down at the lower end of the town a couple of miners, sick of the scurvy, had painfully clambered on their roof—whether to see the sights or be out of harm's way, no one knew. The stingiest man in Minóok, who had refused to help them in their cabin, carried them food on the roof. A woman made and took them the Yukon remedy for their disease. They sat in state in sight of all men, and drank spruce tea.

By one o'clock in the afternoon the river had risen eight feet, but the ice barrier still held. The people, worn out, went away to sleep. All that night the barrier held, though more ice came down and still the water rose. Twelve feet now. The ranks of shattered ice along the shore are claimed again as the flood widens and licks them in. The cheechalkos' cabins are flooded to the eaves. Stout fellows in hip-boots take a boat and rescue the scurvy-stricken from the roof. And still the barrier held.

People began to go about their usual avocations. The empty Gold Nugget filled again. Men sat, as they had done all the winter, drinking, and reading the news of eight months before, out of soiled and tattered papers.

Late the following day everyone started up at a new sound. Again miners, Indians, and dogs lined the bank, saw the piled ice masses tremble, heard a crashing and grinding as of mountains of glass hurled together, saw the barrier give way, and the frozen wastes move down on the bosom of the flood. Higher yet the water rose—the current ran eight miles an hour. And now the ice masses were less enormous, more broken. Somewhere far below another jam. Another long bout of waiting.

Birds are singing everywhere. Between the white snow-drifts the Arctic moss shows green and yellow, white flowers star the hills.

Half the town is packed, ready to catch the boat at five minutes' notice. With door barred and red curtain down, Maudie is doing up her gold-dust for the Colonel to take to Dawson. The man who had washed it out of a Birch Creek placer, and 'blowed it in fur the girl'—up on the hillside he sleeps sound.

The two who had broken the record for winter travel on the Yukon, side by side in the sunshine, on a plank laid across two mackerel firkins, sit and watch the brimming flood. They speak of the Big Chimney men, picture them, packed and waiting for the *Oklahoma,* wonder what they have done with Kaviak, and what the three months have brought them.

'When we started out that day from the Big Chimney, we thought we'd be made if only we managed to reach Minóok.'

'Well, we've got what we came for—each got a claim.'

'Oh, yes.'

'A good claim, too.'

'Guess so.'

'Don't you *know* the gold's there?'

'Yes; but where are the miners? You and I don't propose to spend the next ten years in gettin' that gold out.'

'No; but there are plenty who would if we gave 'em the chance. All we have to do is give the right ones the chance.'

The Colonel wore an air of reflection.

'The district will be opened up,' the Boy went on cheerfully, 'and we'll have people beggin' us to let 'em get out our gold, and givin' us the lion's share for the privilege.'

'Do you like the sound o' that?'

'I expect, like other people, I'll like the result.'

'We ought to see some things clearer than other people. We had our lesson on the trail,' said the Colonel quietly. 'Nobody ought ever to be able to fool us about the power and the value of the individual apart from society. Seems as if association *did* make value. In the absence of men and markets a pit full of gold is worth no more than a pit full of clay.'

'Oh yes; I admit, till the boats come in, we're poor men.'

'Nobody will stop here this summer—they'll all be racing on to Dawson.'

'Dawson's "It," beyond a doubt.'

The Colonel laughed a little ruefully.

'We used to say Minóok.'

'I said Minóok, just to sound reasonable, but, of course, I *meant* Dawson.'

And they sat there thinking, watching the ice-blocks meet, crash, go down in foam, and come up again on the lower reaches, the Boy idly swinging the great Katharine's medal to and fro. In his buckskin pocket it has worn so bright it catches at the light like a coin fresh from the mint.

No doubt Muckluck is on the river-bank at Pymeut; the one-eyed Prince, the story-teller Yagorsha, even Ol' Chief—no one will be indoors today.

Sitting there together, they saw the last stand made by the ice, and shared that moment when the final barrier, somewhere far below, gave way with boom and thunder. The mighty flood ran free, tearing up trees by their roots as it ran, detaching masses of rock, dissolving islands into swirling sand and drift, carving new channels, making and unmaking the land. The water began to fall. It had been a great time: it was ended.

'Pardner,' says the Colonel, 'we've seen the ice go out.'

'No fella can call you and me cheechalkos after today.'

'No, sah. We've travelled the Long Trail, we've seen the ice go out, and we're friends yet.'

The Kentuckian took his pardner's brown hand with a gentle solemnity, seemed about to say something, but stopped and turned his bronzed face to the flood, carried back upon some sudden tide within himself to those black days on the trail, that he wanted most in the world to forget. But in his heart he knew that all dear things, all things kind and precious—his home, a woman's face—all, all would fade before he forgot those last days on the trail. The record of that journey was burnt into the brain of the men who had made it. On that stretch of the Long Trail the elder had grown old, and the younger had forever lost his youth. Not only had the roundness gone out of his face, not only was it scarred, but such lines were graven there as commonly takes the antique pencil half a score of years to trace.

'Something has happened,' the Colonel said quite low. 'We aren't the same men who left the Big Chimney.'

'Right!' said the Boy, with a laugh, unwilling as yet to accept his own personal revelation, preferring to put a superficial interpretation on his companion's words. He glanced at the Colonel, and his face changed a little. But still he would not understand. Looking down at the chaparejos that he had been so proud of, sadly abbreviated to make boots for Nig, jagged here and there, and with fringes now not all intentional, it suited him to pretend that the 'shaps' had suffered most.

'Yes, the ice takes the kinks out.'

'Whether the thing that's happened is good or evil, I don't pretend to say,' the other went on gravely, staring at the river. 'I only know something's happened. There were possibilities—in me, anyhow—that have been frozen to death. Yes, we're different.'

The Boy roused himself, but only to persist in his misinterpretation.

'You ain't different to hurt. If I started out again tomorrow—'

'The Lord forbid!'

'Amen. But if I had to, you're the only man in Alaska—in the world—I'd want for my pardner.'

'Boy—!' he wrestled with a slight bronchial huskiness, cleared his throat, tried again, and gave it up, contenting himself with, 'Beg your pardon for callin' you "Boy". You're a seasoned old-timer, sah.' And the Boy felt as if some Sovereign had dubbed him Knight.

In a day or two now, from north or south, the first boat must appear. The willows were unfolding their silver leaves. The alder-buds were bursting; geese and teal and mallard swarmed about the river margin. Especially where the equisetæ showed the tips of their feathery green tails above the mud, ducks flocked and feasted. People were too excited, "too busy," they said, looking for the boats, to do much shooting. The shy birds waxed daring. Keith, standing by his shack, knocked over a mallard within forty paces of his door.

It was eight days after that first cry, 'The ice is going out!' four since the final jam gave way and let the floes run free, that at one o'clock in the afternoon the shout went up, 'A boat! a boat!'

Only a lumberman's bateau, but two men were poling her down the current with a skill that matched the speed. They swung her in. A dozen hands caught at the painter and made fast. A young man stepped ashore and introduced himself as Van Alen, Benham's

'Upper River pardner, on the way to Anvik.'

His companion, Donovan, was from Circle City, and brought appalling news. The boats depended on for the early summer traffic, *Bella,* and three other N. A. T. and T. steamers, as well as the A. C.'s *Victoria* and the *St. Michael,* had been lifted up by the ice 'like so many feathers,' forced clean out of the channel, and left high and dry on a sandy ridge, with an ice wall eighty feet wide and fifteen high between them and open water.

'All the crews hard at work with jackscrews,' said Donovan; 'and if they can get skids under, and a channel blasted through the ice, they *may* get the boats down here in fifteen or twenty days.'

A heavy blow. But instantly everyone began to talk of the *May West* and the *Muckluck* as though all along they had looked for succour to come up-stream rather than down. But as the precious hours passed, a deep dejection fastened on the camp. There had been a year when, through one disaster after another, no boats had got to the Upper River. Not even the arrival from Dawson of the Montana Kid, pugilist and gambler, could raise spirits so cast down, not even though he was said to bring strange news from outside.

There was war in the world down yonder—war had been formally declared between America and Spain.

Windy slapped his thigh in humorous despair.

'Why hadn't *he* thought o' gettin' off a josh like that?'

To those who listened to the Montana Kid, to the fretted spirits of men eight months imprisoned, the States and her foreign affairs were far away indeed, and as for the other party to the rumoured war—*Spain?* They clutched at school memories of Columbus, Americans finding through him the way to Spain, as through him Spaniards had found the way to America. So Spain was not merely a State historic! She was still in the active world. But what did these things matter? Boats mattered: the place where the Klondykers were caught, this Minóok, mattered. And so did the place they wanted to reach—Dawson mattered most of all. By the narrowed habit of long months, Dawson was the centre of the universe.

More little boats going down, and still nothing going up. Men said gloomily:

'We're done for! The fellows who go by the Canadian route will get everything. The Dawson season will be half over before we're in the field—if we *ever* are!'

The 28th of May! Still no steamer had come, but the mosquitos had—bloodthirsty beyond any the temperate climates know. It was clear that some catastrophe had befallen the Woodworth boats. And Nig had been lured away by his quondam master! No, they had not gone back to the gulch—that was too easy. The man had a mind to keep the dog, and, since he was not allowed to buy him, he would do the other thing.

He had not been gone an hour, rumour said—had taken a scow and provisions, and dropped down the river. Utterly desperate, the Boy seized his new Nulato gun and somebody else's canoe. Without so much as inquiring whose, he shot down the swift current after the dog-thief. He roared back to the remonstrating Colonel that he didn't care if an up-river steamer *did* come while he was gone—he was goin' gunnin'.

At the same time he shared the now general opinion that a Lower River boat would reach them first, and he was only going to meet her, meting justice by the way.

He had gone safely more than ten miles down, when suddenly, as he was passing an island, he stood up in his boat, balanced himself, and cocked his gun.

Down there, on the left, a man was standing knee-deep in the water, trying to free his boat from a fallen tree; a Siwash dog watched him from the bank.

The Boy whistled. The dog threw up his nose, yapped and whined. The man had turned sharply, saw his enemy and the levelled gun. He jumped into the boat, but she was filling while he baled; the dog ran along the island, howling fit to raise the dead. When he was a little above the Boy's boat he plunged into the river. Nig was a good swimmer, but the current here would tax the best. The Boy found himself so occupied with saving Nig from a watery grave, while he kept the canoe from capsizing, that he forgot all about the thief till a turn in the river shut him out of sight.

The canoe was moored, and while trying to restrain Nig's dripping caresses, his master looked up, and saw something queer off there, above the tops of the cotton-woods. As he looked he forgot the dog—forgot everything in earth or heaven except that narrow cloud wavering along the sky. He sat immovable in the round-shouldered attitude learned in pulling a hand-sled against a gale from the Pole. If you are moderately excited you may start, but there is an excitement that 'nails you.'

Nig shook his wolf's coat and sprayed the water far and

wide, made joyful little noises, and licked the face that was so still. But his master, like a man of stone, stared at that long gray pennon in the sky. If it isn't a steamer, what is it? Like an echo out of some lesson he had learned and long forgot, "Up-bound boats don't run the channel: they have to hunt for easy water." Suddenly he leaped up. The canoe tipped, and Nig went a second time into the water. Well for him that they were near the shore; he could jump in without help this time. No hand held out, no eye for him. His master had dragged the painter free, seized the oars, and, saying harshly, 'Lie down, you black devil!' he pulled back against the current with every ounce he had in him. For the gray pennon was going round the other side of the island, and the Boy was losing the boat to Dawson.

Nig sat perkily in the bow, never budging till his master, running into the head of the island, caught up a handful of tough root fringes, and, holding fast by them, waved his cap, and shouted like one possessed, let go the fringes, caught up his gun, and fired. Then Nig, realizing that for once in a way noise seemed to be popular, pointed his nose at the big object hugging the farther shore, and howled with a right goodwill.

'They see! They see! Hooray.'

The Boy waved his arms, embraced Nig, then snatched up the oars. The steamer's engines were reversed; now she was still. The Boy pulled lustily. A crowded ship. Crew and passengers pressed to the rails. The steamer canted, and the captain's orders rang out clear. Several cheechalkos laid their hands on their guns as the wild fellow in the ragged buckskins shot round the motionless wheel, and brought his canoe 'longside, while his savage-looking dog still kept the echoes of the Lower Ramparts calling.

'Three cheers for the *Oklahoma!*'

At the sound of the Boy's voice a red face hanging over the stern broke into a broad grin.

'Be the Siven! Air ye the little divvle himself, or air ye the divvle's gran'fatherr?'

The apparition in the canoe was making fast and preparing to board the ship.

'Can't take another passenger. Full up!' said the Captain. He couldn't hear what was said in reply, but he shook his head. 'Been refusin' 'em right along.' Then, as if reproached by the look in the wild young face, 'We thought you were in trouble.'

'So I am if you won't—'

'I tell you we got every ounce we can carry.'

'Oh, take me back to Minóok, anyway!'

He said a few words about fare to the Captain's back. As that magnate did not distinctly say 'No'—indeed, walked off making conversation with the engineer—twenty hands helped the new passenger to get Nig and the canoe on board.

'Well, got a gold-mine?' asked Potts.

'Yes, *sir.*'

'Where's the Colonel?' Mac rasped out, with his square jaw set for judgment.

'Colonel's all right—at Minóok. We've got a gold-mine apiece.'

'Anny gowld in 'em?'

'Yes sir, and no salt, neither.'

'Sorry to see success has gone to your head,' drawled Potts, eyeing the Boy's long hair. 'I don't see any undue signs of it elsewhere.'

'Faith! I do, thin. He's turned wan o' thim hungry, grabbin' millionaires.'

'What makes you think that?' laughed the Boy, poking his brown fingers through the knee-hole of his breeches.

'Arre ye contint wid that gowld-mine at Minóok? No, be the Siven! What's wan gowld-mine to a millionaire? What forr wud ye be prospectin' that desert oiland, you nad yer faithful man Froyday, if ye wasn't rooned intoirely be riches?'

The Boy tore himself away from his old friends, and followed the arbiter of his fate. The engines had started up again, and they were going on.

'I'm told,' said the Captain rather severely, 'that Minóok's a busted camp.'

'Oh, *is* it?' returned the ragged one cheerfully. Then he remembered that this Captain Rainey had grub-staked a man in the autumn—a man who was reported to know where to look for the Mother Lode, the mighty parent of the Yukon placers. 'I can tell you the *facts* about Minóok.' He followed the Captain up on the hurricane-deck, giving him details about the new strike, and the wonderful richness of Idaho Bar. 'Nobody would know about it today, but that the *right* man went prospecting there.' (One in the eye for whoever said Minóok was 'busted,' and another for the prospector Rainey had sent to look for—) 'You see, men like Pitcairn have given up lookin' for the Mother Lode. They say you might as well look for Mother Eve; you got to make out with her descendants. Yukon gold, Pitcairn says, comes from an older rock series than this'—he stood in the shower of sparks constantly spraying from the smoke-stack to the fireproof deck, and he waved his hand airily at the red rock of the Ramparts—'far older than any of these. The gold up here has all come out o' rock that went out o' the rock business millions o' years ago. Most o' that Mother Lode the miners are lookin' for is sand now, thirteen hundred miles away in Norton Sound.'

'Just my luck,' said the Captain gloomily, going a little for'ard, as though definitely giving up mining and returning to his own proper business.

'But the rest o' the Mother Lode, the gold and magnetic iron, was too heavy to travel. That's what's linin' the gold basins o' the North—linin' Idaho Bar *thick.*'

The Captain sighed.

'Twelve,' a voice sang out on the lower deck.

'Twelve,' repeated the Captain.

'Twelve,' echoed the pilot at the wheel.

'Twelve and a half,' from the man below, a tall, lean fellow, casting the sounding-pole. With a rhythmic nonchalance he plants the long black and white staff at the ship's side, draws it up dripping, plunges it down again, draws it up, and sends it down hour after hour. He never seems to tire; he never seems to see anything but the water-mark, never to say anything but what he is chanting now, 'Twelve and a half,' or some variation merely numerical. You come to think him as little human as the calendar, only that his numbers are told off with the significance of sound, the suggested menace of a cry. If the 'sounding' comes too near the steamer's draught, or the pilot fails to hear the reading, the Captain repeats it. He often does so when there is no need; it is a form of conversation, non-committal, yet smacking of authority.

'Ten.'

'Ten,' echoed the pilot, while the Captain was admitting that he had been mining vicariously 'for twenty years, and never made a cent. Always keep thinkin' I'll soon be able to give up steamboatin' and buy a farm.'

He shook his head as one who sees his last hope fade.

But his ragged companion turned suddenly, and while the sparks fell in a fresh shower, 'Well, Captain,' says he, 'you've got the chance of your life right now.'

'Ten and a half.'

'Just what they've all said. Wish I had the money I've wasted on grub-stakin'.'

The ragged one thrust his hands in the pockets of his chaparejos.

'*I* grub-staked myself, and I'm very glad I did.'

'Nobody in with you?'

'No.'

'Nine.'

Echo, 'Nine.'

'Ten.'

'Pitcairn says, somehow or other, there's been gold-washin' goin' on up here pretty well ever since the world began.'

'Indians?'

'No; seems to have been a bigger job than even white men could manage. Instead o' stamp-mills, glaciers grindin' up the Mother Lode; instead o' little sluice-boxes, rivers; instead o' riffles, gravel bottoms. Work, work, wash, wash, day and night, every summer for a million years. Never a clean-up since the foundation of the world. No, sir, waitin' for us to do that—waitin' now up on Idaho Bar.'

The Captain looked at him, trying to conceal the envy in his soul. They were sounding low water, but he never heard. He looked round sharply as the course changed.

'I've done my assessment,' the ragged man went on joyously, 'and I'm going to Dawson.'

This was bad navigation. He felt instantly he had struck a snag. The Captain smiled, and passed on the sounding: 'Nine and a half.'

'But I've got a fortune on the Bar. I'm not a boomer, but I believe in the Bar.'

'Six.'

'Six. Gettin' into low water.'

Again the steamer swung out, hunting a new channel.

'Pitcairn's opinion is thought a lot of. The Geologic Survey men listen to Pitcairn. He helped them one year. He's one of those extraordinary old miners who can tell from the look of things, without even panning. When he saw that pyrites on Idaho Bar he stopped dead. "This looks good to me!" he said, and, Jee-rusalem! it *was* good!'

They stared at the Ramparts growing bolder, the river hurrying like a mill-race, the steamer feeling its way slow and cautiously like a blind man with a stick.

'Seven.'

'Seven.'

'Seven.'

'Six and a half.'

'Pitcairn says gold is always thickest on the inside of an elbow or turn in the stream. It's in a place like that my claim is.'

The steamer swerved still further out from the course indicated on the chart. The pilot was still hunting a new channel, but still the Captain stood and listened, and it was not to the sounding of the Yukon Bar.

'They say there's no doubt about the whole country being glaciated.'

'Hey?'

'Signs of glacial erosion everywhere.'

The Captain looked sharply about as if his ship might be in some new danger.

'No doubt the gold is all concentrates.'

'Oh, is that so?' He seemed relieved on the whole.

'Eight and a half,' from below.

'Eight and a half,' from the Captain.

'Eight and a half,' from the pilot-house.

'Concentrates, eh?'

Something arresting, rich sounding, in the news—a triple essence of the perfume of riches.

With the incantation of technical phrase over the witch-brew of adventure, gambling, and romance, that simmers in the mind when men tell of finding gold in the ground, with the addition of this salt of science comes a savour of homely virtue, an aroma promising sustenance and strength. It confounds suspicion and sees unbelief, first weaken, and at last do reverence. There is something hypnotic in the terminology. Enthusiasm, even backed by fact, will scare off your practical man, who yet will turn to listen to the theory of 'the mechanics of erosion' and one of its proofs—'up there before our eyes, the striation of the Ramparts.'

But Rainey was what he called 'an old bird.' His squinted pilot-eye came back from the glacier track and fell on the outlandish figure of his passenger. And with an inward admiration of his quality of extreme old-birdness, thc Captain struggled against the trance.

'Didn't I hear you say something about going to Dawson?'

'Y—yes. I think Dawson'll be worth seeing.'

'Holy Moses, yes! There's never been anything like Dawson before.'

'And I want to talk to the big business men there. I'm not a miner myself. I mean to put my property on the market.' As he said the words it occurred to him unpleasantly how very like McGinty they sounded. But he went on: 'I didn't dream of spendin' so much time up here as I've put in already. I've got to get back to the States.'

'You had any proposition yet?' The Captain led the way to his private room.

'About my claim? Not yet; but once I get it on the market—'

So full was he of a scheme of his own he failed to see that he had no need to go to Dawson for a buyer.

The Captain set out drinks, and still the talk was of the Bar. It had come now to seem impossible, even to an old bird, that, given those exact conditions, gold should not be gathered thick along that Bar.

'I regard it as a sure thing. Anyhow, it's recorded, and the assessment's done. All the district wants now is capital to develop it.'

'Districts like that all over the map,' said the old bird, with a final flutter of caution. 'Even if the capital's found—if everything's ready for work, the summer's damn short. But if it's a question of goin' huntin' for the means of workin'—'

'There's time,' returned the other quietly, 'but there's none to waste. You take me and my pardner—'

'Thought you didn't have a pardner,' snapped the other, hot over such duplicity.

'Not in ownership; he's got another claim. But you take my pardner and me to Dawson—'

The Captain stood on his legs and roared:

'I *can't*, I tell you!'

'You can if you will—you will if you want that farm!'

Rainey gaped.

'Take us to Dawson, and I'll get a deed drawn up in Minóok turning over one-third of my Idaho Bar property to John R. Rainey.'

John R. Rainey gaped the more, and then finding his tongue:

'No, no. I'd just as soon come in on the Bar, but it's true what I'm tellin' you. There simply ain't an unoccupied inch on the *Oklahoma* this trip. It's been somethin' awful, the way I've been waylaid and prayed at for a passage. People starvin' with bags o' money waitin' for 'em at the Dawson Bank! Settlements under water—men up in trees callin' to us to stop for the love of God— men in boats crossin' our channel, headin' us off, thinkin' nothin' o' the risk o' bein' run down. "Take us to Dawson!" it's the cry for fifteen hundred miles.'

'Oh, come! you stopped for me.'

The Captain smiled shrewdly.

'I didn't think it necessary at the time to explain. We'd struck bottom just then—new channel, you know; it changes a lot every time the ice goes out and the floods come down. I reversed our engines and went up to talk to the pilot. We backed off just after you boarded us. I must have been rattled to take you even to Minóok.'

'No. It was the best turn you've done yourself in a long while.'

The Captain shook his head. It was true: the passengers of the *Oklahoma* were crowded like cattle on a Kansas stock-car. He knew he ought to unload and let a good portion wait at Minóok for that unknown quantity the next boat. He would issue the order, but that he knew it would mean a mutiny.

'I'll get into trouble for overloading as it is.'

'You probably won't; people are too busy up here. If you do, I'm offerin' you a good many thousand dollars for the risk.'

'God bless my soul! where'd I put you? There ain't a bunk.'

'I've slept by the week on the ice.'

'There ain't room to lie down.'

'Then we'll stand up.'

Lord, Lord! what could you do with such a man? Owner of Idaho Bar, too. 'Mechanics of erosion,' 'Concentrates,' 'a third inter- est'—it all rang in his head. 'I've got nine fellers sleepin' in here,' he said helplessly, 'in *my* room.'

'Can we come if we find our own place, and don't trouble you?'

'Well, I won't have any pardner—but perhaps you—'

'Oh, pardner's got to come too.'

Whatever the Captain said the nerve-tearing shriek of the whistle drowned. It was promptly replied to by the most horrible howls.

'Reckon that's Nig! He's got to come too,' said this dreadful ragged man.

'God bless me, this must be Minóok.'

The harassed Captain hustled out.

'You must wait long enough here to get that deed drawn, Captain!' called out the other, as he flew down the companion-way.

Nearly six hundred people on the bank. Suddenly controlling his eagerness, the Boy contented himself with standing back and staring across strange shoulders at the place he knew so well. There was 'the worst-lookin' shack in the town,' that had been his home, the A. C. store looming importantly, the Gold Nugget, and hardly a face to which he could not give a name and a history: Windy Jim and the crippled Swede; Bonsor, cheek by jowl with his enemy, McGinty; Judge Corey spitting straight and far; the gorgeous bar-tender, all checks and diamonds, in front of a pitiful group of the scurvy-stricken (thirty of them in the town waiting for rescue by the steamer); Butts, quite bland, under the crooked cotton-wood, with never a thought of how near he had come, on that very spot, to missing the first boat of the year, and all the boats of all the years to follow.

Maudie, Keith and the Colonel stood with the A. C. agent at the end of the baggage-bordered plank-walk that led to the landing. Behind them, at least four hundred people packed and waiting with their possessions at their feet, ready to be put aboard the instant the *Oklahoma* made fast. The Captain had called out 'Howdy' to the A. C. Agent, and several greetings were shouted back and forth. Maudie mounted a huge pile of baggage and sat there as on a throne, the Colonel and Keith perching on a heap of gunny-sacks at her feet. That woman almost the only person in sight who did not expect, by means of the *Oklahoma*, to leave misery behind! The Boy stood thinking 'How will they bear it when they know?'

The *Oklahoma* was late, but she was not only the first boat— she might conceivably be the last.

Potts and O'Flynn had spotted the man they were looking for, and called out 'Hello! Hello!' as the big fellow on the pile of gunnies got up and waved his hat.

Mac leaned over the rail, saying gruffly, 'That you, Colonel?' trying, as the Boss of the Big Chimney saw—tryin' his darndest not to look pleased,' and all the while O'Flynn was waving his hat and howling with excitement:

'How's the gowld? How's yersilf?'

The gangway began its slow swing round preparatory to lowering into place. The mob on shore caught up boxes, bundles, bags, and pressed forward.

'No, no! Stand back!' ordered the Captain.

'*Take* your time!' said people trembling with excitement. 'There's no rush.'

'There's no room!' called out the purser to a friend.

'*No room?*' went from mouth to mouth, incredulous that the information could concen the speaker. He was only one. There was certainly room for him; and every man pushed the harder to be the sole exception to the dreadful verdict.

'Stand back there! Can't take even a pound of freight. Loaded to the guards!'

A whirlwind of protest and appeal died away in curses. Women wept, and sick men turned away their faces. The dogs still howled, for nothing is so lacerating to the feelings of your Siwash as a steam-whistle blast. The memory of it troubles him long after the echo of it dies. Suddenly above the din Maudie's shrill voice:

'I *thought* that was Nig.'

Before the gangway had dropped with a bang her sharp eyes had picked out the boy.

'Well I'll be—See who is that behind Nig? Trust *him* to get in on the ground-floor. *He* ain't worryin' for fear his pardner'll lose the boat,' she called to the Colonel, who was pressing forward as Rainey came down the gangway.

'How do you do, Captain?'

The man addressed never turned his head. He was forcing his way through the jam up to the A. C. Store.

'You may recall me, sah; I am—'

'If you are a man wantin' to go to Dawson, it doesn't matter who you are. I can't take you.'

'But, sah—' It was no use.

A dozen more were pushing their claims, every one in vain. The *Oklahoma* passengers, bent on having a look at Minóok, crowded after the Captain. Among those who first left the ship, the Boy, talking to the purser, hard upon Rainey's heels. The Colonel stood there as they passed, the Captain turning back to say something to the Boy, and then they disappeared together through the door of thc A. C.

Never a word for his pardner, not so much as a look. Bitterness fell upon the Colonel's heart. Maudie called to him, and he went back to his seat on the gunny-sacks.

'He's in with the Captain now,' she said; 'he's got no more use for us.'

But there was less disgust than triumph in her face.

O'Flynn was walking over people in his frantic haste to reach the Colonel. Before he could accomplish his design he had three separate quarrels on his hands, and was threatening with fury to 'settle the hash' of several of his dearest new friends.

Potts meanwhile was shaking the Big Chimney boss by the hand and saying, 'Awfully sorry we can't take you on with us;' adding lower: 'We had a mighty mean time after you lit out.'

Then Mac thrust his hand in between the two, and gave the Colonel a monkey-wrench grip that made the Kentuckian's eyes water.

'Kaviak? Well, I'll tell you.'

He shouldered Potts out of his way, and while the talk and movement went on all round Maudie's throne, Mac, ignoring her, set forth grimly how, after an awful row with Potts, he had adventured with Kaviak to Holy Cross. 'An awful row, indeed,' thought the Colonel, 'to bring Mac to that;' but the circumstance had little interest for him, beside the fact that his pardner would be off to Dawson in a few minutes, leaving him behind and caring 'not a sou markee.'

Mac was still at Holy Cross. He had seen a woman there—'calls herself a nun—evidently swallows those priests whole. Kind of mad, believes it all. Except for that, good sort of girl. The kind to keep her word'—and she had promised to look after Kaviak, and never let him away from her till Mac came back to fetch him.

'Fetch him?'

'Fetch him.'

'Fetch him where?'

'Home!'

'When will that be?'

'Just as soon as I've put through the job up yonder.' He jerked his head up the river, indicating the common goal.

And now O'Flynn, roaring as usual, had broken away from those who had obstructed his progress, and had flung himself upon the Colonel. When the excitement had calmed down a little, 'Well,' said the Colonel to the three ranged in front of him, Maudie looking on from above, 'what you been doin' all these three months?'

'Doin'?'

'Well—a—'

'Oh, we done a lot.'

They looked at one another out of the corners of their eyes and then they looked away.

'Since the birds came,' began Mac in the tone of one who wishes to let bygones be bygones.

'Och yes; them burruds was foine.'

Potts pulled something out of his trousers pocket—a strange collapsed object. He took another of the same description out of another pocket. Mac's hands and O'Flynn's performed the same action. Each man seemed to have his pockets full of these—

'What are they?'

'Money-bags, me bhoy! Made out o' the fut o' the 'Lasky swan, God bless 'em! Mac calls 'em some haythen name, but everybuddy else cahls 'em illegant money-bags!'

* * * * *

In less than twenty minutes the steamer whistle shrieked. Nig bounded out of the A. C., frantic at the reception of the insult; other dogs took the quarrel up, and the Ramparts rang.

The Boy followed the Captain out of the A. C. store. All the motley crew that had swarmed off to inspect Minóok, swarmed back upon the *Oklahoma*. The Boy left the Captain this time, and came briskly over to his friends, who were taking leave of the Colonel.

'So you're all goin' on but me!' said the Colonel very sadly.

The Colonel's pardner stopped short, and looked at the pile of baggage.

'Got your stuff all ready!' he said.

'Yes.' The answer was not free from bitterness. 'I'll have the pleasure of packin' it back to the shack after you're gone.'

'So you were all ready to go off and leave me,' said the Boy.

The Colonel could not stoop to the obvious retort. His pardner came round the pile and his eyes fell on their common sleeping-bag, the two Nulato rifles, and other 'traps,' that meant more to him than any objects inanimate in all the world.

'What? you were goin' to carry off my things too?' exclaimed the Boy.

'That's all you get,' Maudie burst out indignantly—'all you get for packin' his stuff down to the landin', to have it all ready for him, and worryin' yourself into shoe-strings for fear he'd miss the boat.'

Mac, O'Flynn, and Potts condoled with the Colonel, while the fire of the old feud flamed and died.

'Yes,' the Colonel admitted, 'I'd give five hundred dollars for a ticket on that steamer.'

He looked in each of the three faces, and he knew the vague hope behind his words was vain. But the Boy had only laughed, and caught up the baggage as the last whistle set the Rampart echoes flying, piping, like a lot of frightened birds.

'Come along, then.'

'Look here!' the Colonel burst out. 'That's my stuff.'

'It's all the same. You bring mine. I've got the tickets. You and me and Nig's goin' to the Klondyke.'

The Cremation of Sam McGee

BY ROBERT SERVICE

THERE ARE STRANGE THINGS DONE IN THE MIDNIGHT SUN
By the men who moil for gold;
The Arctic trails have their secret tales
That would make your blood run cold;
The Northern Lights have seen queer sights,
But the queerest they ever did see
Was that night on the marge of Lake Lebarge
I cremated Sam McGee.

Now Sam McGee was from Tennessee, where the cotton
blooms and blows.
Why he left his home in the South to roam round the Pole
God only knows.
He was always cold, but the land of gold seemed to hold
him like a spell;
Though he'd often say in his homely way that he'd "sooner
live in hell."

On a Christmas Day we were mushing our way over the
Dawson trail.
Talk of your cold! through the parka's fold it stabbed like a
driven nail.

If our eyes we'd close, then the lashes froze, till sometimes
    we couldn't see;
It wasn't much fun, but the only one to whimper was Sam
    McGee.

And that very night as we lay packed tight in our robes
    beneath the snow,
And the dogs were fed, and the stars o'erhead were dancing
    heel and toe,
He turned to me, and, "Cap," says he, "I'll cash in this trip,
    I guess;
And if I do, I'm asking that you won't refuse my last request."

Well he seemed so low that I couldn't say no; then he says
    with a sort of moan:
"It's the cursed cold, and it's got right hold till I'm chilled
    clean through to the bone.
Yet 'taint being dead, it's my awful dread of the icy grave
    that pains;
So I want you to swear that, foul or fair, you'll cremate my
    last remains."

A pal's last need is a thing to heed, so I swore I would
    not fail;
And we started on at the streak of dawn, but God! he
    looked ghastly pale.
He crouched on the sleigh, and he raved all day of his
    home in Tennessee;
And before nightfall a corpse was all that was left of
    Sam McGee.

There wasn't a breath in that land of death, and I hurried,
    horror driven,
With a corpse half-hid that I couldn't get rid, because of a
    promise given;
It was lashed to the sleigh, and it seemed to say: "You may
    tax your brawn and brains,
But you promised true, and it's up to you to cremate those
    last remains."

Now a promise made is a debt unpaid, and the trail has its
      own stern code.
In the days to come, though my lips were dumb, in my
      heart how I cursed that load.
In the long, long night, by the lone firelight, while the
      huskies, round in a ring,
Howled out their woes to the homeless snows—O God!
      how I loathed the thing.

And every day that quiet clay seemed to heavy and
      heavier grow;
And on I went, though the dogs were spent and the grub
      was getting low;
The trail was bad, and I felt half mad, but I swore I would
      not give in;
And I'd often sing to the hateful thing, and it hearkened
      with a grin.

Till I came to the marge of Lake Lebarge, and a derelict
      there lay;
It was jammed in the ice, but I saw in a trice it was called
      the "Alice May."
And I looked at it, and I thought a bit, and I looked at my
      frozen chum:
Then, "Here," said I, with a sudden cry, "is my
      cre-ma-tor-eum."

Some planks I tore from the cabin floor, and I lit the boiler
      fire;
Some coal I found that was lying around, and I heaped the
      fuel higher;
The flames just soared, and the furnace roared—such a
      blaze you seldom see;
And I burrowed a hole in the glowing coal, and I stuffed in
      Sam McGee.

Then I made a hike, for I didn't like to hear him sizzle so;
And the heavens scowled, and the huskies howled, and the
      wind began to blow.

It was icy cold, but the hot sweat rolled down my cheeks,
       and I don't know why;
And the greasy smoke in an inky cloak went streaking
       down the sky.

I do not know how long in the snow I wrestled with
       grisly fear;
But the stars came out and they danced about ere again I
       ventured near;
I was sick with dread, but I bravely said: "I'll just take a
       peep inside.
I guess he's cooked, and it's time I looked,". . . then the
       door I opened wide.

And there sat Sam, looking cool and calm, in the heart of
       the furnace roar;
And he wore a smile you could see a mile, and he said:
       "Please close that door.
It's fine in here, but I greatly fear you'll let in the cold
       and storm—
Since I left Plumtree, down in Tennessee, it's the first time
       I've been warm."

There are strange things done in the midnight sun
       By the men who moil for gold;
The Arctic trails have their secret tales
       That would make your blood run cold;
The Northern lights have seen queer sights,
       But the queerest they ever did see
Was that night on the marge of Lake Lebarge
       I cremated Sam McGee.

Luck

BY MARJORIE PICKTHALL

THERE WERE FOUR BUNKS in the shanty, and three of them were filled.

Ohlsen lay in one, a great bulk under the Hudson Bay Company blankets, breathing like a bull; in the next was Forbes, with eyes as quick as a mink's, and now red rimmed from snow blindness, twinkling from time to time over his yellowish furs. Nearest the door was Lajeune, singing in his sleep. In one corner an old Indian cowered, as little regarded as the rags and skins in which he was hidden; and Desmond sat by the stove, drinking to his luck, fingering it and folding it.

It was all there in a bag—raw gold, pure gold, the food of joy. At the weight of it in his rough palm, Desmond chattered and chuckled with delight. He had sat there talking and laughing for hours, while the glow of the stove grew darker and the cold crept in. Little blots of snow from the snow-shoes, first melting, had turned again to dark ice on the floor; the red light clung to them until each little circle seemed to be one of blood. Outside the world trembled under the shafts of the bitter stars; but Desmond, with the very fuel of life in his hand, was warm.

Dreams ran in his brain like a tide and dripped off his tongue in words. They were strangely innocent dreams of innocent things; sunlight on an old wall, honey, a girl with sandy eyebrows, and yellow ducklings.

"And maybe there'll be a garden, with fruit you can pick off the bushes. 'Twas under a thorn-bush she used to stand, with the wind snapping her print gown. Or maybe I'll see more of the world first in an easy fashion, never a drink scarce, and no man my better at it. I know how a gentleman should behave. Are you hearing me, boys?"

Ohlsen breathed as slowly and deeply as a bull. Forbes blinked a moment over the greasy furs and said, "I'm hearing you." Lajeune gave a sudden little call in his sleep, like a bird.

"They're all asleep, like so many hogs," said Desmond, with a maudlin wonder; "they don't care. Two years we've struggled and starved together in this here freezing hell, and now my luck's come, and they don't care. Well, well."

He stared resentfully at the bunks. He could see nothing of Ohlsen but blanket, yet Ohlsen helped him to a new outfit when he lost everything in a snow-slide. Forbes was only an unheeding head of grimy fur, yet once he had pulled Desmond out of a log-jam. And Lejeune had nursed him laughingly when he hurt his foot with a pick. Yet now Lejeune cared nothing; he was asleep, his head flung back, showing his smooth, lean throat and a scar that ran across it, white on brown. Desmond felt hurt. He took another drink, strode over to the bunk, and shook him petulantly.

"Don't ye hear when a friend talks t'ye?"

Lajeune did not move, yet he was instantly awake. His eyes, so black that they showed no pupil, stared suddenly into Desmond's muddled blue ones. His right hand gripped and grew rigid.

Desmond, leaning over him, was sobered by something in the breathless strain of that stare. He laughed uneasily.

"It's only me Jooney. Was you asleep? I'm sorry."

He backed off bewildered, but young Lajeune smiled and yawned, showing his red tongue curled like a wolf's.

"Still the gold, my friend?" he asked, drowsily.

"I—I can't seem to get used to it, like," explained Desmond: "I have to talk of it. I know I'm a fool, but a man's luck takes him all ways. You go to sleep, young Jooney. I won't talk to you no more."

"Nor before your old savage in the corner, *hein?*"

Desmond glanced at the heap of rags in the corner.

"Hom? What's the matter? Think he'll steal it? Why, there's four of us, and even an Injun can have a corner of my shack for an hour or two tonight. I reckon," finished Desmond, with a kind of gravity, "as my luck is making me soft. It takes a man all ways."

Lajeune yawned, grinned, flung up his left arm, and was instantly asleep again. He looked so young in his sleep, that Desmond was suddenly moved to draw the blanket over him. In the dim light he saw Forbes worn and grizzled, the wariness gone out of him, a defeated old man with horrible eyes. Ohlsen's hand lay over the edge of the bunk, his huge fingers, curved helplessly, like a child's. Desmond felt inarticulately tender to the three who had toiled by his side and missed their luck. He piled wood on the stove, saying, "I must do something for the boys. They're good boys."

At the freshened roar of the stove the old Indian in the corner stirred and lifted his head, groping like an old turtle in the sunlight. He had a curious effect of meaningless blurs and shadows. Eye and memory could hold nothing of his insignificance. Only under smoked and puckered lids the flickering glitter of his eyes pricked in a meaning unreadable. Desmond looked at him with the wide good nature born of his luck.

"I ain't going to turn ye out, Old Bones," he said.

The eyes steadied on him an instant, and the old shadow spoke fair English in the ghost of a voice.

"Thanks. You give grub. I eat, I warm, I rest. Now I go."

"Jest as ye like. But have a drink first." He pushed over the dregs of the whiskey bottle.

The old man seized it; seemed to hold it to his heart. While he could get whiskey he might drink and forget; when he could get it no more, he must remember and die. He drank, Lethe and Paradise in one, and handed back the bottle.

"How," he said. "You good man. Once I had things to give, now nothing. Nothing but dreams."

"Dreams, is it, Old Bones?"

The eyes were like cunning sparks.

"Dreams, yes," he said with a stealthy indrawing of breath. "You good man. I give you three dreams. See."

With a movement so swift the eye could hardly follow it, he caught three hot wood-coals from the ash under the stove and flung them on the floor at Desmond's feet. He bent forward, and under his breath they woke to a moment's flame. The strangeness of his movements held Desmond, and he also bent forward, watching. He had an instant's impression that the coals were burning him fiercely somewhere between the eyes, that the bars of personality were breaking, that he was falling into some darkness that was the darkness of death. Before his ignorance could find words for his fear, the old Indian leaned back; the fire fled, and the spent coals were no more than rounds of empty ash, which the old man took in his hands.

"Dreams," he said, with something that might have been a laugh. He blew the ash like little grey feathers toward the sleeping men in the bunks. His eyes were alive, fixed on Desmond with a meaning unreadable. He thrust his face close. "You good man. You give me whiskey. I give you three dreams, little dreams—for luck."

Desmond was staring at the little floating feathers of wood ash. As they slowly sank and settled, he heard the door close and felt a sharp stab of cold. The old Indian had gone: Desmond could hear his footsteps dragging over the frozen crust of the snow for a little while. He got up and shook himself. The drink had died out of him; he felt himself suddenly and greatly weary of body and mind. The fire would last till morning. "Dreams—dreams, for luck!" he muttered, as he rolled into the fourth bunk. He was ready for sleep. And as he lay down and yielded to the oncoming of sleep, as a weed yields to the tide, he knew of a swift, clear, certainty that he would dream.

II

He opened his eyes to the pale flood of day; Lajeune was cooking pork and making coffee; Ohlsen was mending snow shoes; Forbes bent over his bunk, black against the blind square of the frozen window, feeling blindly with his hands, and snuffling a little as he spoke:

"We'd ha' let you sleep on, but we wanted to know what you'd be doing. Will ye stay here with me and rest—I'm all but blind the day—or will ye go into Fort Recompense with Jooney here and the dogs, and put the dust in safety? Or will ye try the short cut across the pass with Ohlsen?"

Desmond stretched, grunted, and hesitated. He felt curiously unwilling to decide. But Forbes was waiting, his yellow fingers twitching on the end of the bunk.

"Oh, I dunno," he said. "What's the hurry? Well—I guess I'll try the pass with Ohlsen."

"Right." Ohlsen nodded his heavy head, for he seldom spoke. He had the physique men always associate with a kind and stupid fidelity. Desmond said of him, "Them that talks most ain't the best at heart." Desmond said it to himself as he rolled out of the bunk for breakfast.

Forbes stayed in his bunk, and made little moaning animal noises while he fed. Lajeune bubbled over with quick laughter. Desmond beamed on everyone and talked of his luck. Ohlsen sat immovable, working his jaws like an ox, watching Desmond with his small, pale eyes.

He did not speak as they drew on their furs and packed the gold; nor as they turned out of the shack, shutting the door swiftly behind them, and faced the stinging splendour of the windy winter day. The cold had lessened with the sunrise, but what cold there was the wind took and drove to the bone. The air was filled with a glittering mist of blown snow, and all the lower slopes of the hills and the climbing spruce forests were hidden. Above the *poudre* the mountains lifted like iron in the unpitying day, and every snowfield and glacier was crowned with a streaming feather of white against a hard turquoise sky.

"You think we'll get through?" asked Desmond doubtfully.

"Ay t'ank so." Ohlsen was striding heavily, tirelessly, just behind his shoulder. His grey eyes, still fixed on Desmond, were like little bits of glacier ice inset above his high cheek bones.

"We may."

"We may. It ain't far." Desmond was talkative. "This gold weighs heavy. I like the colour o' gold. Ohlsen, you got any children?"

"Ay, got two kids."

"Wisht I had. Maybe I will, though—little boy 'n' gal, with kind o' gold hair. See here, you ever had a garden?"

"No."

"I've me garden on me back here, hey? With them blue things that smell, and hens. You come and see me, Ohlsen, and you'll have the best there is."

"T'anks. Ay like fresh eggs."

"So do I. And apples. Say Ohlsen, I'm sorry this luck ain't for you."

Ohlsen did not answer or slacken his heavy, stooping stride against the wind. The curved hills opened slowly, swung aside. The spruce stood up, came nearer, and closed in around them like the outposts of a waiting army. The wind roared through the trees like a flood of which the surf was snow.

"Do you think we'll do it?" shouted Desmond again and Ohlsen answered:

"Ay t'ank so."

In a little while the trees were a dark mass beneath them, and they were out on the bare heights, fighting with the wind for every foothold. Desmond staggered under it, but Ohlsen seemed untiring, climbing very close at his shoulder. The glare of the sun seared their eyes, but they had no heat of it. In all the vast upheaval of the hills, in all the stark space of the sky, there was no warmth, no life.

Something took Desmond by the throat.

"We'll not do it," he cried, to Ohlsen. "Let's turn back."

For answer Ohlsen unstrapped the heavy pack of gold, fastened it on his shoulders, and went on. This time he was ahead, and his huge body sheltered Desmond from the wind.

"I been drinking too much," thought Desmond; "and here's Ohlsen having to do my work for me. It ain't right."

They were on a high ridge, and the wind was at its worst. On the left lay a precipice, and the dark masses of the spruce. On the right the depths were veiled with glittering silver now and then shot through with the blue-green gleam of a glacier. It was fair going for a steady head, but the wind was dangerous. It took Desmond, as with hands, and thrust him to his knees at the narrowing of the ledge. He slipped a little. The dark grey ice, white veined, gave him no hold. He lost his head, slipped a little farther, and the white driven foam of snow and cloud above the glacier was suddenly visible. He called to Ohlsen.

Ohlsen could not have heard, yet he turned and came slowly back. Desmond could have raged at him for his slowness if his lips had not been so stiff and dry. Inside his fur mitts his hands were suddenly wet. Gently he slid a little farther, and the wind-driven white below was plainer, cut through with turquoise as with a sword. He shut his eyes. And when he opened them Ohlsen had stopped and was standing quietly watching him.

Desmond shrieked hoarsely, for he understood. Between the two drove the torrent of the wind, shutting slayer and all but slain into a separate prison of silence. But even the wind did not stir Ohlsen; he stood like a grey rock, watching Desmond. Presently he leaned forward, hands on knees, his back humped grotesquely under the pack, as the cruel or the curious might watch the struggles of a drowning kitten. Desmond was shaken to his fingers by the terrible thudding of his heart. He could not make a sound. Earth and sky flashed away. There remained only the grey inhuman shape beyond the barrier of the wind.

Presently that also flashed away. Yet, as Desmond fell, he was aware of light, a great swift relief, for he knew that he dreamed.

Then came darkness.

III

It was a darkness glittering with stars. Such stars as the men of the South, the men of the cities, never see. Each was a blazing world hung in nothingness, rayed with sapphire and rose. Now and then the white ice-blink ran over and died beyond them in the spaces where even stars were not. Desmond was lying on his back, staring at them through a cranny in his sleeping-bag. He knew where he was, yet in his brain was a sort of cold confusion. He seemed to hear Forbes speaking.

"Will ye stay here with me and rest—I'm all but blind the day—or will ye go into Fort Recompense with Jooney here and the dogs, and put the dust in safety? Or will ye try the short cut across the pass with Ohlsen?"

"And here I am, half-way to the fort, and sleeping out with Jooney and the dogs," Desmond muttered; "but I can't remember coming."

Yet, as he turned in his sleeping-bag, his knowledge of his whereabouts was exact. He was in a stony little gully beyond Fachette, where high banks cut off the wind and ground willows gave firing. The huskies were asleep and warm in deep drift under the bank, after a full meal of dried salmon.

"I'll say this for young Jooney," said Desmond, drowsily, "he's got some sense with dogs."

Lajeune was beside him, asleep in another bag. Between them was the pack of gold and the sledge harness. And the great plain, he knew, ran north and south of the very lip of the gully, silver under the stars, ridged and rippled by the wind, like white sand of the sea. The wind was now still. The earth was again a star, bright, silent, and alone, akin to her sisters of the infinite heavens.

"There ain't so much gold in a place like this here," Desmond whispered, resentfully, to the night, "but jest you wait till I get south-east again." He was filled with blind longing for red brick, asphalt, and crowded streets; even the hens and ducklings were not enough. He hungered in this splendour of desolation for the little tumults of mankind. It seemed as if the stars laughed.

"There ain't nothing my gold won't get me," said Desmond more loudly. His breath hung in little icicles on the edges of his spy-hole. It was cruelly cold. He drew his hood closer round his head, and thrust it out of the bag.

Lajeune was gone.

He did not feel afraid; only deadly cold and sick as he struggled to his feet. Under their shelter of canvas and snow he was alone; everything else was gone. He fell on his hands and knees, digging furiously in the trodden snow, like a dog.

The gold was gone also.

"My luck," whispered Desmond, stupidly. "My luck."

He was still on his knees, shaping a little rounded column of snow; suppose it might be Lajeune's throat, and he with his hands on each side of it—so. Lajeune's dark face seemed to lie beneath him, but it was not touched with fear, but with laughter. He was laughing, as the stars had laughed, at Desmond and his luck. Desmond dashed the snow away with a cry.

He scrambled out of the gully. The dog-trail was easy to read, running straight across the silvery plain. He began to run along it.

As he ran he admired Lajeune very much. With what deadly quietness and precision he must have worked! The gully and the deserted camp were a grey streak behind him, were gone. He was running in Lajeune's very foot-prints, and he was sure he ran at an immense speed. The glittering levels reeled away behind him. A star flared and fell, staining the world with gold. Desmond had forgotten his gold. He had forgotten food and shelter, life and death. He could think of nothing but Lajeune's brown throat with the scar across it. That throat, his own hands on each side of it, and an end for ever to the singing and the laughter.

He thought Lajeune was near at hand, laughing at him. He felt the trail, and searched. The dark face was everywhere, and the quick laughter; but silence was waiting.

Again he knelt and groped in the snow; but he could feel nothing firm and living. He tore off his mitts, and groped again, but there was only the snow, drifting in his fingers like dust. Lajeune was near at hand, yet he could not find him. He got up and began to run in circles. His feet and hands were heavy and as cold as ice, and his breath hurt; but Lajeune was alive and warm and lucky and laughing.

He fell, got up, and fell again. The third time he did not get up, for he had caught young Lejeune at last. The brown throat was under his hands, and the stricken face. He, Desmond, was doing all the laughing, for Lajeune was dead.

"My luck, Jooney, my luck," chuckled Desmond.

His head fell forward, and the dry snow was like dust in his mouth. Darkness covered the stars.

IV

In the darkness and the shadow something moved. Desmond was in his own bunk at the shack. There seemed to be an echo of words in the air, yet he knew that he had slept for some time. He was not asleep now. Yet, sleep lay on him like a weight, and he could not move.

Forbes was silent, too. He was quite clear that he was alone with Forbes, and that the other two had gone prospecting beyond Fachette. Forbes had asked him, "Will ye stay here with me and rest, —I'm all but blind the day,—or will ye go in to Fort Recompense with Jooney here and the dogs, and put the dust in safety? Or will ye try the short cut across the pass with Ohlsen?" And he knew he had chosen to stay in the shack with Forbes.

It was night. The shack was dark, save for the red glow of the stove, and something moved very softly in the dusk and the shadow.

Desmond weighted with sleep, could not move; but he listened. Someone was shuffling very softly and slowly round the wall of the shack, pausing at the bunks. It was Forbes. He was snuffling to himself, as some little soft-nosed animal might snuffle, and feeling in his blind way with one yellowed hand.

Desmond was amused. "If I was to yell out, old Scotty'd have a fit," he thought. He decided to wait until Forbes was quite near, and then yell, and hear the old man curse. Old Forbes' cursing was the admiration of the camps. Desmond lay very still and listened.

Forbes was coming nearer, feeling his way as if over unseen ground, and whimpering to himself very softly. Desmond could hear the scratch, scratch, of his long-clawed fingers as he slipped his hand over the empty bunk near the door. He was silent and still for a minute, then the shuffling came again.

"I'll wait till he's at the foot o' my bunk," thought Desmond, grinning foolishly, "and then I'll bark like a dog. Used to do it in school when I was a kid and scare the teacher. Lord! how a bit of luck does raise a man's spirits!" He lay very quiet, grinning to himself in the dark.

Forbes' blind, bent head showed, swaying slightly against the dull, red glow of the farther wall. A tremulous touch, as light as a falling leaf, fell on Desmond's foot, and suddenly he was stricken with the black, dumb terror of dreams; for he knew there was death in the touch of that hand.

The walls reeled about him, shot with streaks of red. He could feel the hand hovering lightly at his knee. The blind man's soft, whimpering breathing sounded close above him. But he could not move. His whole life was centred in the quivering nerves which recorded the touch of the blind man's hand.

It travelled very slowly and lightly up his body, and lingered above his heart. His life gathered there also like a cold flame. And he could not move.

Visions rose before him. The gold was under his head; and he heard again the sound of wind in a garden among tall flowers, and thud of ripe apples falling, soft croons, and cluckings of hens, a whirring of the wings of doves. He saw a straight girl in a stiff print dress, with very blue eyes under brows and lashes the colour of sea-sand. He saw two children with hair the colour of gold.

The blind man moaned and bent waveringly near, his right hand gathered to his breast.

The flowers of the hollyhocks were gold, and the little ducks were gold, and gold sunlight lay on the gold hair of the children. "Gold," said Desmond, faintly—"gold; my luck." The blind hand crept upward. Like a blown flame, the golden visions flickered and went out.

Desmond awoke, fighting upward out of darkness and the dreams of the night. He felt reality coming back to him as a tide comes back to a beach, and opened his eyes on a glad world. His terrors fell away from him. He came near to thanking God. Dark words he had dreamed, dark deeds, but they were not true. Thank God! they were only dreams. He stirred in the bunk, sat up, and brushed a white feather of wood-ash from his sleeve. Only dreams!

Lajeune was cooking pork and making coffee; Ohlsen was mending snow shoes; Forbes bent over his bunk, black against the frozen window, feeling blindly with his hands and snuffling a little as he spoke:

"We'd ha let you sleep on, but we wanted to know what you'd be doing. Will ye stay with me and rest—I'm all but blind the day—or will ye go into Fort Recompense with Jooney here and the dogs, and put the dust in safety? Or will ye try the short cut across the pass with Ohlsen?"

He stopped suddenly. Desmond shrank back slowly against the wall of the bunk, his eyes staring on them as a man stares on death, a fleck of froth on his lips. There was no sound in the shack but the quick breathing of four men.

Routine Patrol

BY JAMES B. HENDRYX

CORPORAL DOWNEY, ACE of the North–West Mounted Police non-coms in the Yukon, glanced uneasily at the glittering, distorted sun, low-hung in the sky to the southward. There was an unfamiliar, unreal look to it; and an unnatural feel to the dead, still air. Before him stretched the unending windings of the river, flanked to the northward by high sparsely timbered hills, and to the southward by flat tundra and low rolling prairie, even more sparsely timbered.

At late sunrise the wind had died and it had grown steadily colder. For two days past his Government map had been useless, vague dottings showing the supposed course of the river. His working map, hand-drawn in Dawson by a breed who had helped Stan Braddock pack his stock of trade goods and liquor to the new camp of Good Luck, had been doubted at Selkirk. Two men who professed to have been to Good Luck insisted that the breed had located the camp on the wrong branch of the Pelly. They drew Downey a new map. Another argued that the breed's map might be right, but doubted that any one could cover the ground in eight days even on the hard, wind-packed snow. An old Indian, who had trapped the country to the eastward a dozen years before, drew a crude map that coincided with neither of the others. In disgust Downey had pulled out of Selkirk, leaving those knowing ones wrangling among themselves.

The dogs slowed. Even Topek, the lead dog, was traveling listlessly, his muzzle low to the unbroken snow. Tight-curled tails had lost their gimp, and breath plumes frosted shaggy coats. Downey, himself, was conscious of a growing lassitude. He swore unconvincingly at the dogs, but the long-lashed whip remained coiled in his mittened hand, and the dogs paid no heed.

Somewhere on the heights to the left a tree exploded with the frost. Again Downey glanced across the rolling prairie toward the sun. White specks danced before his eyes—specks that resolved themselves into false suns that danced their silent mockery in the ice-green sky above the cold dead waste of snow.

In a dull, detached way, he estimated that it was one o'clock. The conclusion seemed of no importance, and of no importance seemed the slow pace of the dogs as he walked on and on behind the sled. Vaguely his mind reverted to his maps—the breed's map, and the others. He shivered with a chill not born of the cold—for he realized that, to his dulled senses, the maps, too, seemed of no importance. Pulling himself together with an effort, he cracked his whip and swore loudly at the dogs. His voice sounded curiously flat and unfamiliar, and the animals plodded on without increasing their pace, proud tails at half-cock. Downey, too, plodded on without bothering to coil his whip, the long walrus lash dragging behind him, his eyes on the unbroken snow that covered the river ice. Since leaving Selkirk he had seen no tracks. No moose, nor caribou—not even a wolf nor a fox had crossed the river. And this fact, too, seemed of no importance even though he was low on meat—for himself; and for his dogs. Tonight they would get the last of the frozen fish—then no more till Good Luck. Perhaps they would never reach Good Luck. The matter seemed of no importance beyond being a good joke on the dogs. Downey realized that he was chuckling inanely.

The lopsided, brassy sun touched the horizon and as the officer looked, the false suns leaped and danced—a dance of hideous mockery on the rim of the frozen world. "I've heard of it," he mumbled, striving to control his brain—"the white death—it comes in the strong cold—but it ain't the cold—the air goes dead, or somethin'—some of the old timers claim it's a lie—but others claim a man dies or goes crazy. . . . Well, if a man goes crazy, or dies, what the hell?" A delicious lassitude permeated his brain—a pleasant, warming numbness—and he slogged on.

The leader swung abruptly from the river and headed up a small feeder that emerged from a notch in the hills; "Hey, you, Topek! Gee, Topek, gee!" But the leader paid no slightest heed to the command, and Downey grasped the tail-rope as the superb brute threw his weight into the collar, tightening the traces. By his very strength and power he dragged his lagging team mates into a faster pace. "Whoa, Topek! Down! Damn you—down!"

Ignoring the command, the big dog plunged on, head up, ears cocked expectantly ahead. Tightening his grip on the tail-rope, the officer followed. He glanced over his shoulder toward the southward. The brief March sun had set. No false suns danced crazily before his eyes—only long plumes of blue-green light were visible, radiating from a bright spot on the horizon to the zenith above his head. His glance shifted to Topek. Topek, the best lead dog in the police service, deserting the trail! Ignoring commands! What did it mean? Downey heard his own voice babbling foolishly: "Gone crazy-crazy with the white death—dogs and men both—they go crazy or die, if they don't camp. Or, maybe Topek knows a new trail—no one else knows this damn country—maybe Topek knows. Might as well die up one crick as another. Hi, Topek—mush!"

The high hills closed in abruptly, shutting out the weird light of the blue-green plumes. Naked rock walls rose sheer to jagged rims outlined high above against the sky. The canyon, a mere cleft in the living rock, was scarce fifty feet from wall to wall. The new snow was softer here—protected from the sweep of the wind by the high walls. Dully Downey realized that, despite the shifty footing, and the increased drag of the sled in the softer snow, the pace was fast. Drooping tails once more curled over shaggy backs as each dog threw his weight into the collar. Gone was the languor that had marked the brief daylight hours of travel. It was as though Topek had inspired his team —was inspiring Corporal Downey, too. Slowly, but consciously, as one awakening from a horrible dream, the officer realized that the dangerous brain lethargy that had gripped him on the river was losing its hold. He shook his head to clear it of the last remnant of fogginess, and his voice rang sharp and hard through the narrow corridor as he shouted words of encouragement to the dogs.

One mile—two—and the canyon suddenly widened to a hundred yards and terminated abruptly in a dead end—a sheer rock wall at the base of which stood a grove of stunted spruce.

"Fire-wood, anyway," the officer muttered, as he glanced about him in the semi-darkness. Topek headed straight for the copse and disappeared, his team mates following, pulling the sled which came to a halt partially within the timber a few yards from where Downey stood. Rumbling, throaty growls issued from the copse, and the officer hurried forward to see the huge lead dog, his muzzle low against the door of a small pole-and-mud cabin, lips curled back to expose gleaming white fangs as growl after growl issued from the depths of the mighty chest.

Making his way around the sled, Downey was about to speak to the dog when the great brute settled back on his haunches, pointed his sharp muzzle to the sky, and howled. Loud and eerie the ululation rose until as if at a signal, each of the other six dogs of the team followed the example of their leader until the horrid cacophony rolled and reverberated in an all-engulfing hullabaloo of strident noise. Then, as suddenly as it had begun, the deafening hubbub ceased, and at a word of command, the dogs sank onto their bellies, reaching out here and there to snap up mouthfuls of snow.

For some moments the officer stood peering into the gathering darkness. A neatly piled rank of firewood, an ax standing against the wall beside the door, a pair of snowshoes hanging from a peg driven into the wall all spoke of occupancy. Yet—not a track was to be seen. No one had passed in or out of the cabin since the latest fall of snow.

Pulling the thong that raised the crude wooden latch bar, Downey pushed the door open and stepped into the absolute blackness of the room. Shaking off a mitten, he shuddered slightly as he groped in his pocket for a match—the interior seemed colder even than the outside air, seemed fraught with a deadly chill that struck to the very marrow of his bones. Closing the door, he scratched the match upon its inner surface, and as the light flared up he started back in horror at sight of the dead man who lay upon his back in the middle of the floor, his glassy, frozen eyes staring straight up into his own. The match burned Downey's fingers and he dropped it, plunging the room into darkness. Reaching for another, he scratched it and, stepping over the still form on the floor, held the flame to the wick of a candle-stub that protruded from the neck of a bottle on the rude pole table.

When the flame burned steadily, flooding the room with mellow light, Downey thrust his hand, already stiff from cold, back into his mitten, picked up the bottle and, stepping to the dead man's side, stood gazing down into the marble-white face—the face of an old man. An unkempt white mustache and a scraggly white beard somewhat stained by tobacco juice masked the lower half of his face. Thin white hair edged the brow, and as Downey stood staring in fascination into the frozen eyes, a peculiar sensation stole over him. He felt that the man wanted to speak—that behind those frozen eyeballs a spark of brain still lived—that the man had something to tell him—something of vast importance.

"Poor devil," muttered the officer, his glance shifting to the blue-black revolver that lay close beside the outflung right hand, and back to the ugly hole in the man's right temple. "He couldn't take it no longer. The North got him. The strong cold—or maybe the white death that some claim is a lie." He turned abruptly away and returned the bottle to the table. "An' it'll be gettin' me, too, if I don't get a fire goin'. It's sixty below in here right now—or I miss my guess."

Stepping to the stove, he started in surprise. "Why the hell," he wondered aloud as he applied a match to the bark beneath the kindlings that showed through the open door, "would he lay his fire an' then blow his brains out without lightin' it?"

With the fire roaring in the stove Downey stepped outside, unharnessed his dogs, tossed them a frozen salmon apiece, and carried his own grub and the remainder of his meager supply of dog food into the cabin.

The room was beginning to warm. The candle flared and flickered, having burned to the bottle neck and, rummaging on a shelf, Downey found another and lighted it. Filling his tea pail with snow, he placed it on the stove and turned his attention to an exploration of the tiny room. He found sufficient flour, tea, sugar, and salt to last a man two months. There was also an ample supply of desiccated vegetables, and a bag of beans. A plate on the table held several good cuts of caribou steak frozen to the hardness of iron.

Beside the cheap alarm clock on the shelf from which he had taken the candle, Downey found a small box containing a number of dynamite caps part of a box of rifle ammunition, for which there seemed to be no rifle. He found no revolver ammunition, nor any box in which such ammunition had been packed.

Beneath the pole bunk he found half a case of dynamite and a coil of fuse. Also, dozens of samples of hard rock—quartz for the most part, many of them showing flecks of free gold.

On the table, pushed back against the wall, was an Indian-tanned caribou skin from which had been cut several pieces of a uniform pattern, evidently for the purpose of fashioning the small pouches commonly used in the country as receptacles for gold dust.

In a corner, where they had been carelessly tossed, lay a pair of worn mokluks of the same size and pattern as those on the feet of the dead man. Downey noted with interest that on one of these boots dust had collected on the inside and out, while the other was nearly free from dust.

He replenished the fire, dropped a pinch of tea into the snow water, and set the plate of caribou steaks on the stove to thaw. Again he turned his attention to the dead man, and again as he stared down into the frozen eyes, the strange feeling stole over him that the man wanted to speak to him—to impart a matter of importance.

Dismissing the fancy with a frown of annoyance, the officer stooped closer. "Too bad, old timer, that you can't talk," he muttered. Prob'ly want to tell me how you missed out on the mother lode. But —whatever it is'll have to keep a long, long time, I guess."

Examination of the wound disclosed powder marks on the surrounding skin, and its position indicated that it could easily have been inflicted by a pistol held in the man's right hand. Blood had flowed from it, trickling down just in front of the ear, and had dripped from the stained white beard, freezing as it fell, to form a tiny red pyramid, or inverted cone upon the floor. "Done it when the strong cold was on," Downey muttered, "or that blood wouldn't have froze as it dripped. But not this spell of the strong cold. He hasn't left the shack since the last snow—an' that must be a week, or more."

Picking up the revolver, he noted that it was of .41 caliber, and that it held five loaded cartridges and an empty shell. "Funny he'd shoot himself with plenty of grub on hand, an' enough giant, an' caps, an' fuse to last him quite a while," he mused aloud, as is the wont of lone men. "Might be he got just one disappointment too many. But them old timers is used to disappointments. They've got a sort of hopelessly hopeful faith that they'll hit it next week, er next month, er next year. It's what keeps em' goin'—that faith in the mother lode."

Clearing a space along the wall near the stove, Downey stooped to lift the corpse. As he raised the outflung right arm from the floor a low exclamation escaped his lips. He lowered the body, and for long moments knelt there—staring. For, gripped between the thumb and finger of that iron-hard right hand was an unlighted-match! "A man can't shoot himself in the right temple with a gun held in his left hand," he murmured slowly. "An' he can't hold a gun in his right hand—when that hand is grippin' a match." His glance strayed to the face of the corpse, and he started nervously. For, as a drop of grease guttered down the length of the candle, the flame flared, and in the flickering light the frozen left eye seemed to wink knowingly. The officer grinned into the glassily staring eyes. "I get you, old timer," he said. "You sure put it acrost—what you wanted to tell me. This ain't suicide—it's murder."

Arranging the body close against the wall, Downey turned his attention to a more minute examination of the room. An hour later he fried the caribou steaks, seated himself at the table, and devoured a hearty meal. "Things had a wrong look, in the first place," he mused. "What with a revolver, an' no extry shells for it. An' some rifle shells on the shelf, an' no rifle. An' that pair of mukluks—one all covered with dust, an' the other without no dust on it to speak of. But I guess, now, I've got the picture—someone comes along, an' the old timer invites him in. He lays his fire, an' just as he's about to light it, the other shoves the revolver almost against his head an' pulls the trigger. Then he makes a quick search an' finds the old man's cache of gold in one of them mukluks—the one without the dust. There'd be seven pokes of it, accordin' to that caribou hide—maybe eight, ten thousand dollars. Then he beat it without lightin' the fire. He wasn't takin' no chances in bein' caught in this box canyon if someone should come along. A man can't never tell what he's goin' to run up against on one of these routine patrols."

In the morning Downey inventoried the old man's effects, lifted his body to the bunk and covered it with a blanket, requisitioned a quarter of caribou meat to augment his meager supply of dog food, and struck off down the canyon. The strong cold persisted, but the curious dead feel was gone from the air, and the dogs bent to their work with a will. Later in the day a light breeze sprang up and the temperature moderated considerably.

On the third day thereafter the outfit pulled into the camp of Good Luck, situated at the precise location the breed had indicated on his map, Stepping into Stan Braddock's saloon, Downey was greeted by Old Bettles and Camillo Bill, two sourdoughs who had thrown in with the Good Luck stampede.

"Hello, Downey!" cried Bettles, "yer jest in time to have one on me! What in hell fetches you up to Good Luck? So fer, we've got along fine without no police."

Corporal Downey winked at Camillo Bill as he filled the glass Stan Braddock spun toward him with professional accuracy. "The inspector sent me up here to see why two able-bodied men would be hangin' around a saloon in the daytime, instead of workin' their claim," he replied.

"Well, ain't a man got a right to celebrate his birthday?" grinned the oldster.

Camillo Bill laughed: "Bettles, he celebrates his birthday every month."

"Shore I do! Every month except Feb'ry. Why wouldn't I? It was a damn important day fer me. I was born on the thirtieth—so every time the thirtieth comes around, I celebrate. What I claim—a man overlooks lot of bets if he don't celebrate his birthday only onct year."

"Guess that's right," Downey agreed. "How's things goin'?"

"Oh, not so bad. Good Luck ain't no Bonanza nor Hunker. But she's a damn sight better'n a lot of other cricks men are stickin' to. Most of the boys is takin' out a lot better'n wages."

"Heard any complaints? Any cache robbin', or claim jumpin' goin' on?"

Stan Braddock shook his head: "Nope. Here it is damn near April, an' we've gone through the winter without no crime that anyone knows of—an I'd have heard it in here, if anythin' out of the way had be'n goin' on. Some of the boys is in here every night."

"They's be'n three deaths" supplemented Bettles, "but they was all of 'em common ones. A rock squushed one fella where it fell on him, an' the other two died of some sickness they got. There ain't no doctor in camp, but we figger it was their guts went back on 'em, er mebbe their heart. We buried 'em decent, an' saved their names an' their stuff fer the public administrator. Two of 'em didn't have much, but one done pretty well fer hisself. It's all in Stan's safe, there—he'll turn it over to you."

"How many men do you figure wintered in Good Luck?"

"Couple hundred wouldn't miss it far," Braddock replied.

"Mostly chechakos, I s'pose."

"Yeah," said Camillo Bill. "Good Luck's jest like all the other camps. What with the damn chechakos crowdin' into the country, it's gittin' so us old timers can't hardly git enough of us together no more fer a decent stud game."

"Speakin' of old timers," said Downey, casually, "who's the old fella that located in a box canyon about three days back down the river?"

"He must mean old Tom Whipple," Bettles opined. "This here canyon runs in from the north, an' dead ends a couple of mile up, don't it?"

"That's the one."

"Yeah, that's old Tom. He's kinda batty—like all them hard-rock men—allus huntin' the mother lode. I know'd Tom first, must be fifteen, sixteen year ago—on Birch Crick, over on the American side. He wouldn't pay no 'tention to the placer stuff in the crick beds. Stuck to the hard rock—shootin' an' peckin'—peckin' an' shootin'— pryin' a little flake gold out of his samples with the p'int of his belt knife. He passed up all the good cricks—Forty Mile—Bonanza— Hunker—Dominion. We tried to git him to quit foolin' around amongst the rocks an' git in on some of the cricks—but it wasn't no use. He was old, then—too old, I guess, to learn him new tricks. He'd look at us like we didn't have all our buttons—like he was kinda takin' pity on us, er somethin'. 'That damn stuff in the crick beds ain't nothing but float,' he'd say. 'I wouldn't fool away my time on it. It's all got to come from the mother lode. Find the mother lode— that's where the gold is,' he'd tell us. 'An' the mother lode's in the hills —not in the crick beds.'

"There can't no one claim old Tom ain't got faith. He stuck to his idee when we was pannin' out two, three dollars to the pan on Birch Crick, an' up to seven, eight dollars on Forty Mile, an' then twenty an' a hundred on Bonanza. He watched us gittin' rich right in under his nose—but he wouldn't fool with it. An' he's stickin' to the same idee yet, up on the head of that canyon."

"A damn sight more faith than sense—that's what he's got, if you ask me," opined Camillo Bill. "Gold's where you find it, whether it's in the cricks, er on the hills."

"Didn't he ever make a strike," Downey asked.

Bettles shook his head: "Nope. Jest keeps on shootin' down rock, an' peckin' with his pick, an' pryin' with his knife. Don't cost him nothin' much to live. Never has nothin' to do with wimmin er licker—never blow'd an ounce in his life. Beans, an' tea, an' flour, an' sugar—a little chawin' terbacker, an' ca'tridges fer that old rifle of his —that's all he needs."

"But, keepin' at it long as he has, an' not spendin' no more'n what he spends he'd be bound to have some dust cached away some-wheres, wouldn't he?"

"Oh, chances is, he's got some—prob'ly enough to keep him the rest of his life, when he gits too old to fight the rocks. I doubt an' he kin show ten thousan' in dust fer God knows how many years he's worked."

"You spoke of an old rifle," said Downey. "Would you know that gun if you saw it?"

"Shore, I'd know it. So would Camillo, here, an' Moosehide Charlie, an' Swiftwater Bill. It's a Marlin. He bust the stock, one time on Birch Crick, an' we wired it up fer him with some wire we ontwisted out of a chunk of cable. But—what you so int'rested in old Tom Whipple fer?"

"Didn't own a revolver that you know of?" persisted Downey, ignoring the question. "A forty-one calibre six-gun?"

"Hell, no! What would old Tom be doing with a revolver? He allus travelled light. I seen him 'long about Christmas. Come up here draggin' a hand-sled after a load of grub an' giant. I kidded him about not havin' no dogs, an' he claimed it cost too much to feed 'em, an' he didn't need none. Claimed he sold off all his dogs two years back, when he located where he's at. There wasn't no Good Luck then—Tom had the country all to hisself. Claimed he's right up agin the mother lode, this time, an' would never have to make another move. Told me he'd be into it, come spring, fer shore—an' then he'd show us what damn fools we was fer muckin' around in th' gravel. Pore old cuss—he'll keep on huntin' the mother lode till the last day he kin stand on his legs— an' allus it'll be jest ahead of him. If he'd throw'd in on the stampedes, like we done, he could of had as much dust as the best of us—more, 'cause he's a hard worker, an' he don't never spend nothin'. It's too damn bad. A fella with faith like that ort to win."

Stan Braddock smiled, and set out a fresh bottle. "I don't look at it that way, Bettles," he said, as the glasses were filled. "A man like that wouldn't never be satisfied with placer gold—no matter how much he took out. He'd always figure he was a fool fer passin' up the mother lode. An' what good would a lot of dust do him, anyhow— livin' like he does? I'm telling you, he's a damn sight happier'n the most of us. He's got enough to keep him, an' he's got his faith—an' he'll have it till he dies. If a man knows he's goin' to be the richest man in the world next week, er next month, er next year, he's bound to be happy. What happens to him in the meantime don't matter. Ain't that so, Corporal?"

Corporal Downey nodded slowly, as he toyed with his glass on the bar: "Yes," he said, "I guess maybe yer right."

Men began to drift into the saloon, and Braddock became busy with bottles and glasses. The officer turned to Bettles: "This last snow—when did it come?"

"'Bout a week ago. It snowed fer two days."

"An' before that you'd had a spell of the strong cold?"

"I'll tell the world we did! Worst I ever seen. She hit fifty below fer twelve days, hand runnin'." He paused and indicated a man who had just entered and was limping painfully to the bar. "There's a bird kin tell you more about it than me. It ketched him comin' in—froze all his toes an' one of his heels. He's in a hell of a shape, without no doctor in camp. Them toes had ort to come off."

"Chechako?"

"Yeah—rawer'n hell. Claims he come in over the White Pass an' split off from his pals at Selkirk, when he heard about this strike."

Corporal Downey regarded the man intently as he hobbled to the bar and elevated a clumsily swathed foot to the rail. He was a large man, unprepossessing and ill-kempt, with a month's growth of beard. He called for whiskey without inviting others to join him, and when Braddock set out the bottle, he filled his glass to the brim and emptied it at a gulp. He repeated the performance and tossed a pouch to the bar.

"He ain't be'n able to do much work since he got here, has he?" Downey asked. "Ain't taken out much dust?"

"Hell, no!" Camillo Bill replied. "He moved into Bill Davis's shack—it was Bill got squished by the rock. Me an' Bettles went down there yesterday to see if we could do somethin' fer him, an' the stink in there was somethin' fierce. Them toes of his has started to rot. We offered to cut 'em off fer him—but the damn fool wouldn't let us. By God, if they was my toes they'd come off—if I had to do it myself with an ax! But, that's the way with a damn chechako. They don't know nothin'—an' never will. He cussed the hell out of us when we told him he'd be dead in a month with the blood pizen."

Corporal Downey watched Stan Braddock pick up the sack the man had tossed onto the bar and shake a few yellow flakes of gold into the scales. "Kind of queer, ain't it?" he observed, "that a chechako jest in over the pass, an' not in shape to take out any dust after he got here, should be spendin' dust?"

Old Bettles looked up quickly. "Why—why—shore it is!" he agreed.

"Damn if it ain't," said Camillo Bill. "Where would he git it?"

"I believe," replied Downey, "that I know."

The man had turned from the bar and hobbled to a chair on the opposite side of the room as Downey slipped to the scales just as

Braddock lifted the little pan to transfer the gold to the till. He thrust out his hand, palm up. "Pour it in there, Braddock. I want to have a look at it," he ordered, and when the man complied, he returned to where Bettles and Camillo Bill waited under one of the big swinging lamps. Eagerly, the three examined the yellow grains, as the officer prodded them about with a forefinger. "Ever see any stuff like it?" he asked, abruptly.

"Them flakes is sort of sharp edged," ventured Camillo Bill. "They don't show no water wear."

"That," replied Downey, "is because they didn't come out of a crick bed. They was pried out of rock samples—with the point of a belt knife, maybe."

"You mean!" exclaimed Bettles, his eyes suddenly widening, "that—"

The officer silenced him with a wink, and a glance toward the chechako who sat sprawled in his chair, his eyes on his bandaged foot. "Yeah," he replied, in an undertone. "Old Tom Whipple was murdered an' robbed in his cabin in that box canyon. It happened durin' the last spell of the strong cold—there was no tracks in the new snow. Whoever done it stole Whipple's dust, an' his rifle. The three of us'll jest sift down to this chechako's shack, now. Besides Whipple's old rifle I think we'll find his dust, in caribou-hide sacks—six of 'em, besides the one the chechako's packin' on him. An' when we rip 'em apart, I think we'll find that the pieces was cut out of a hide I fetched along out of Whipple's shack. We'd ort to find some forty-one-caliber revolver ammunition, too. Forty-ones ain't common. It's the gun the murderer left to make it look like Whipple killed himself. When we find them things, I'll arrest that bird—an' I'll have enough evidence to hang him higher than hell."

"It'll be all right with me," growled Camillo Bill, as the three stepped out onto the hard-packed snow, "if we can't find no evidence whatever in his shack. Hangin's too good fer a damn cuss that would murder old Tom Whipple—which Tom had prob'ly took him in to save him from the strong cold. I'd ruther see him left here to rot from his toes clean up to his chin!"

"How come you turned off up that canyon if there wasn't no tracks in the snow?" queried Bettles, as Downey spoke to his dogs who had lain down in the harness, wrapped snugly in their bushy tails.

"That was pure accident," the officer replied. "The air had gone dead. There was a peculiar feel to it an' there was false suns dancin' in the sky. I felt sort of weak an' light headed—like nothin' mattered—an' I guess the dogs felt it, too. Anyhow, my lead dog turned off up this canyon, an' I couldn't head him off. Like I said— nothin' seemed to matter—one crick seemed as good as any other— so I let 'em go."

Old Bettles nodded: "The white death reachin' fer you, eh? Some claim it's a lie—that there ain't no sech thing. But don't you believe 'em, Downey. I know."

"You tellin' me?"

"Where'd you git that lead dog?" the oldster asked, after a moment's pause, his eyes on the great brute who stood alert, awaiting the word of command.

"Down in Dawson, a year ago. Best lead dog in the country. It's funny he'd leave the trail fer a side crick."

"Not so damn funny as you think," Bettles replied. "I know that dog. He's Topek. Old Tom Whipple raised him from a pup."

Grist for the Newsmill

BY STROLLER WHITE

WHEN THE STROLLER reached Dawson, in the heart of the Klondike gold fields, late in the year 1898, he found many of the same class of people he had previously known in Skagway. In fact, many of them were the same individuals, and their activities were producing much the same line-up of news the Stroller had become familiar with in Skagway. But there was this major difference between the two towns: Skagway was open to shipping the year around, so there was a continuous flow of news from the outside world with which to fill the columns of the newspapers. Dawson, on the other hand, was virtually isolated for long periods during the winter.

Mail came over the winter trail from Skagway once a month—when it could make it. The longest period between mails after regular service was established, as the Stroller remembers it, was thirty-three days—late in the year 1899. There was also the Dominion telegraph line which carried press dispatches, at the rate of eight cents a word, when the line was working. But it was out of commission much of the time. Most of the line ran through wilderness country and a tree might fall across the wire or a moose would tangle his horns in it forty or fifty miles from anywhere. Then the linemen would have to hike out to locate the break and repair it, and this required from a day to a week and sometimes longer.

One result of this lack of mail and telegraph service was that much of the news in the Dawson papers was necessarily home grown and hand picked. There were three daily papers in Dawson for some time, with a great deal of rivalry among them for the attention of the newspaper-buying public, their circulation depending heavily on individual sales both on the streets of the town and out along the maze of creeks where the miners worked. Sales were promoted by the use of large and sensational headlines in all the papers, and the front page of the paper on which the Stroller was employed regularly carried three headlines, of three lines each and in the largest type in the shop. Composing these headlines was something of a problem on this paper because of the scarcity of the letter "K" in the 72-point font, only three being available. This was a serious handicap as in those days there was at least one King of the Klondike on every street corner in Dawson and they were frequently in the headlines. The Koyukuk country, over on the Alaska side of the line, was also much in the news just then, but fortunately and so far as the Stroller knows there was never a King of the Koyukuk. Even more fortunately, the Ku Klux Klan never became active in either the Klondike or the Koyukuk.

Fires and the Dawson Police Court furnished a good deal of local news, as the Stroller has previously mentioned, and another prolific source of copy was the Dawson theaters, of which there were several. There was lively competition among both the owners of the theaters and the actors and performers who appeared on their stages for newspaper space, and in that quarter at least the news reporters were esteemed and even respected. There were exceptions, however, and in such instances the reporters, although employed on rival papers and always eager to "scoop" the other fellows, stood together in upholding the dignity of their profession. Any ham-and-egg actor or actress who slighted a member of the Fourth Estate was at once taboo with the whole lot and usually was very soon minus an engagement as well.

But entertainers who were known as good scouts and who were inclined to "tote fair" with the reporters not only graced the front page frequently but received favorable stories under unfavorable circumstances. For example, if Cad Wilson or Nellie Holgate (who became the model for Rex Beach's Cherry Mellott) or any of the numerous footlight favorites became all bruised up as a result of falling down stairs or something—usually something—the reporters would explain that the bruises were caused by the gold nuggets which showered the bruisee when she responded to a third encore with "Just Tell Me That You Love Me and I Will Know the Rest." Or when Freddie Breen, a standby at the Standard Theatre, appeared on the stage thoroughly spiflicated and incapacitated in half a dozen other ways and was greeted with groans, the news stories told how the inimitable comedian had so perfectly impersonated a Rube actor that many in the audience were taken in and believed it was natural instead of put on.

But "Cecil Marian essayed to sing" was as good as Cecil was accorded in any of the papers; not that she was a poor singer but because she had cultivated an uppish attitude towards news reporters. Bessie Chandon carried a violin under her arm all the way from San Francisco to Dawson and her coming was widely and loudly heralded. But she snubbed the newsmen and after her first appearance the papers agreed that "Miss Chandon is not a violinist, or even a promising violin pupil."

It was reported in the papers as a happy social event when Fred Maurettis, a low comedian, fat and good-natured, assumed the garb of a priest and united Jim Hall and one of the Drummond sisters in fake bonds of matrimony. Jim, believing the rite to be the genuine article, presented his supposed bride with two thousand dollars in cash and everybody drank to their happiness in Mumm's Extra Dry at $25 a quart—at Jim's expense. What Jim said two days later when he came to was never printed. But the papers came to Jim's aid some months later when a number of his friends made an affidavit that he was of unsound mind in order to prevent him securing a license to wed Grace Anderson whose specialty was a barefoot dance. Perhaps the papers should have stayed out of it, but in consequence of their action the license was issued and they were married. Jim, who had cleaned up something like a million dollars on Eldorado Creek, purchased the Auditorium Theatre and gave it to Grace as a wedding present and they lived happily for a month, maybe six weeks. But right or wrong, the marriage and the bride's subsequent venture into the theatrical field as a manager were grist for the newsmill and made interesting copy, and that was what was essential to the papers if they were not to appear with blank pages.

Ranking as an equal of the theater as a news source was politics, especially municipal and territorial politics, since Dawson was too far from Ottawa to take much interest in Dominion affairs except on such occasions as Ottawa meddled with Dawson affairs. It was in 1901 that the Yukon Territorial Council delegated to Dawson the authority to form a municipal government and this she proceeded to do by electing a mayor and seven city councilmen. The initial meeting of the new council was something of an eye-opener to the electorate, for its first act was to vote an annual salary of $5,000 for the mayor and $3,600 for each of the councilmen, while a young lawyer who had boosted for the winning ticket was named city attorney, also at $3,600 a year.

One result of this action was to make seats on the aldermanic board much sought after, and each spring thereafter brought forth from twenty-five to forty candidates, all of them willing to sacrifice themselves pro bono publico. It happened that five of the seven members of the first Dawson City Council lived on Third Street, and by a majority vote of the council they decided to macadamize that street. This not only made it the most valuable business location in town but enhanced the value of abutting property, and the Stroller came close to being lynched for referring to it in a news story as "Aldermanic Avenue." But the Stroller desisted when the post of Official Reporter was created for him with emoluments, hereditaments and appurtenances nearly equal to the salary of the mayor.

Territorial political conventions in the Yukon were always lively affairs and the Stroller vividly recalls one held at the town of Caribou, which was on Dominion Creek. Just why it was held there, the Stroller does not know, as Caribou was forty-five miles from Dawson and about the same distance from any given point, and the only way to reach it was by a stage which scaled the dizzy dome separating Hunker and Dominion Creeks, at $20 per scale. The convention met in the Gold Belt Hotel, a place which fitted the description Sam Dunham gave the late Ed Levante's roadhouse at Eagle:

> The latchstring always hung outside
> And you didn't have to knock;
> He had no knocker on the door
> And he hadn't any lock.
> But when you ordered porterhouse
> He dished up caribou,
> And when you craved a whiskey straight
> He served you hoochinoo.

The landlord at the Gold Belt Hotel was handicapped by having lost his bartender the day before the convention opened, but he was fortunately able to enlist the services of a neighbor and the convention was able to proceed. This neighbor had a place of business across the street from the hotel, advertised by a sign which read UNDERTAKING,

EMBALMING & ICE CREAM PARLOR but he did well enough as a bartender, or at least a bartender for a political convention.

The convention, which lasted for three days and would have lasted longer but that the delegates needed sleep, was what was termed a howling success; at any rate, there was a great deal of howling. The caliber of the delegates may be indicated by a brief but impassioned speech made by one of them who opposed a resolution favoring a miners' lien law.

"Lean law," he shouted. "Wat'sa matter you fellows? What's this here country coming to, anyway? We don't need no lean law for miners. Make 'em stand up straight!"

The convention broke up in a row with an assortment of black eyes and general contusions and every candidate nominated by it was defeated in the election six weeks later. It may have been the convention, too, that put the kibosh on the town of Caribou, which went into a decline shortly afterward and never recovered, although it was in the center of a busy mining district. The next time the Stroller saw the place, while nestled in a fur robe as he passed through on the stage the following winter, owls were hooting in the garret of the Gold Belt Hotel and the services of the embalmer-ice cream vendor were no longer in demand.

But although Caribou wasted away and finally disappeared, Dawson remained lively and continued to grow and that was where most of the news-gathering centered. Even in Dawson, however, there were times when fires were few, court cases became dull and routine, the theater went stale and politics was dormant. At such times the reporters fell back on that old stand-by, the personal interview. And a favorite subject, when a reporter had a couple of columns to fill and not much of anything to put in them, was a man known as Captain Jinks. He was always available; at times, in fact, he was over-available. But what really endeared him to the reporters was the fact that he did not give two whoops whether he was quoted correctly or incorrectly so long as he was quoted and his name was displayed prominently.

Captain Jinks did not mine gold, sell goods, tend bar, deal cards, spin a roulette wheel or follow any of the other occupations common to Dawson in that day, and how he managed to live was something of a mystery although there were rumors of a regular remittance from somewhere Back East. But he did live, and fairly well, too, and he occupied himself by being a chairman. He was a natural-born chairman and he followed that calling faithfully, with time out only for newspaper interviews. Whenever the occasion required a chairman, Captain Jinks was on hand for the job, and if the occasion did not arise frequently enough to suit him, he assisted in churning them up.

It was a rare day when the governor of Yukon Territory was not visited by a delegation seeking something or other. Many wrongs, most of them imaginary, existed and required righting: the price of miners' licenses was too high; fees for recording claims were exorbitant; it was a shame the way the gamblers were lined up every thirty days and fined $50 and costs; Uncle Hoffman was charging forty percent a month on loans to members of the perfesh, and so forth. All of these things and many others were called to the attention of the governor by delegations which were invariably headed by Captain Jinks. And before, after and between such calls, Captain Jinks was available, and eager, for interviews by the reporters.

He was a boon to the news reporters in another way, too, as he was always the chairman of meetings pertaining to schools, hospitals and other civic affairs. From the point of view of the reporters he was a good chairman because he never called anybody to order and never did anything to quiet the disturbances which usually arose at such meetings. A meeting that did not develop at least one good fist fight was considered a total loss by the reporters, but there were few such losses when Captain Jinks presided. And to top off his sterling qualities, he was religiously inclined; so much so that he never took a drink, except for his stomach's sake. But his stomach required much attention and he was never known to refuse something for its sake; it made a demand every time there was anything in sight, which in those days in Dawson was very frequently.

At times when Captain Jinks' stomach treatments incapacitated him temporarily and other news was scarce, the reporters were thrown upon their own resources of imagination and ingenuity, and the results were sometimes astounding. There was, for example, the time the cold weather turned a large quantity of liquor to water. The facts were simple: In the fall of 1899 a shipment of liquor valued at about $30,000 was caught by the ice and frozen in about a hundred miles up the river from Dawson. A watchman was placed in charge and it remained there all winter. When navigation opened in the spring the shipment was delivered to the consignees at Dawson, but when the casks were opened they contained water and nothing but water.

Ordinarily this would not have been worth more than a paragraph in the papers, but times were dull and the reporters blew it up into a marvel unrivaled since the Biblical water into wine stunt. The facts were examined from every possible angle and there were long and involved explanations, all of them allegedly scientific. Opinion was solicited from many sources as to whether the change had been gradual or whether it had occurred all at once when the temperature dropped to a certain point, and whether the whiskey, rum and brandy had all turned at the same temperature. All in all, it made a fine, paper-selling series of stories and only one pertinent fact was omitted. The reporters neglected to mention that there was a well-traveled dog sled trail between the liquor cache and Dawson, and that this trail, far from straight to begin with, had grown more and more crooked as the winter progressed.

The Ice Worm Story

BY STROLLER WHITE

THE NORTHLAND IS thundering down the corridors of Time without a distinctive and personal class of literature. There have been meters, furlongs and miles of writing about Alaska and the Yukon, and much of it, especially the meters, has been wholly devoid of metre or much of anything else save words—a multiplicity of words. What is needed is something in the way of literature on which the brand of the North is so defined and distinctive that it may not be mistaken. That there is much in the North to inspire high class writing is beyond question, but with very few exceptions the writers who could produce such literature have never been accorded the encouragement their efforts deserved.

Back in the early and glorious years when the words "Alaska" and "Klondike" were heralded from the river unto the ends of the earth, hundreds of writers and would-be writers invaded the Northland. Some of them brought talent, while many brought nothing except the clothes in which they stood. But they came from all corners of the globe, bringing letters of introduction from Lord Strathcona or the editor of the Prune Growers' Journal. They came singly and in pairs and flocks, male and female, young, middling and superannuated. Many of them had never actually written a line for publication in their lives. Others were never sober if they could beg, borrow or purloin the price to be otherwise, and in those free and easy days they were generally otherwise.

The Stroller remembers as fairly typical of the lot a man who came from London and wrote a large part of the alphabet after his name. He had a two-storey forehead, carried seventeen lead pencils, and talked learnedly of telepathic communications which came to him direct from Mother Nature every time he took a sneak into the brush where there was naught to disturb the telepathic intake. It was his announced intention to write short stories and market them locally to meet his temporal needs, meanwhile corralling the information for a book that would revolutionize the literature of Christendom. His theory may have been sound, but it fell down when he attempted to put it into practice. The market for the kind of stories he turned out was very bearish around Dawson, and before long there came demand from the region below his belt for nourishment, demands that refused to lie low. The result was a triumph of matter over mind and he got a job as a dishwasher at the Silver Tip Cafe and his literary life washed down the drain with the soapsuds.

The hundreds of writers who came north at that time had two things in common. They were all intent upon giving to the Northland a kind of literature that would stand out through the ages as though carved on the azure dome of heaven and painted red. And they would all look offended if you did not invite them over to the Dutchman's to have something, at four-bits per something.

Their intentions were noble, but nothing much ever came of them. The male contingent was absorbed in one way or another, most of it finding employment in menial positions such as reporters on newspapers, cuspidor wrestlers in the saloons, or boosters at the black-jack tables. And the women, bless 'em, mostly married miners or prospectors and were led from the alter to the washtub, where their literary aspirations evaporated in the steam or faded out with the dye in the denim.

The Stroller, in his own meek and cow-eyed manner, once made an attempt to inflict some distinctly northern literature on the unsuspecting world, and for a time he congratulated himself that he had succeeded. It happened this way:

It was a cold winter morning in Dawson and the newspaper business was at a very low ebb. There had been no mail for nearly a month and the telegraph line had been out of commission for more than a week. In consequence, no news was forthcoming from the great world outside, while local news was scarce as to quantity and insipid as to quality. The editor was pacing the office and alternately moaning and tearing his hair. The paper, he announced, had reached bedrock; the only way it could sink lower would be to fold up and go out of business entirely.

"Go out and rustle up some news," he demanded. "Get me something that will make headlines and sell papers."

The Stroller and Casey Moran had been hovering around the office stove all morning and churning their brains for excuses to remain there, for the temperature outdoors had dropped to seventy degrees below zero, Fahrenheit.

"You call yourselves reporters," the editor stormed. "Why an old squaw with a rusty nail and piece of board could write a better story than the two of you today. Now get out!"

It was apparent that the temperature of the editor had reached 212 degrees above zero, Fahrenheit, and since he was known to have a flash point of 213 degrees, Casey and the Stroller scrambled into their parkas and got.

Casey wandered off into the ice fog and eventually returned with his justly famed contribution to archaeology, the discovery of Noah's Ark on a mountain top in Alaska. The Stroller headed for Tom Chisholm's Aurora Saloon. This was the one known as the big Aurora, for Tom had five other Auroras, six in all, the big Aurora being in Dawson and the five little Auroras out on the creeks where the miners worked. Tom believed in going after trade, and he got it. One reason for his success in getting trade was that he encouraged his customers to run accounts, and as the trade did not need much encouragement along that line, he soon built up a wonderful business. Of course, Tom eventually went broke, but that did not worry the trade. He still had the accounts, didn't he?

But all of that came later, and on this particular morning the trade at the Aurora, both cash and on account, was very slow. On more than one occasion the Stroller had received inspiration while rubbing the fine brass rail in the Aurora with the sole of his boot, but on this morning, although he rubbed and rubbed, nothing came of it. Nor did anything come of the inspiring beverage carefully poured for him by Tom's kindly bartender, who did not neglect the squirt of lemon. The Stroller next tried Bill McPhee's Northern and then Sam Bonnifield's Bank Saloon, but the brass rails there were no more productive and at last he could no longer postpone his return to the newspaper office.

As the Stroller trudged along the deserted Dawson street that morning, empty-handed and empty-headed, he heard somewhere behind him in the ice fog the squeak, squeak, squeak of a sled runner on the dry and powdery snow. And that sound gave him a faint glimmering of an idea. So, after Casey's Ark story had been polished up and a headline composed for it, the Stroller got busy on filling his own allotted space. He wrote a simple and straightforward story in which he reported that the extremely low temperatures had combined with the recent heavy fall of blue snow to bring thousands and thousands of ice worms out of their beds in the glaciers surrounding Dawson to bask in the frigidity. They had crawled forth in such numbers, in fact, that their chirping was keeping the people of Dawson awake nights, and if the temperature did not rise soon to send the ice worms back into cold storage, something drastic would have to be done.

Casey's Noah's Ark story was a sensation and the Stroller's story made something of a hit as he realized the following day when he entered the Northern Saloon and saw a large placard which read: "Ice Worm Cocktails, $1." The bartender spotted the Stroller at about the same moment and beckoned him closer.

"Better try one," said the bartender. "It's on the house."

While a crowd gathered to watch, the bartender carefully lifted the cover from a bowl of the finest cut glass, and there, embedded in a chunk of ice, were the ice worms, white and succulent. The bartender chipped off a piece of the ice and with a pair of silver tongs delicately drew forth one of the luscious creatures. He dropped it into a tall glass along with the ice and added other suitable ingredients.

As the bartender handed the glass to the Stroller, he drew close and whispered anxiously, "We couldn't catch any of the real thing so we had to fake 'em. We made holes in the ice with a gimlet, poked spaghetti in the holes and let it swell. Think they'll pass for the real thing?"

The Stoller tasted, smacked his lips and pronounced it the finest ice worm cocktail it had ever been his pleasure to imbibe. "Be sure always to use the youngest and freshest ice worms you can get," he advised the bartender. "Their bouquet when infants is superb." And during the remainder of the day the gentleman in the white coat could scarcely build ice worm cocktails fast enough to satisfy the demand.

The Stroller's little story was reprinted in other papers both in this country and abroad and brought a great response. The Scientific Research Society in London asked for details on the habits and environment of the ice worm and requested that specimens be forwarded by mail. The Department of Agriculture in Washington, D.C., wrote to the Stroller for further information on the creatures, and this was gladly furnished, free of charge and suitably embellished in keeping with the dignity of the department seeking it. The Stroller gloried in his position as the world's foremost authority on the ice worms.

Then some smart aleck of a writer employed by the *Philadelphia Ledger* butted in and got the Stroller in bad with the Department of Agriculture by reprinting the original story and following it with these lines:

> Oh, liar, we adore thee
> In humble awe
> And pray that heaven bless thee
> With tardy thaw.
> Blue snow we all admire
> But seldom see;
> For news of it, Oh, liar,
> We turn to thee.
> Our ice worms, too, are dumb;
> No chirp have they;
> But in our ice are some
> Bad germs, I say.
> To Yukon, land august
> Where zeros burn,
> The local liar must
> With envy turn.

Talk about being squelched, cast down and mortified! The Stroller was so deeply wounded that despite the fact that the Northland literally exudes inspiring subjects and opportunities, he has never since attempted to elevate its literature from the slime-covered slough of mediocrity in which it reposes.

Liar indeed! The Stroller will take his oath, now or any other time, that never has he seen blue snow or heard an iceworm chirp when the thermometer stood above seventy degrees below zero, Fahrenheit.

The Law of The Yukon

BY ROBERT SERVICE

THIS IS THE LAW OF THE YUKON, AND EVER SHE MAKES IT
     PLAIN:
"Send not your foolish and feeble; send me your strong and
     your sane.
Strong for the red rage of battle; sane, for I harry them sore;
Send me men girt for the combat, men who are grit to
     the core;
Swift as the panther in triumph, fierce as the bear
     in defeat,
Sired of a bulldog parent, steeled in the furnace heat.
Send me the best of your breeding, lend me your
     chosen ones;
Them will I take to my bosom, them will I call my sons;
Them will I gild with my treasure, them will I glut with
     my meat;
But the others—the misfits, the failures—I trample under
     my feet.

Dissolute, damned and despairful, crippled and palsied and
     slain,
Ye would send me the spawn of your gutters—Go! take
     back your spawn again.

"Wild and wide are my borders, stern as death is my sway;
From my ruthless throne I have ruled alone for a million
      years and a day;
Hugging my mighty treasure, waiting for man to come:
Till he swept like a turbid torrent, and after him swept—
      the scum.
The pallid pimp of the dead-line, the enervate of the pen,
One by one I weeded them out, for all that I sought
      was—Men.
One by one I dismayed them, frighting them sore with
      my glooms;
One by one I betrayed them unto my manifold dooms.
Drowned them like rats in my rivers, starved them like curs
      on my plains,
Rotted the flesh that was left them, poisoned the blood in
      their veins;
Burst with my winter upon them, searing forever their sight,
Lashed them with fungus-white faces, whimpering wild in
      the night;
Staggering blind through the storm-whirl, stumbling mad
      through the snow,
Frozen stiff in the ice pack, brittle and bent like a bow;
Featureless, formless, forsaken, scented by wolves in
      their flight,
Left for the wind to make music through ribs that are
      glittering white;
Gnawing the black crust of failure, searching the pit of despair,
Crooking the toe in the trigger, trying to patter a prayer;
Going outside with an escort, raving with lips all afoam;
Writing a cheque for a million, drivelling feebly of home;
Lost like a louse in the burning . . . or else in the tented town
Seeking a drunkard's solace, sinking and sinking down;
Steeped in the slime at the bottom, dead to a decent world,
Lost 'mid the human flotsam, far on the frontier hurled;
In the camp at the bend of the river, with its dozen
      saloons aglare,
Its gambling dens ariot, its gramophones all ablare;
Crimped with the crimes of a city, sin-ridden and bridled
      with lies,

In the hush of my mountained vastness, in the flush of my
        midnight skies.
Plague-spots, yet tools of my purpose, so natheless I suffer
        them thrive,
Crushing my Weak in their clutches, that only my Strong
        may survive.

"But the others, the men of my mettle, the men who
        would 'stablish my fame,
Unto its ultimate issue, winning me honor, not shame;
Searching my uttermost valleys, fighting each step as
        they go,
Shooting the wrath of my rapids, scaling my ramparts
        of snow;
Ripping the guts of my mountains, looting the beds of
        my creeks,
Them will I take to my bosom, and speak as a mother speaks.
I am the land that listens, I am the land that broods;
Steeped in eternal beauty, crystalline waters and woods.
Long have I waited lonely, shunned as a thing accurst,
Monstrous, moody, pathetic, the last of the lands and
        the first;
Visioning camp-fires at twilight, sad with a longing forlorn,
Feeling my womb o'er-pregnant with the seed of cities
        unborn.
Wild and wide are my borders, stern as death is my sway,
And I wait for the men who will win me—and I will not
        be won in a day;
And I will not be won by weaklings, subtile, suave and mild,
But by men with the hearts of vikings, and the simple faith
        of a child;
Desperate, strong and resistless, unthrottled by fear or defeat,
Them will I gild with my treasure, them will I glut with
        my meat.

"Lofty I stand from each sister land, patient and wearily wise,
With the weight of a world of sadness in my quiet,
        passionless eyes;
Dreaming alone of a people, dreaming alone of a day,

When men shall not rape my riches, and curse me and
      go away;
Making a bawd of my bounty, fouling the hand that gave—
Till I rise in my wrath and I sweep on their path and I
      stamp them into a grave.
Dreaming of men who will bless me, of women esteeming
      me good,
Of children born in my borders, of radiant motherhood,
Of cities leaping to stature, of fame like a flag unfurled,
As I pour the tide of my riches in the eager lap of the world."

This is the Law of the Yukon, that only the Strong shall thrive;
That surely the Weak shall perish, and only the Fit survive.
Dissolute, damned and despairful, crippled and palsied
      and slain,
This is the Will of the Yukon,—Lo! how she makes it plain!

Editor Ted Stone has been gathering the lore of the North American West for over twenty years. As editor of Red Deer Press's Roundup Books, he has compiled such best-sellers as *100 Years of Cowboy Stories*, *A Roundup of Cowboy Humor*, *The Complete Cowboy Reader* and *Riding the Northern Range: Poems from the Last Best-West*. Ted Stone is also the best-selling author of *Cowboy Logic: The Wit & Wisdom of the West* and *It's So Cold on the Prairies: Wit & Wisdom About Winter*.